SHERLOCK HOLMES AND
THE SHAKESPEARE LETTER

The Sherlock Holmes Mysteries by Barry Grant

THE STRANGE RETURN OF SHERLOCK HOLMES
SHERLOCK HOLMES AND THE SHAKESPEARE LETTER

SHERLOCK HOLMES
AND
THE SHAKESPEARE
LETTER

Barry Grant

This first world edition published 2010
in Great Britain and in the USA by
SEVERN HOUSE PUBLISHERS LTD of
9–15 High Street, Sutton, Surrey, England, SM1 1DF.
Trade paperback edition first published
in Great Britain and the USA 2011 by
SEVERN HOUSE PUBLISHERS LTD.

British Library Cataloguing in Publication Data

Grant, Barry.
    Sherlock Holmes and the Shakespeare letter.
    1. Holmes, Sherlock (Fictitious character) – Fiction.
    2. Watson, John H. (Fictitious character) – Fiction.
    3. Shakespeare, William, 1564–1616 – Correspondence –
    Fiction. 4. Terrorists – Scotland – Fiction. 5. Detective
    and mystery stories.
    I. Title
    823.9'2-dc22

ISBN-13: 978-0-7278-6946-3   (cased)
ISBN-13: 978-1-84751-279-6   (trade paper)

All Severn House titles are printed on acid-free paper.

Severn House Publishers support The Forest Stewardship Council [FSC],
the leading international forest certification organisation. All our titles that
are printed on Greenpeace-approved FSC-certified paper carry the FSC logo.

Mixed Sources
Product group from well-managed
forests and other controlled sources
www.fsc.org Cert no. SA-COC-1565
© 1996 Forest Stewardship Council

Typeset by Palimpsest Book Production Ltd.,
Falkirk, Stirlingshire, Scotland.
Printed and bound in Great Britain by the
MPG Books Group, Bodmin, Cornwall.

For Lily

ONE
London Blues

The old Afghan bullet made my shoulder ache, gloomy winter still lingered, and my companion had sunk into a blue funk. Each morning after breakfast he would sit staring at the desk drawer containing the cocaine authorized by Scotland Yard 'for emergencies only'. He would stare a long while, sometimes almost trembling, apparently longing to take up the syringe and inject himself. Then a sea change would sweep over him and he would begin pacing, sighing, flinging himself desperately first into one chair then another. 'How strange,' he would cry, 'that London is awash with crimes and conundrums, yet no one calls!'

I could only give him the sort of trite advice that everyone gives and no one believes. 'Be patient, Holmes,' I would say. 'Something will turn up.'

Eventually he would settle down to his daily routine, preparing himself for the call when it came. From noon till nightfall he would sit by our fireside reading books and newspapers, surfing the Web, striving to educate himself in all aspects of twenty-first century culture. He was especially keen on studying the biological sciences but he studied everything, including physics, literature, economics, psychology and movie history. While he worked he clung to the pipe that had been found with him in the Swiss glacier, the old meerschaum that he had purchased in Holland in 1910. It was always in his pocket or his mouth. But Holmes followed doctor's orders and never lit it. The unrelenting Dr Coleman did not intend to let his spectacular experiment in stem-cell manipulation and organ regrowth – the 'grand resuscitation' as Holmes sarcastically styled it – go up in smoke.

On the day our terrifying adventure began my shoulder was throbbing unmercifully when I awoke, and was throbbing even more by the time I had finished my second cup of coffee. So I popped two pain pills, left Holmes staring at the cocaine drawer, and descended into the feeble light of a wintry London morn.

As I strode along Baker Street towards the Underground I suddenly felt better. The hurrying crowds stirred my spirits, and the fresh-faced young beauty at the coffee kiosk made me smile. Motion is always good medicine, and as I hurried about London that day I found many a pleasure. The only mistake I made was the matinee I chose, a play called *Madame de Sade*. But even unsatisfactory plays can be instructive if viewed in the right spirit, and I felt in fine fettle as I stepped from the theatre into the early dark of a winter's eve. A storm had blown up. I huddled beneath the marquee to fasten my flapping coat. Tremendous blasts of rain and snow were lashing along Charing Cross Road, turning the street into a blurry Impressionist night scene: stalled traffic, tilting buildings, people struggling against wind. I clutched my unopened umbrella in one hand and my plastic shopping bags in the other, ducked my head, and ran for the nearby Underground entrance. Soon I was gliding in comfort deep beneath the stormy streets.

As I changed trains at Piccadilly I noticed a TRAVEL SCOTLAND poster featuring a massive castle beneath a lofty crag – one of those scenes that conjure dreams of adventure and romance. I had been urging Sherlock Holmes to take a journey to stir his spirits, and suddenly it occurred to me that he might find Scotland intriguing. I couldn't remember him saying he'd ever been there. I decided I would suggest it to him.

By the time I emerged at Baker Street the storm had miraculously vanished, and an eerie fog had descended upon the city. Even familiar roads were suddenly mysterious. Halos glowed round street lamps and my footfalls echoed so oddly that I looked back twice to see if someone was following me. A brisk walk brought me to our first-floor flat where, just as I expected, I found Sherlock Holmes sitting cosy by the fire.

He sprang from his chair. 'I am dreadfully sorry, my dear Watson—'

'Wilson.'

'—but I haven't organized supper.'

'Not to worry,' I said, as I put my shopping bags on the table and laid out the contents of my overcoat pockets. 'I have brought you a *Cook's European Timetable* – Spain or Switzerland, Sweden or Scotland, it's all here. Have you ever been to Scotland?' I plunked the bright red book on to the table.

'Ah, thank you,' said Holmes. 'Reading it will be a feast, for

I love a train journey.' He nervously felt in his side jacket pocket, then touched his lapel pocket.

'Lose your pipe?'

'Crushed it. Very silly of me.'

'Crushed it!' I cried.

'When the resident porter delivered a package for you this afternoon, I forgot I had my pipe in my hand. I opened the door, dropped the pipe, stepped on it – and there is the result.' He pointed to a pile of white powder and fragments on the mantle. 'I have begun to wonder about my mental faculties, Wilson. I fear they are disintegrating.'

'You are thinking on too many channels simultaneously – that's your only problem,' I said.

He handed me a large padded envelope. On the outside of it was inscribed a note from my old friend, Percy Ffoulkes:

> *James,*
> *   You forgot your mobile phone in the restaurant. Luckily I spotted it. Hope you decided on* The Dream. *Still not sure about tonight.*
> *   Percy*

'What luck,' I said, slipping my mobile out of the envelope and into my pocket. 'I have had a wonderfully lucky day, Holmes. And my shoulder no longer aches.'

'Excellent!' said he. 'But 'tis a shame you were disappointed in *Madame de Sade*.'

'Oh, please!' I said with some impatience. 'How can you possibly know what play I saw, or what I thought of it!'

'Sorry,' he murmured.

'There *are* limits,' I said. 'Your little flights of deductive guesswork make me feel as if I'm being spied upon.'

'My apologies,' said he. 'Won't happen again.'

'Of course it will happen again,' I said, with a sigh. 'You cannot help yourself.'

'It is just that without real work, Wilson, these little flights of guesswork, as you call them, are the only deductive mental exercise I get. How I wish a real problem would come my way!' He rushed to the window and looked down at the street, as if expecting a problem to suddenly appear under the street lamp. Then he took a deep breath and flung himself back into his wingtip chair by the fire, and he sat rigidly, his thin arms on the chair arms. He leant far back and gazed up at the ceiling. His whole body was tense, like a compressed spring.

During the past month I had witnessed him striking that same desperate pose repeatedly. I knew that even a hundred and twenty years ago Holmes had been subject to fits of impatience, anxiety and depression whenever his mind was deprived of impenetrable mysteries to solve. His mental apparatus was like an exquisitely tuned sports car that only runs on very high octane fuel – a fuel consisting, in his case, of a steady stream of baffling crimes and scientific conundrums. Anything less potent than this caused his body to stall and his brain to switch off. Now, as he sat by the fire in that strange posture of total frustration, he looked at once so comical and so pathetic that suddenly I laughed and said, 'All right, Holmes, my good friend, do your worst! Since you imagine you can deduce my activities this day, you are welcome to try. Come! Let us put you to the test!'

He raised his forearms and placed his fingertips together, almost as if praying. 'You mustn't expect too much detail.'

'And why not?' said I.

'You removed your shoes before coming in, which robs me of very important clues.'

'Come now, Holmes,' said I, as I busied myself making two American martinis. 'No dallying. Tell me what I've done today – if you can.'

He closed his eyes, as if meditating on deep matters.

I dropped the olives into our drinks with a happy heart, for Holmes seemed at a loss, and this suited me. It is not pleasant to feel one's life is as transparent as a martini glass.

'With so few clues, I cannot deduce a great deal,' he said.

'Excuses, excuses,' said I, gaily giving the glasses a swirl.

'Still, your activities are not entirely obscure to me. This morning on your way to the Baker Street Underground you stopped at the chemist's to refill your pain pill prescription, and while in the shop you thought of your old Eton schoolmate, Percy Ffoulkes. This prompted you to phone him and make a luncheon date. At the Underground station you stopped at the coffee kiosk, bought a chocolate eclair and a cup of coffee, then took the Underground south to Piccadilly where you got off and walked to Sothran's bookshop in Sackville Street. You bought a book, then strolled east to The Cat's Potato Restaurant in Wardour Street where you met Percy Ffoulkes for lunch. Over your meal you talked about his niece. You also spoke about the theatre. You left the restaurant and, still puzzling over which play to see, you crossed Charing Cross Road and walked up Long Acre to Stanfords where you purchased *Cook's European Timetable* in hopes it would spur me to take a journey. You then walked back to Wyndham's theatre and bought a ticket for *Madame de Sade*. You didn't care much for the play but nonetheless you stayed for the whole of it, and afterwards you came directly home via the Underground. That's all I can say with certainty.'

'Outrageous,' I said quietly, trying not to sound bitter. But I felt betrayed. 'To spy on a friend is not decent, Holmes. Not even in jest.'

'Spy?'

'I presume you have used my mobile phone to track me. It is all very amusing, of course – and I forgive you. But it is an intrusion.' I handed him the martini. 'I presume you found a way to turn on my phone remotely, and to listen in on my conversations. Did you also manage to track me through the streets of London with the GPS function?'

'No,' said he. 'I've heard such things can be done, but I don't know how to do them.'

I picked up my glass. 'Cheers . . .'

'Cheers.' He took a sip.

'So, you followed me, or what?'

'I have not left the flat all day. My method, alas, was the ancient one: careful observation followed by rigorous logic and a dollop of imagination.' He got out of his chair and wandered listlessly towards the fire. 'But evidently the same result can now be accomplished through sheer technology. Doubtless that is why my talents are nowadays so little required.'

'Absurd!' said I, feeling suddenly ashamed for having accused him. 'The penetrating eye, the well-stocked mind, the creative spirit – these qualities will always be necessary to solve life's mysteries.'

'I used to think so, but I wonder . . .' He was in a mood.

'So how *did* you track me, *sans* technology, Mr Sherlock Holmes?'

He turned by the fireplace; the fire flickered behind his pant legs. 'Elementary, my dear Watson.'

'Wilson.'

He took a deep breath, rubbed his eyes with thumb and forefinger. 'I meant *Wilson*, of course. My brain cells may be degenerating. I have a theory why this might be so, and also a theory how I might slow the process by adding chemicals to my diet. This morning I designed several experiments . . .'

'For heaven's sake, Holmes, leave any medical fiddling to the doctors!' I said. 'We all forget things at a certain age. And you are not sixty-four, despite what your new passport proclaims. You are, by some reckonings, a hundred and fifty-four. What do you expect, my good fellow? Perfection?'

He tossed his head back and laughed. 'Well, I *do* remember your name. Truly.'

'Call me Watson, call me Wilson, call me anything but crazy. I am honoured to be confused with your old friend,' said I. 'As to your logical faculties, they appear to me highly tuned, for your description of my activities today was – I hate to admit it – perfectly correct. It is a mystery to me how you do it . . . and I often wish you wouldn't. But I know it all will seem quite simple when you explain it. So carry on, Holmes. Destroy the magical illusion while I throw a couple of salmon fillets into the pan.'

He stuck his hands into his trousers pockets and leant in the kitchen doorway. As the fish began to sizzle, he presented his explanation. 'This morning,' he said, 'I saw you take your last two pain pills, yet when you returned this evening – after the chemist's shop had closed – you set a full bottle of those same pills on the side table. Ergo, on your way to the Baker Street station this morning you stopped at your usual chemist to get a refill. Three days ago you told me that the niece of Percy Ffoulkes had nearly died of an overdose of pain pills and sleeping pills, so it was quite impossible that you could be in a chemist's shop buying pain pills and not think of your old Eton schoolmate and his unfortunate niece. The package Percy Ffoulkes sent around proves you called him and made a luncheon date.'

'Quite obvious.'

'This evening you pulled from your pocket a crumpled napkin of the sort they serve at the coffee kiosk, and it had smears of chocolate and yellow on it – hence, it is evident you bought a chocolate eclair with lemon filling to go with your habitual cup of coffee before boarding the train. You also laid a bag from Sothran's of Sackville Street on the table, with a book in it –

ergo, this morning you got off at Piccadilly Underground Station and walked to Sothran's in Sackville Street where you browsed – after your usual fashion – before buying a book. That left you just time enough to walk along Shaftesbury Avenue to Wardour Street and your favourite little restaurant, The Cat's Potato. Last week you treated me to a meal there and I was very pleased by the Bendicks mints they served afterwards – mints which were identical to the two gold-wrapped Bendicks mints you took from your coat pocket this evening.'

'All this is disappointingly obvious. As I knew it would be. You are a magician, Holmes. It isn't wise to reveal your tricks.'

He laughed. 'It is also obvious that you next went to Stanfords to buy my *Cook's*, since you had no other time to do it. The Stanfords plastic bag is pretty straightforward evidence.'

'True. But this morning I told you I was probably going to see *A Midsummer Night's Dream*. What makes you think I didn't?'

'A dry umbrella, for one thing. And what you did not mention, for another.'

I seasoned the fish with oregano. 'Carry on, Holmes.'

'At the time the matinees let out this afternoon there was a tremendous downpour of rain and snow over the city – yet your umbrella was perfectly dry in its sheath when you arrived home. Wyndham's, where *Madame de Sade* is playing, is only a few yards from the Underground – closer to an Underground station than any other theatre in London. And you had also mentioned you were considering going to that play. The theatre where *A Midsummer Night's Dream* is playing lies many blocks from an Underground station. Had you gone there you would have used your umbrella. Clearly, you went to *Madame de Sade* at Wyndham's Theatre and afterwards darted into the nearby Underground station. By the time you reached Baker Street the rain had stopped. And as to your opinion of the play? Whenever you enjoy a performance you bring home an illustrated programme to add to your extensive collection. You didn't bring home a programme, so clearly you regarded the production as a disappointment.'

'But the dry umbrella seems flimsy proof,' I said. 'I might have taken a taxi after seeing Shakespeare's play.'

'Not plausible,' said he. 'To imagine you saw *A Midsummer Night's Dream* is quite impossible.'

'Impossible?' said I. 'I am shocked you pretend to be so sure!'

He laughed. 'Even a brave soul such as yourself – an ex-war correspondent fresh from Afghanistan's dangerous plains – could hardly be so blasé that you would not have mentioned the bomb that exploded during the second act of this afternoon's performance.'

'A bomb!'

'According to the BBC, one of Titania's fairies had just begun to sing of *spotted snakes and thorny hedgehogs* when his lute appeared to explode. He tumbled from his perch to the boards eight feet below, and people rushed in from the wings to help him. Bedlam ensued. The play went on after a little delay. No one seriously hurt.'

'An exploding lute!' I said.

'Curious,' mused Holmes. 'It is only the third time in history I've heard of a stringed instrument blowing up.'

'And what were the other two?' I asked, as I turned the fish.

'There was a case in 1840 in which a cello exploded during a Mozart opera in Salzburg. Three players were killed. The attack was attributed to anarchists who objected to the Habsburgs.'

'Your knowledge of crime amazes me, Holmes.'

'The other instance was a month ago in the Green Park pedestrian subway, right here in London. A street musician's electric guitar exploded. Perhaps you remember? At first people thought it was a terrorist attack, and panic ensued.'

'I do remember. As I recall, there was speculation it was merely some sort of electrical short-circuit in the guitar.'

'The cause was never officially determined. Strange that two stringed instruments should meet the same fate within a month. Tiny explosions.'

'Coincidence.'

'Perhaps so . . .' He took another sip.

When we sat down to eat, he became moody again, seemed to fade. He grew more dismal, distant, depressed and disengaged. I tried to interest him in a variety of topics, with little success. 'I think we should get a dog, Holmes. Imagine a hound lying by our hearth this very moment, ready to take us for a walk – just what a couple of older chaps like ourselves need. Stir the blood. You ever have a dog?'

He looked bemused, smiled faintly. 'When I was a child we had one – a great friendly mutt called Sir Launcelot. He liked scones.'

There the conversation dropped. For when I mentioned the possibility of rescuing a pup from the local animal shelter, Holmes didn't seem to hear me. He was already elsewhere. Neither could I interest him in the paintings of Velasquez, the politics of Barack Obama, or the possibility of an excursion to a local pub.

'He'll have a devilish time getting out,' he said, suddenly.

'Who?'

'Obama. Afghanistan. Difficult to get out of that country in one piece.'

'Quite right.'

'Alexander the Great was the last who managed it. The Russians couldn't do it. We couldn't do it. When I was young they were still talking about the retreat from Kabul back in '42, the greatest humiliation ever suffered by the British Army – whole army slaughtered, all but one man.'

'As I recall, Dr Brydon was the survivor. He was wounded, his horse wounded, his sword blade broken off by a jezail bullet, yet he reached Jalalabad, and safety – but only *just*.'

Holmes tossed back his head and gazed at the clock on the mantelpiece:

'*When you're wounded an' left on Afghanistan's plains,*
An' the women come out to cut up your remains,
Jest roll to your rifle an' blow out your brains,
An' go to your Gawd like a soldier.'

'Excellent recitation!' said I. 'Have you memorized much Kipling?'

Holmes didn't seem to hear my question. By the end of the meal he had vanished into himself. He looked so gloomy and hopeless that I was induced to mention something that I had absolutely resolved – for fear of raising false hopes – *not* to mention. 'At lunch today,' said I, 'Percy Ffoulkes hinted that he might need to consult you.'

Holmes looked up expectantly. 'About his niece, I presume?'

'I think so. He spoke to me only in the vaguest terms. But I am sure it is a serious matter. I could see the poor fellow was suffering. Mind you, Holmes, he was not certain that he would come by. He was merely considering doing so. He is very worried about her.'

Holmes's face brightened momentarily. 'I would be very glad

to see him,' he said. He leant back in his chair, and felt in his pocket for a pipe that wasn't there.

I took the dinner plates into the kitchen and set them in the sink. Scarcely had I done so when my phone rang. It was Percy. He said he was in a car out front. His niece was with him. Might they come up?

TWO
Rachel Random

'She has a bold stride,' said Holmes, looking down at the street through our large front window. 'I can hardly believe she is the sort of a woman who would resort to killing herself with sleeping tablets and pain pills.'

'Do you presume to plumb her character from a second-storey glimpse?' I said.

'Idle speculation,' he replied, with a laugh.

'And what else do you dare deduce from this distance?'

He slipped his hands into his pockets as he gazed down. 'Very little.'

'I am relieved,' I said.

'All that is certain,' he said, 'is that she plays squash, is a serious cyclist, reads voraciously, is fond of dogs, allows herself to be pampered by men, is left-handed, and has recently travelled to the continent.'

'You frighten me, Holmes.'

'All quite obvious,' he replied.

The bell rang. A moment later Percy Ffoulkes and a striking young redhead stood framed in our doorway. The woman immediately introduced herself as Rachel Random. I hung her stylish mauve coat on the coat tree, and I draped Percy's blue wool topcoat and white scarf next to it. He was still the same good-looking, compact, energetic and affable fellow that he had been in the old days at university – the sort of chap people find immediately attractive. This evening he seemed subdued as he handed me a package. 'A small gift of brandy, James. Bought it at auction several years ago. Hope you like it.'

'My heavens,' I said, looking at the label. 'It's a hundred years old, isn't it?'

'About that.' He swept the air with the back of his hand as if to brush away my reluctance to accept so lavish a gift.

I set the bottle on the side table, carefully.

As my old friend and his niece walked in to meet Holmes, they struck me as a most handsome couple – perfectly matched in style and manner. He was sixty-two, she perhaps thirty-five. We all sat down by the dancing hearth, and their faces shone with excitement and concern.

'Mr Holmes, I am sorry to impose on you so late in the evening,' said Percy. 'I rather desperately need your help, and that is my only excuse.'

'You need no excuse,' said Holmes. 'Had you not introduced me to Wilson last autumn in Wales – at that critical moment when I was recuperating from years in the glacier, and he from Afghanistan's wounds – I fear I would have had difficult days. Your old friend has helped me restart my career, and consequently I am very much in your debt.'

'What a terrible tangle that Black Priest affair was!' said Percy. 'I followed it in the newspapers. You are to be congratulated for handling it so subtly, Mr Holmes.'

'It was my first murder case in more than ninety years,' he replied, 'and solving it was a pleasure. But since then my services have been in very small demand.' His eyes were alight with expectation. 'But, please, be good enough to tell us what brings you to see me this evening.'

'My niece and I have become entangled in a most unusual crime,' said Percy. 'I certainly hope matters can be set right.'

'Pray give me the details,' urged Holmes.

'The long and the short of it, Mr Holmes, is that a letter has been stolen – a letter written and signed by William Shakespeare.'

Holmes lurched a little in his chair.

I too was startled.

'I know how improbable my tale must sound,' said Percy. 'Apart from a few signatures on legal documents, nothing hand-written by William Shakespeare has ever been discovered – not a single letter, script or poem in four hundred years. Nothing. But several months ago a good friend of mine, Professor Hugh Blake of Oxford, confided to me that he had discovered a letter written and signed by Shakespeare. It was purportedly composed in Florence in March of 1592, and it was addressed to a woman named Emilia. Everything about the document appeared to Hugh to be perfectly genuine. But he felt he could not so much as whisper of his discovery until he was absolutely certain of the letter's authenticity. He told no one but his wife and me. He felt he simply could not present to his peers a letter that would rock the foundations of scholarship and put the whole civilized earth in an uproar if there were any chance that it might prove to be a fake.'

'Quite so, quite so,' said Holmes.

'Sir Hugh found the letter in a pile of papers at an art dealer's shop in Florence, and purchased it for a song. When he got back to England he closeted himself at his manor in the Cotswolds and did everything in his power to ascertain the letter's authenticity in absolute secrecy. He had the paper analysed in a laboratory. The paper was found to have been made in Italy in the late sixteenth century. He thoroughly analysed the contents of the letter, including the words used, the spellings, the subjects alluded to, the people and places mentioned in it, and so forth. He then checked his own judgement – without ever revealing the existence of the letter – with that of Shakespeare scholars around the world, asking them a number of questions. Their answers all suggested that the letter was one which Shakespeare certainly could have written. A month ago Sir Hugh came to the point when he could do no more to verify the authenticity of the letter without actually revealing its existence to the scholarly community – revealing it, that is, to the scrutiny of all those experts worldwide who will, quite naturally, be anxious to examine it. But Hugh is a worrier. Even at school – we were at Oxford together – he was a worrier. I suggested to him that he might consider, as one last precaution, submitting the letter to my niece. I told him that Rachel has worked for two major auction houses, is an expert in holograph letters, and now works for a firm in New Bond Street that specializes in authenticating documents of all kinds. I assured him that she, in strictest secrecy, would match the writing of the letter to Shakespeare's known signatures, analyse the ink, and perform a number of other forensic tests to help determine if the letter is what it pretends to be. Hugh agreed that this would be a good idea. Seven days ago he brought the letter to Lashings and Bedrock, Ltd, in New Bond Street, and turned it over to my niece. And that is where the trouble began. This affair has caused my niece so much consternation that for a while I really believed she had tried to commit suicide with a cocktail of sleeping pills and pain pills — '

'But that wasn't it at all,' broke in Rachel Random. 'I certainly did not try to kill myself!'

She had been sitting very straight in her chair, listening intently as her uncle spoke. She was a statuesque young woman with very red hair and very green eyes. Her skin was smooth as soap, and it was exceptionally white, except for a few freckles on the nose. She gave an impression of boldness. Yet she exuded such femininity, particularly when she spoke, that the impression of boldness was diluted. She gave the immediate impression of being exceptionally beautiful – an impression no doubt enhanced by the fact that she was wrapped in a tight-fitting green dress. I felt, at first, that her face was as beautiful as that of any cover girl. Then I realized that this was not so, that the nose was a little too prominent, and that much of her beauty came from the animation of her face and the energy of her moods.

'I admit I had a little too much wine on the night after the letter was stolen,' she said. 'As a result, I forgot which medications I had already taken. I had injured my wrist playing squash, and I took a pain pill for that. Then I took a sleeping pill to get some rest. But evidently I took each dose twice, or three times, and that made me very sick.'

'Gave us all a scare,' said Percy.

'I suppose I ought to tell you exactly what happened, Mr Holmes,' she said.

'Pray do so, and omit no details.' said Holmes. He sat in a state of utter quiescence and concentration, his wrists limp and thin hands falling bent over the ends of the chair arms. 'Even the most seemingly inconsequential detail can sometimes be crucial in the solution of a case.'

'I will do my best to omit nothing,' she said. 'Exactly one week ago today my uncle Percy phoned me and said that a friend of his would soon contact me about a very important matter. My uncle asked me to do everything in my power to accommodate his friend's needs. A little later that day Sir Hugh Blake phoned and informed me that he had an old letter that might be of very great importance. He asked if I would be willing to examine it. We made an appointment for that very afternoon, and at exactly four thirty he stepped into my office. When I closed the door he informed me, in hushed tones, that he believed he had a letter in his hand that had been written by William Shakespeare. I dare say, you could have knocked me off my chair by simply *blow*ing at me. I knew Professor Blake had a worldwide reputation as a Shakespeare scholar. If anyone else had made this claim to my face, I might have laughed out loud – or at least smiled. But in this case, I could only try to keep my pulse rate down. The letter was in an envelope about eight and a half inches long and five and a half inches wide. I drew the letter out very carefully, laid it on my table, unfolded it, and cast my eye over it. To my casual glance everything looked perfectly authentic. But, of course, many further tests would be required before I could say anything definite. Nonetheless, I suddenly felt as though I were handling a holy relic. I carefully slipped the letter back into its envelope and laid it on the table. Professor Blake and I talked a little longer. He told me nothing further about the letter I was to examine, neither its provenance nor what tests it had already been subjected to. He stood up and shook my hand, and he said, "Please take good care of it." And at about ten minutes past five o'clock Sir Hugh left my office. From my office door I could see him go towards the elevator. I presume he got into the elevator and left the building.'

Rachel Random paused in her narrative, leant forward, and drew something out of her purse. 'I thought this might help you to visualize our building, Mr Holmes. It is a little sketch I made of our office layout.'

'You are very thorough,' said Holmes, taking the foolscap sheet.

'It is my job to be thorough,' she replied. 'When Sir Hugh Blake left, there were just three of us remaining in the building: Paul, our receptionist; Mr Gaston, whose office is nearest mine; and me. Mr Lashings had already left, and Mr Bedrock had not come to work that day for he was on holiday in Spain.'

'What happened next?'

'I sat down at my desk and ate a sandwich left over from my lunch. I felt the most urgent need to look at the letter and determine whether it was real. At the same time I was reluctant to begin – perhaps for fear of what I'd find. I was in a very strange state of mind, Mr Holmes. After having boosted my energy with the sandwich and a pickle, I decided I would freshen up and begin work immediately. I left the Shakespeare letter in

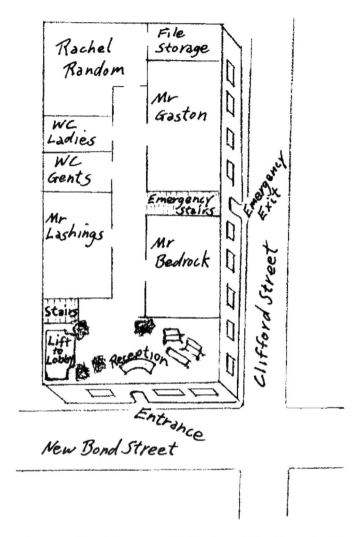

its envelope on the table where Sir Hugh and I had been looking at it. I stepped out of my office and went into the WC just next door.'

'Did you lock your office when you went to the WC?' asked Holmes.

'No. I didn't even close the door. I presumed the letter was perfectly safe in its anonymous manila envelope on my table, especially since no one but me, my uncle, Sir Hugh and his wife even knew of its existence.'

'That makes sense,' Holmes nodded. 'And then?'

'I had been in the WC for perhaps a minute and a half, and

I had just turned on the water faucet when I heard a terrible shout. I rushed into the hallway but saw nothing. I heard a clatter of footsteps, then heard Paul's voice shouting "Stop!" from the emergency staircase that leads down to Clifford Street. A moment later the emergency door alarm went off. A few moments after that Mr Gaston's head appeared in his doorway. "What's going on?" Mr Gaston asked. Paul soon emerged from the emergency stairwell and cried, "Someone just ran out of the building." He looked rather distracted and wild, and he said to me, "Who was in your office, Rachel?"

"'No one," I answered.

'But already a cold feeling had come over me, Mr Holmes. Already I seemed to know what had happened. I hurried to my office and looked on the table: the envelope containing the letter was gone. I searched the desk and the floor behind the desk, thinking it might have fallen. I could not believe it had vanished. And yet from the moment the alarm sounded I knew perfectly well that the Shakespeare letter was gone, stolen – gone before I had kept it in my care for even half an hour. You cannot imagine how I felt, Mr Holmes! How I feel!'

Rachel Random stopped speaking. She looked shaken. I felt sorry for her.

'What made Paul think someone had been in your office?' asked Holmes.

'The sound of footsteps,' she said. 'Paul usually does not stay after hours, but this night he stayed late to catch up on some filing. He found a file that I had asked for earlier in the day, and he brought it to my office – just at the time I was in the WC. But when he tossed it on to the desk top, it slid right off on to the floor behind. So he knelt down and collected the papers that had slid out of the file folder. At that moment he heard a sound behind him, someone hurrying out the door. Paul got up and ran across the room into the hallway. He saw no one, but he heard footsteps rushing down the emergency exit staircase. So he hurried to the staircase and chased whoever it was. As he went around the first turning he heard the outer door open somewhere below him – and then the alarm went off. When Paul reached the bottom of the stairs he looked out the door in hopes of seeing someone running, but he saw only the usual street crowds flowing by. So he closed the door and came back up. That's when he met me and Mr Gaston in the hallway, and told us what had happened.'

'Why was Mr Gaston there after hours?' asked Holmes.

'He comes to work a bit later than the rest of us, and so he always stays until five forty-five.'

'Did you call the police?'

'Immediately. Detectives very soon arrived. I put on my coat and went with one of them to headquarters at New Scotland Yard, where I told him everything I have told you.'

'And nothing has been learnt of the letter since it vanished a week ago?'

'Nothing that I know of. I suppose the police are working on it.'

Holmes sprang to his feet and stood in front of the fire, looking at the plan of the office that she had given him. 'According to your diagram, the storage room can be entered only through your office. Could someone have been hiding there?'

'Not possible. I went into that room for a pad of paper at four o'clock or so. No one was there. Besides, I can't imagine how a stranger would get into the building. The only entrance is through the front, and someone is at the desk all the time. Mr Bedrock is very particular about security. Important books, manuscripts and documents are always on the premises.'

Holmes walked to the window and looked out at the square. 'The case has some singular and, indeed, startling features,' he said. 'Will you be at your office tomorrow, Ms Random?'

'Eight to five,' said she.

She and Percy rose. As I helped Rachel into her stylish coat, she turned to me suddenly and said, 'A month ago I was on a motoring holiday in Germany and everything seemed perfect – isn't it strange how quickly fortune changes!'

Percy touched her arm. 'Never worry, my dear. Mr Holmes will take care of everything – depend upon it!'

'I have every confidence,' she said. Again she turned to me. 'Who is that lovely old lady I met out front, with the two poodles? Luckily, I always carry dog biscuits for such meetings!'

'That would be Mrs Cleary,' I said. 'She lives in the ground floor flat beneath us.'

'Good night, Mr Wilson – and thank you, Mr Holmes,' she said.

When they had left I walked to the front window and looked down. Rachel Random had parked her bright red car beneath the streetlamp. Her uncle opened the driver's door for her. Very

clearly on the rear window shelf I could see a scattering of books
. . . and a squash racquet in its case. The car was this year's
model. It had a GB sticker on the back, which of course suggested
she had driven it abroad. Standing up in the rack on top was a
road bicycle. 'I am beginning to learn your methods, Holmes,'
I said.

Long after our guests had left us, Holmes still paced about,
revved by the fuel of this seemingly inexplicable crime. I almost
hoped he would not solve it too quickly. He was more cheerful
than I'd seen him in weeks.

Before we retired, I opened the old bottle of brandy that Percy
had brought, and I poured us each a small splash. I toasted
Holmes and wished him success in his search for the Shakespeare
letter. He sipped the brandy, and smiled with pleasure at the
first sip. Then he put the brandy glass to his nose, sniffed it
curiously. A haunted look crept into his eyes.

'How do you like it?' I asked.

He did not answer.

'Are you all right, my good fellow?'

Holmes leapt from his chair and pointed out the window.
'Look out! It's coming!' he cried.

'Holmes!' I said.

But he did not hear me. He was staring out the window into
the emptiness of night, with a look of fear on his face.

THREE
Vanished Without Trace

B y the time I arose the following morning, Holmes was already
up and had the coffee made and the bread in the toaster. He
took a sip and placed his cup on to its saucer, producing a
musical sound like a bell tinkling and eggshell breaking.

'The sound of fine China,' said I.

'The sound of a nervous hand,' said he.

'My heavens, what have you to be nervous about!'

'Never have I been presented with a case so important. It is
a great responsibility.'

'Come now!' I replied. 'I have read all your cases as reported by Dr Watson. To whatever height this case may lead you, surely it will lie far below the summit of your achievement. To take but one example, you eliminated Moriarty, the most powerful criminal of his age. What could be more important than that?'

Holmes brandished his toast in the air like a flag. 'I rid the world of Moriarty, 'tis true. And undoubtedly he was the greatest criminal mastermind of the nineteenth century – unless you count Napoleon as a criminal. I hope it is not immodest to add that I have intervened to save many a royal house of Europe from foundering on the rocks of scandal.'

'Precisely my point,' said I.

'Yet in those cases, Wilson, I was dealing with tiny bubbles in the sea of time – bubbles important to the people involved, but to few others. Shakespeare, by contrast, is not a bubble but a tidal wave, a cataclysm that for four hundred years has heaved whole oceans upward, shaken the shores of the world, and stirred the souls of multitudes. His work is universal, colossal, and as near to eternal as anything earthly is likely ever to be. His only competition is God . . . and perhaps Beethoven.'

'I deduce that you are an admirer of Shakespeare,' said I.

'A single letter written by Shakespeare's hand would be worth more to the world than all the papers of the Habsburgs, the Mings, the Tudors, the Romanoffs, and the Liberal Party.'

I was astonished at this outburst. I could only laugh. 'I don't think I've ever seen you so passionate.'

'Even ninety years frozen in a glacier has not numbed my enthusiasm for Shakespeare, though I fear it has dulled certain other of my delights. Think, Wilson, what it may mean to have a letter from Shakespeare's own hand! It may solve a multitude of quibbles about the authorship of the plays, and about the little-known life of the poet. Would not the world be overjoyed to learn that William Shakespeare, far from being an untravelled country boy, had in fact taken the grand tour of Europe? Would not everyone be pleased—'

'Everyone but the Baconites.'

'—to learn that William Shakespeare actually visited those Italian towns in which he set so many of his plays? One letter from Florence would open the doorway to continents of plausible speculation. *A Midsummer Night's Dream* was set in Athens – and who could say, if we had a letter written by Shakespeare in Florence, that he had not travelled some hundreds of miles further to Athens as well? Who could say that he had not visited Denmark, and walked the parapets at Elsinore long before he set Hamlet a'walking and a'talking there? Such a letter would be published in every language. It would be not merely a love letter to Emilia Bassano, but a love letter to all the world.'

'You even know the lady's last name?'

'I have glanced at recent Shakespearean studies. A man called Rowse has convinced me that *very likely* Shakespeare had an affair with Emilia Bassano, who was from a family of Italian court musicians in London. Very likely it was she who was the "Dark Lady" of the sonnets.'

'You astonish me.'

'Shakespearean scholarship began to interest me late in life, because of something you just mentioned, the Baconites and others like them – people who believed Bacon or someone else wrote Shakespeare's plays. Around the turn of the century a great many people were debating this question. It became a kind of madness, this notion that someone else wrote the plays of Shakespeare. One day an acquaintance, who believed me to be one of the world's better detectives . . .'

'You are too modest!'

'. . . asked me to solve the problem logically. I therefore wrote an essay on the subject. I believe my essay proves conclusively that William Shakespeare of Stratford-upon-Avon did write the plays attributed to him. But rational argument cannot hope to penetrate the madness of that tribe of Shakespeare doubters whose views are based entirely on faith and not at all on facts. If such a person has stolen the letter, alas! I fear he may destroy it.'

'Surely no one would *destroy* it, Holmes!'

'You are an optimist,' said he, with a laugh. 'Men throughout history have done whatever is necessary to suppress opinions that do not agree with their own, burning not only books but the heretics who wrote them.'

'I would like to have read your essay.'

'The typescript may have been stored at Scotland Yard along with the other things that dear old Watson saved from my cottage in Sussex – my revolver, syringe, violin, magnifying glasses, and so on. I'll ask Lestrade to check.'

'I knew you had written monographs on various technical

topics, such as techniques for identifying cigar ash,' I said. 'But I had no idea you had written on literary topics.'

'Ah!' cried Holmes. 'My interest in literature arose from something Dr Watson wrote in his first memoir of my exploits. He laid before the public a list labelled "Sherlock Holmes – his limits". The first item on that list was *Knowledge of Literature – nil*. That entry was immediately followed by two equally damning ones: *Knowledge of philosophy – nil* and *Knowledge of astronomy – nil.*'

'I recall that list,' I said. 'Vaguely.'

'Poor old Watson didn't realize how deeply he had wounded me. I secretly resolved to expand my knowledge in all those areas in which he had rated me a "nil". Truth to tell, Watson was right. In the extremism and certainty of my youth I had been convinced that a focused intensity was the *ne plus ultra* of success. I had foolishly determined to focus only on realms of knowledge that appeared to be immediately useful in solving crimes. More mature reflection suggested to me that all realms of knowledge are linked, and that there is no fact, however small, that may not some day be needed in order to solve one of life's mysteries.'

'Your knowledge of Sheridan's *The Rivals* certainly helped you to solve the Black Priest murder,' said I.

'Exactly the sort of thing I mean,' said Holmes, throwing down his napkin and bounding to his feet. 'And now I must be off to have a look at the scene of the crime. If you are free, Wilson, perhaps you would like to come along? I couldn't help but notice that last evening you paid particular attention to the considerable charms of Rachel Random.'

'Come, now, Holmes!' said I. 'She is barely more than half my age. Surely you do not think I am so foolish as—'

'Duty calls!' said Holmes, and he darted towards the front hall, swung on his overcoat, pocketed his small digital camera, grabbed his thin black gloves, clapped his Greek fisherman's cap on to his head at a rakish angle, then turned to me with a look all briskness and business. 'Ready, Wilson?'

Not long afterwards we were hurrying through the elegant bustle of New Bond Street. Limousines lurked like polished shadows. Women in *très chic* clothing stalked from window to window like large shore birds. By and by I spotted a little brass plate announcing LASHINGS AND BEDROCK, LTD. We opened the glass door and stepped into a tiny lobby. Holmes tried the staircase door but it was locked. He winked at me as he pointed to the security camera in the ceiling. He pushed the lift button. A voice asked us our names. The lift door slid open. A moment later we stepped out into a reception room filled with potted plants and sunlight.

The receptionist rose from his half-moon desk and approached us. He was a tall young man in his early thirties, sandy hair, blue eyes, wide shoulders, slim hips. He wore a blousy blue silk shirt, low-cut blue jeans, and a wide brown belt with a brass buckle. A gold chain hung lightly around his neck. In his left hand he held a large bottle of Evian water. He plunked the water bottle amidst the potted plants as he neared us. He limped a little. 'I'm Paul Primrose – so glad you found us, Mr Holmes, Mr Wilson! Please, you may ask me any questions at all. Mr Lashings has instructed us to be entirely at your service.'

'Very good of him,' said Holmes. 'To begin, did you see the person who ran out of the building?'

'I did not. By the time I reached the bottom of the staircase, he had already vanished amidst the crowds in the street. He, she, whoever.'

'Did you smell anything as you ran down the stairwell?'

'Smell anything?' Primrose tilted his head in surprise.

'Perfume, deodorant, food . . .'

Primrose touched his nose. 'Not a very good smeller, I'm afraid.'

'You were in Ms Random's office when you heard someone running?'

'Just picking up a dropped file, yes.'

'Could the person have come out of one of the WCs rather than out of her office?'

'No, I am certain someone was in the room with me, behind the Chinese screen. Oh . . . here's Rachel.' He waved to her.

Rachel Random came smiling towards us. 'I am so glad you came, Mr Holmes.'

She wore light blue slacks. Her dark blue blouse was accented by a gold bracelet and gold necklace.

'Doesn't she look gorgeous!' exploded Paul Primrose. 'I dressed her.'

'Indeed?' said Holmes, looking at him.

'You misunderstand me!' cried Primrose, clapping his palm to his cheek.

'Paul is my fashion consultant.' said Rachel. 'He accompanies me to shops to pick out nice things, and then he alters my clothes. He is like my big sister.'

'Snip, snip,' said Paul, making a scissors motion with his right hand. 'I am a clothes designer by training, a receptionist by necessity. I hope to start my own fashion boutique within a year. *Paul's of Piccadilly* – how does that sound?'

'Excellent,' I said.

'Or perhaps, *Primrose Printemps*?' He tilted his head and smiled expectantly.

Mr Lashings emerged from the front office. He was a hard-looking man with an elegant edge, a man of fifty or so with black hair, a gaunt and chiselled face, and a slightly pained expression that was both fascinating and forbidding. He raised a brow. 'Mr Holmes, I presume?' Lashings shook Holmes by the hand. 'Sir Hugh Blake phoned this morning and asked that we cooperate with you fully.'

'Excellent,' said Holmes.

'Frankly,' said Lashings, 'I think the recovery of this missing document might be entirely trusted to the efforts of the Metropolitan Police.'

'Ah, the *efforts* of the boys in blue are always impressive,' said Holmes.

This elliptical comment gave Lashings pause. He glanced at his watch.

'Were you aware,' asked Holmes, 'that the Shakespeare letter was in your establishment?'

'I knew nothing of it whatever. And I thought that very odd.'

'In what way?'

'I have known Sir Hugh Blake for many years. Why would he keep this project secret from me? I very much doubt, Mr Holmes, that there ever *was* a Shakespeare letter.'

'An authentic one, you mean?'

'It seems to me most unlikely.'

'But you do agree that a document of some sort was stolen from your establishment?'

'So they tell me.'

'Have you any idea how someone might have entered these premises unseen?'

'I have puzzled over that very question, Mr Holmes. The windows are double-glazed and permanent, and cannot be opened. The emergency staircase exit is always locked. The staircase door in the lower front lobby is also always locked, and the lift will not operate unless our receptionist pushes the button to allow it to rise. Every visitor is, therefore, met by our receptionist.'

'I understand that your partner, Mr Bedrock, was away on the day of the incident,' said Holmes. 'Did any office staff go into his office that day?'

'I don't know.'

'So someone could have been hiding in there all day?'

'It does not seem likely. His office is locked.'

'Who has a key to the office, other than Mr Bedrock?'

'We all have a key to every office. One key fits all. Sometimes it is necessary to go into a colleague's office.'

'When is the janitorial work done here?'

'Every morning between seven-thirty and eight. But someone is always here when they come, and here when they go. They have no key to the premises.'

'Thank you,' said Holmes.

'That is all?'

'For now. I shall let you know if I need anything more.'

'Very good,' said Lashings. He tilted stiffly at the waist, as if imitating a nineteenth-century military bow, then hurried away – heels clicking on the polished hallway.

Rachel Random led us to her office and pointed towards a large Chinese screen behind the ceiling-mounted document camera. 'Someone might have hidden behind that screen – Uncle Percy collects Chinese art and gave it to me. But I think I would have noticed. A small sound, or something, would have alerted me.'

Holmes opened the door to the storage room and in a moment was down on his hands and knees, examining the floor with the help of a pocket torch. He returned to Ms Random's office and examined it equally thoroughly. He next examined both the women's and the men's WC, then the hallway. The hallway was straight, well-lit. Opening into it were the doors to the four offices – Bedrock's, Lashings's, Gaston's and Random's – plus the doors to the two WCs, and also the door to the emergency exit stairs. Holmes descended the emergency stairs, then crawled slowly back up on his hands and knees, examining the floor with a small magnifying glass as he did so. He reached the landing and crawled out into the main hallway just as Mr Gaston stepped out of his office and looked down. 'My God, sir, what are you doing! Are you *smelling* the floor!'

'Mr Holmes is investigating the recent theft,' said Rachel.

Holmes slipped his magnifying glass into his pocket as he got to his feet. 'Mr Gaston? I am Sherlock Holmes.'

Gaston stepped back a pace. 'Holmes?' He adjusted his thick spectacles. He was a short and stocky man with short-cropped black hair.

'Was your door open when the incident occurred?' asked Holmes.

'Yes, it was.' He pushed his glasses back on his nose.

'In the minutes before the incident occurred, did you observe Mr Primrose walking past your door towards Ms Random's office?'

'He glided by in his usual bird-like manner. Whistling.'

'Whistling?'

'Very irritating.'

'And later did you hear anything?'

'I heard someone running.'

'One person?'

'At the time I thought it was one.'

'Then what happened?'

'I saw Paul pass my door.'

'Was he carrying anything?'

'A bottle of water.'

'In which hand?'

Gaston pushed the glasses back on his nose and rubbed the back of his neck, as if he were getting a headache. 'Since we are being so precise, Mr Holmes, he carried the water with his left hand. With his right hand he was pointing at something.'

'Then I take it he wasn't running terribly fast, since you noticed all this.'

'Mr Holmes, the police have already questioned me. I have answered many questions.'

'Did they ask these particular questions?'

'Not these particular questions, no.'

'Ah, I thought not,' said Holmes.

'You asked if he was running,' said Gaston, holding his hands in front of him in frustration, as if he were holding a small box. 'Let me revise my answer. I will say he was moving quickly. But he was limping, which slowed him. He hurt his leg recently.'

'How long have you worked for this company?'

'Five years.'

'Were you aware that Ms Random had in her possession, on that late afternoon, a letter purported to be extremely valuable?'

'I was aware of no such thing.'

'No one ever mentioned this to you?'

'Not till afterwards.'

'So you heard the footsteps, you saw Mr Primrose passing your door at a goodly clip, and he was carrying a bottle of water in his left hand and he was pointing at something with his right hand.'

'Yes.'

'Then what happened?'

'I hurried here to the door to see what was going on. I heard Paul shout from the emergency stairwell. A moment later the alarm went off.'

'What did Paul shout?'

'I think he shouted "Wait!"'

'How did Mr Primrose appear when he came up the stairs again?'

'Flustered.'

'Did he say anything to you?'

'He said that someone had just run out of the building through the emergency exit.'

Holmes thanked Mr Gaston. Gaston pushed the glasses back on his nose, took a deep breath and waddled back into his office with an injured and frustrated air.

It was nearly noon when we left the hermetically sealed premises of Lashings and Bedrock. The weather had turned dry and blowy and cold. A few fat and shining clouds were sailing over the city like ships. I was glad the weather forecasters had proclaimed the unseasonably cold weather would soon be over. We pressed our way briskly along New Bond Street, past Sotheby's, and soon we were shouldering our way through the crowds in Oxford Street. Holmes turned north and pointed to a pub.

'Excellent idea,' said I.

Over a ploughman's lunch and a pint of beer, he asked, 'Wilson, what do you make of it?'

'Well,' said I, 'it appears to be a very easy case – apart from the question of who did it, how they did it, their motive for doing it, what they might have done with the letter, and how they knew about the letter in the first place. Those are the only points that puzzle me.'

Holmes smiled wryly and watched foam sliding down the side of his beer glass. 'My investigation of the premises revealed only that the Bedrock and Lashings janitorial crew do excellent work. Even the emergency staircase had been cleaned and polished. I could detect not a flake or fleck of evidence anywhere – not a boot mark, not a hand print on the outer door, nothing. In the seven days since the crime was committed, all physical evidence appears to have been obliterated completely.'

'I am surprised.'

'Such a thing has never happened to me before. Always I have been able to find *some*thing.' He took a deep breath and gazed across the small round table at me with strange intensity. 'Has it ever occurred to you, Wilson, that I am not quite myself these days?'

'Certain of your outbursts have worried me,' I replied. 'Still, problems are to be expected, are they not? You were warned that there might be anomalies. I think you are doing fine.'

'I wonder.'

'According to Dr Coleman, everything about you is precisely as it was in 1914, at the very moment that the avalanche buried and quick-froze you on the glacier under Jungfrau. I see no reason why we shouldn't believe him. Let us not make a problem where there is none.'

And that was as much of truth as I could wrestle into my words at that awkward moment. Truth is not always as plain as one hopes it would be. The other truth was that I had sometimes had doubts, not as to whether the resuscitation had been a brilliant success – obviously it had – but as to whether it would last. I had frequently read about the successes of modern cell technology, but just as frequently had read of its failures, of how cloned animals were afterwards found to have fatal defects, of how animal organs regrown from stem cells – as Holmes's were – often proved faulty . . . whereupon the newly resuscitated animals malfunctioned and died. Such things had been haunting my imagination ever since I had met Holmes four and a half months earlier and had learnt the startling story of how, in a final service to King George V, he had attempted to halt the Great War by carrying a personal message from the King to Kaiser Wilhelm. The whole project had come to wreck when a German agent, tracking Holmes across a glacier in Switzerland, had foolishly fired shots that brought down an avalanche. From the very beginning I had been sensitive to any little sign that Holmes might have been failing in body or mind after his terrible ordeal of freezing and thawing. But I reminded myself that whenever you begin looking for symptoms you find them, whether they exist or not. I comforted myself with the thought that very likely I was only imagining certain non-sequiturs in Holmes's conversation, certain lapses in his behaviour. After all, he had always been an unusual individual, a man of quirks.

'The scene of the crime has been wiped clean,' said Holmes. 'Therefore I must start at the other end, with the criminal.'

'The only people likely to have stolen the letter,' I said, 'are the ones who knew it existed.'

'You are a logician, Wilson!' He laughed.

'And we have been told that only four people knew: Sir Hugh and his wife Lotte, plus Percy and Rachel.'

Holmes swigged off the last of his lager and set down his glass. 'Are you game for a journey to Gloucestershire tomorrow?'

'The Cotswolds are lovely at this time of year,' I replied.

FOUR
Widcombe Manor

We drove north out of London on the whirling M40. Holmes sat beside me scanning a morning newspaper with his usual hawk-like attention. As I drove I could not help but ponder his outburst of several nights earlier, that strange cry – *Look out! It's coming!* I felt I had heard those words before. But where? *Déjà vu*. Was it a sign he was disintegrating mentally? I pushed the thought aside.

'It has happened again, Wilson!' he cried, crushing the newspaper down so that he could look over the top of it. 'At Queen Elizabeth Hall last evening two explosions halted the Antoine Capinelli violin concert.'

'What!' I gasped. I pictured Southbank in shambles.

'Only very tiny explosions. Some people described them as loud popping sounds. Capinelli was playing Paganini's famous A minor capriccio when a man in the first row screamed, clapped his hands to his ears, and tumbled to the floor. At the same time a man in the second row doubled over groaning. Capinelli was forced to stop playing while the two injured men were carried from the hall.'

'What was the explanation for all this?'

'None. It is a mystery . . . the third such in recent weeks.'

'The third?'

'Oh, do come along, my dear fellow! Do come along! First the exploding electric guitar in the Green Park pedestrian subway, then the exploding lute in *A Midsummer Night's Dream* – and now this.'

'But Holmes, aren't you leaping . . .' I paused to reformulate my words. I said, 'If Antoine Capinelli's *violin* had exploded, I would see a real similarity. As it is, this case seems rather different.'

Holmes paid no attention to my objection, merely went on with his musings. 'The explosions are always very tiny,' he said. 'That is the strangest aspect.'

'I defer to your better intuition,' said I. 'But a multitude of crimes are committed in London each day. Many are bound to have similarities.'

'The two injured men were music critics,' he said. 'How curious.'

I began to have the uneasy feeling that either I was a bit dull, or Holmes was drifting so far into outer space that I had lost radio contact. I gazed north. 'The spires of Oxford are beautiful this time of day.'

'Quite beautiful,' he agreed.

'I enjoyed Oxford very much,' I said. 'Ffoulkes came up from Eton a few years after I did. We were both at Christ Church. Percy and Hugh Blake were the same age, and they were great friends in those days. I was acquainted with Hugh though we were never close.'

'I didn't know that,' said Holmes, folding the newspaper.

'I haven't seen Hugh Blake for decades. I doubt he'll even recognize me. As I recall he was married soon after graduating from Oxford, and his first wife died rather young. He is now married to Lotte Linger, actress of stage and screen.'

'I saw her in a film several years ago, while I was recuperating in hospital. Very charming woman.'

'Her first husband was Lord Anthony Gray, now deceased.

From Lord Gray she inherited Widcombe Manor estate, where we are now headed. They had two sons. The elder is Alexis Gray, a writer and cultural critic. The younger – I think his name is Bart – does some sort of scientific research at Cambridge. The family is a bit complicated. Hugh is Lotte's third husband. Her second was somebody named Eldon Hideaway . . . appropriately named, for shortly after their marriage he ran off to Istanbul with a belly dancer and hasn't been seen since. Marianne Hideaway, Lotte's daughter by that man, is twenty-three or four, a student at Oxford. She still lives with Lotte and Sir Hugh. Percy Ffoulkes filled me in on all these details.'

Suddenly we found ourselves sliding along the tree-lined drive towards Widcombe Manor, shadows flickering dizzily, the ball of sun bouncing through treetops. The manor house rose into view, seeming to float on a swell of green lawn that swept down to a swan pond. A hundred yards beyond the house was a stone barn.

A maid took our coats. Just as she hung them on the coat tree in the entry hall, a heavy bumblebee swooped in through an open window – the creature made a circle around the coat tree, bumped into a window pane with a soft thud, and vanished outside with a fading buzz. The sound of Hugh Blake's voice greeting us from the hallway brought back vivid memories of times past, but as Hugh approached us I had difficulty seeing, beneath the heavy accretions of age, the slim young man I had known so long ago. After the usual greetings and allusions to days gone by, my old acquaintance led us to his study. He was a big man with large hands and large ears. I had forgotten how retiring he was. He spoke in so restrained a manner, and in so delicately modulated a voice, that had it not been for his substantial physical presence one would have felt he might blow away in a breath of breeze. His desk stood near a tall cathedral window containing two armorial panes of stained glass. He bade us sit on a couch facing the high wall of books. 'It was very good of you to come so far to see us, Mr Holmes,' said Sir Hugh. 'I flatter myself to think that even your namesake, the Holmes of literary fame, might have accepted this case simply because of its importance.'

'I am quite positive he *would* have accepted it,' said Holmes. 'It is assuredly one of the more important cases that have ever surfaced in England, and it is not entirely devoid of interesting features – not least of which is that the letter has disappeared despite the curious fact that almost no one knew it existed. Have you any suspicions who might have stolen it?'

'None.'

'Could any of the scholars you queried about the letter's contents have guessed, from your questions, that such a letter might exist?'

'I do not think so,' said the professor. 'I was very careful as to how I framed my queries to them. Also, few things are *less* likely to occur to a Shakespearean scholar than that a letter by Shakespeare would turn up. Nothing like that has happened in four hundred years. It simply would not cross anyone's mind.'

'I don't mean to press the point, Sir Hugh, but let me ask the question in a slightly different way: can you think of anyone who, *if* they knew of the letter's existence, would be the sort who *might* steal it? I do not ask you to be logical or fair. I only ask for your fleeting impression.'

'Well . . .' Sir Hugh nodded, slowly. 'I can think of only one man who *might* have stolen such a letter.'

'Ah!' said Holmes.

'But I am sure he didn't steal it.'

'But how can you be sure?'

'He is dead.'

'Then you are probably correct,' said Holmes.

'I am thinking of my wife's first husband, Lord Anthony Gray. Poor fellow believed that Francis Bacon wrote the plays, and that the world had grievously wronged the great Francis by not acknowledging this obvious fact. I believe Lord Gray might have stolen such a letter – and done so simply to destroy it. His ego was huge, and he had invested much of it in championing Francis Bacon – all those tracts he wrote, for instance, purporting to prove Bacon's authorship.'

'I have not seen any of them.'

'Privately printed, most of them.'

'If the letter still exists,' said Holmes, 'it certainly can be found – and I will spare no effort to find it. If you don't mind, Professor Blake, I should now like to speak to your wife.'

Hugh Blake rose quickly. 'Let us see where the good lady is hiding.'

He led us down a long hallway that was filled with the haunting, hesitating, surging sound of Debussy's *Clair de Lune*. The music grew louder and more distinct as we walked, and when we passed the music room I looked through an open doorway and saw a beautiful blonde woman playing a grand piano. I paused a moment to look and listen.

'My stepdaughter,' said Sir Hugh, glancing back at me.

The music faded as we neared the far end of the hallway. Sir Hugh ushered us into a large sitting room.

We found Lotte Linger writing letters under lamplight. She sat at a leather-topped, kidney-shaped desk in a dark corner. The moment she saw us she rose and floated towards us, smiling. She bowed slightly as she pressed my hand. She also pressed the reluctantly extended hand of Sherlock Holmes. 'So pleased to meet you both,' said she.

'They would like to ask you a few questions, my dear,' said Sir Hugh.

She gazed at us with very much the same expectant, misty look I had seen so often on her face as she gazed up at her leading men in the movies. 'Is it about the letter?' she asked.

'Precisely,' said Holmes.

'We were told that if anyone in the world can find the letter, *you* can, Mr Holmes.'

'I shall do my best,' he replied.

Lotte Linger was petite, with astonishing light in her crystal blue eyes. I was surprised she was so small a woman. She looked much larger on the screen. 'To think that a letter written by William Shakespeare was only recently in this room!' she said. 'The thought makes me feel quite in awe, and also quite exalted. I should like to have it under my roof once more, Mr Holmes, so that Hugh can properly present it to the whole world – for the whole world's treasure it truly is.'

'How long was the letter in this house?' asked Holmes.

She looked at her husband. 'Six or eight weeks, wasn't it Hugh?'

'About that.'

'And where was it kept?' asked Holmes.

'Locked in my desk in my study,' said Sir Hugh.

'Does anyone other than you have a key to the desk?'

'No one but Lotte,' he said.

'I believe the maid does, my dear,' said Lotte Linger. 'I sometimes have sent her to your desk for the fine stationery. I gave her the second key.'

'I am surprised,' said Sir Hugh.

'And could you give me an idea,' said Holmes, 'of how many visitors have been to the house during the time the letter was here?'

'Oh, I have no idea,' she replied. 'But I will consult my diary and write you a list and send it to you.'

'That would be excellent,' said Holmes. 'Now, Professor Blake, it must have required considerable self-control on your part to refrain from telling any of your colleagues of the existence of the letter.'

'It did indeed,' he replied.

'The only people you have told are Percy Ffoulkes, Rachel Random and your wife.'

'That is correct.'

'And Percy Ffoulkes,' said Holmes, 'has told no one but me and Mr Wilson. And we have told no one.'

'Quite right,' said Hugh Blake.

'And Ms Linger, you have told no one?'

'That is perfectly right, Mr Holmes. No one, other than the children.'

'The children?' said Sir Hugh. There was a tremor of shock in his voice that even his considerable self-control, and his upper-class poise, could not quite suppress.

Lotte Linger turned towards her husband so quickly that the gesture might have been defensive, or mere attentiveness. 'Of course, my dear! Surely there can be no harm in having told my children?'

'I am disappointed,' he said, and bit his lip thoughtfully. 'I had hoped the letter would be kept a secret.'

At that moment a blond young man burst effervescently through the doorway, almost prancing. 'Oh, heavens, Sir Hugh! We have known about the letter for weeks. But I certainly have mentioned it to no one, and I'm sure Marianne and Bart have been equally discreet.'

'I hope so,' said Sir Hugh. 'This is Alexis Gray, my stepson . . . Mr Sherlock Holmes, Mr James Wilson.'

Alexis wasn't quite so young as I had first thought, but his exuberance gave him an aura of youth. His handsome face seemed illumined by light emanating from his full head of blond hair, and he was brightly turned out in a navy blazer and pink shirt, grey slacks. He was perhaps in his forties. 'Sherlock Holmes!'

he cried with a laugh. 'The name is familiar – and even, strangely so, the face.'

'You are a writer, I believe?' said Holmes, with his usual genial reserve.

'I scribble occasionally.'

'Alexis is too modest,' said Lotte Linger. 'He is quite brilliant – and I should like my little bit of credit for that.' She laughed charmingly. 'My role as a mother has been important to me, Mr Holmes, far more important than all my roles as an actress – and more difficult. If you simply turn children into a pasture and lock the gate, you end up with animals. That seems to be the modern method. But I have tried to be both strict and attentive.'

'And you have succeeded, Mother! You were certainly strict . . . when you were present.'

'I was present much of the time, Alexis!'

'You were *a presence* at all times – writ large on the marquee of the world.'

She ignored him, and with a fond laugh she looked towards me and Holmes. 'I was a doting but strict mother. When one of my boys began putting firecrackers into the mouths of frogs, I corrected him harshly.'

'This way,' said Sir Hugh, in a tone suggesting faint impatience with all this banter. He ushered us into the central hall of the house where a party seemed to be in preparation. A large birthday cake rose imposingly on a table near the window. On top of the cake was a statuette of the actor David Garrick in that famous pose of his when, playing Hamlet, he saw the ghost of his father for the first time and spun about in amazement – black cape whirling, black hat falling. The previous year I had almost bought a print of that same famous scene at a shop in Museum Street.

'Then it is your birthday, Sir Hugh?' I said.

'It is,' he replied. 'To have seen Garrick must have been a splendid experience, don't you think! The greatest Shakespearean actor of the eighteenth century, perhaps of all time.'

The young woman with blonde hair was standing near the cake.

'Your Debussy was exquisite,' I said.

'Thank you.'

Sir Hugh introduced her as his stepdaughter, Marianne Hideaway.

She was slender, shapely, with a wide mouth and small nose and expressive eyes. Wonderfully bright and intriguing expressions fled across her face like wind over water. She laid a gift package by the cake.

Alexis Gray hurried to her, in his breathless way, and kissed her forehead. 'Where is your dear friend George Bingly? Does he scorn our festivities?'

She shrugged. 'He apologizes for not being able to come this afternoon. He did not have time.'

Alexis smiled. 'For those we love we find time; for the rest we find an excuse.'

'You are too hard on him,' said Marianne.

'I am too hard on everybody,' said Alexis. He flamboyantly plucked a biscuit from the side table, dipped it in hummus, and popped it into his mouth. He gazed at Marianne with admiration. 'Shouldn't you find a new boy friend?'

'Why would you say such a thing?' She looked a little shocked.

'I always think if you are going to be hurt by somebody, it is best to be hurt by somebody new.'

'I believe you dislike George merely because you dislike his poetry,' said Marianne.

'What better reason?' said Alexis. 'His poems, like most contemporary poems, are pretentious, private, plodding, obscure, self-indulgent, and not in the least memorable.'

'Heavens, Alexis!' said Lotte Linger. 'Most things are not memorable – neither people, nor poems, nor dinners at eight.'

'But *memorable language* is the very definition of poetry!' cried Alexis. 'A poem is language so full of sense that a person *wants* to remember it, and so full of music that he *can*.'

'Such language is rare,' said Lotte.

'Contemporary poetry seldom speaks of topics common people care about, and even more seldom sings. No wonder few read it and none remember it. Stop twenty people on the street and two will be able to quote Keats or Kipling – but none will be able to quote a contemporary cryptogram going under the name of "poem". It is easier to memorize a page of the telephone directory than to memorize a modern poem – and more rewarding. By contrast, who, having twice heard Bacon's lovely – *When to the sessions of sweet silent thought, I summon up remembrance of things past, I sigh the lack of many a thing I sought* – I say, who could not remember those lines?'

'But to compare other poets to Shakespeare – whether you claim The Bard is Bacon or Humpty Dumpty or the Queen of England – is quite silly,' said Sir Hugh. 'It is to compare flies to an eagle.'

'Poems nowadays,' said Alexis, 'should be compared with newspaper copy.'

'That is what I am doing in my new research project,' said Marianne. 'Comparing the language of journalism and poetry.'

'How odd,' said Lotte.

'Mr Wilson is a journalist,' said Sherlock Holmes. 'Perhaps you should talk to him.'

'Might I interview you sometime when I'm in London?' asked Marianne, turning to me brightly.

'It would be my pleasure,' I replied.

Sir Hugh stoked his briar pipe and emptied it, then dipped it into the humidor on the mantle, and packed the tobacco. He scratched a big match, which flared, and he hunched over (as pipe smokers so often do) and took quick deep sucks. A wreath of smoke enveloped his head. Fragrance filled the room.

'Very handsome pipe,' observed Holmes.

Sir Hugh brandished it in the air. 'Made by the incomparable Mr Sedly of Hexham.'

Everyone now gathered for the cutting of the cake.

Lotte held the knife.

Sir Hugh walked near the tall window and stood with a proprietorial air, hands in pockets, pipe dangling from lip, profile outlined in pale light.

Marianne leant to strike a match over the cake candles.

Alexis tilted a bottle of champagne with his right hand, held a glass in his left.

Holmes began to speak to Alexis, 'You mentioned that your mother . . .'

A loud *boom* rocked the room.

The window beside Sir Hugh became a star of jagged shards.

The bowl of Sir Hugh's pipe vanished.

The cake collapsed.

David Garrick exploded into black fragments.

Marianne Hideaway crouched.

Lotte Linger flung up her hands as if playing a scene in a horror film.

Alexis froze like a marble statue.

Holmes alone reacted, turning his head and saying sharply, 'That was a .600 nitro express!'

I reached for my handkerchief and dabbed blood from my cheek – for a fragment of glass had struck me.

Alexis Gray quickly un-petrified and came back to life, and calmly continued pouring himself a glass of champagne. 'Poor brother Bart,' he said. 'Someone ought to tell him to be more careful. He may kill somebody one of these birthdays.'

FIVE
Humble-Bees And Dragonflies

Marianne ran towards the barn. I followed close behind but had a deuce of a time keeping up. The rest of the party were strung out behind us. Marianne vanished through a side door, blonde hair bouncing. I plunged after her into hay-scented air. I passed a screen cage filled with humming bumblebees, then a cage filled with buzzing houseflies. Ahead in a shaft of dusty light I saw an old man lying on the straw-strewn floor beneath an open window. A slender young man knelt beside him. Near them lay a double-barrelled rifle. Apparently the old fellow had been knocked down by the recoil. He was clutching his shoulder and moaning.

'Why did you let him have the elephant gun, Bart!' cried Marianne.

Bart looked up at her. Dark locks fell across his white and angry brow. 'He wanted it,' he said.

'I am all right,' groaned the old man.

Bart Gray stood up and wiped his hands downward on his brown corduroy trousers. Then he wiped them on his Cambridge University sweatshirt. He wore a necklace of flat blue stones. He was good-looking in a haunted sort of way. His dark brown eyes shone with alarm. 'I fear Grandpa's shoulder is broken,' he said.

Marianne knelt to the old man.

A moment later Lotte Linger scurried through the barn door, appraised the situation, pulled out her mobile phone. 'I'm calling an ambulance,' she said.

Alexis sauntered in and picked up the massive rifle. He fondled the fine stock of Turkish walnut. 'If Grandpa had fired both barrels, he'd have killed himself.'

Hugh Blake pressed into the barn with Sherlock Holmes close beside him. 'It was my favourite pipe!' Sir Hugh lamented.

Alexis held up the rifle. 'What odd talents you possess, Mr Holmes! Few men in the world have ever seen a .600 nitro express, and fewer still have heard one. Yet you can instantly identify the sound of one at a hundred yards.'

'I say, that *is* a puzzle, Holmes,' said Sir Hugh, looking bemused. 'How *could* you have done that?'

'Some years ago in India,' replied Holmes, 'I encountered a very curious murder mystery. Its solution depended upon discovering the effect that the report of a .600 nitro express had on a Waterford wine glass when the glass was half-filled with claret, and when the gun was fired precisely thirty-three yards away. To find the answer, I spent a week at Simla experimenting with a .600 nitro express.'

'My uncle hunted tigers in India with that very gun!' croaked the old man, pointing feebly at Holmes.

'Then he was a fool,' said Holmes.

The old man seemed stunned by this blunt reply. He fell backwards as if shot.

'Why talk like *that*,' said Bart Gray, looking hard at Holmes. 'My grandfather is speaking of the old days!'

'So am I,' said Holmes. 'All the hunters I knew in India considered the .600 nitro express too big even for elephants. It had power enough to stop a dinosaur. It was too heavy to manoeuvre quickly, and so it was unsafe to use against tigers.' Holmes gestured towards Bart Gray's sweatshirt, and said, with easy geniality, 'I'm a Cambridge man myself. I'm told you do research there. May I ask, what sort of research?'

With two fingers Bart brushed the lock of hair from his brow. 'I work in biomedical miniaturization,' he said.

'I've never heard of that,' said Holmes.

'Few people have. But all soon will.'

'What does it involve?' asked Holmes.

'Give me a leafer small enough, and I will move the world!' cried Bart Gray.

'What's a leafer?' asked Alexis.

'Why, anything that sits on a leaf,' said Bart.

'My brother is nothing if not cryptic!' said Alexis.

'My whole life is encrypted,' cried Bart. He laughed almost hysterically. 'Even Alexis cannot decipher me!'

Hugh Blake turned his back on this brotherly banter and spoke confidentially to Holmes. 'I need to order a new pipe, Mr Holmes. And I intend to order one for you also – in appreciation for your efforts.'

'I will be profoundly grateful,' said Holmes.

'Cheerio.' Sir Hugh hurried away toward the house to make sure the ambulance was properly directed to the barn.

'Would you gentlemen be interested, at all, in seeing my laboratory?' asked Bart Gray, rather timidly. He seemed suddenly reticent, uncertain.

'I would,' said Holmes.

'That would be interesting,' I agreed.

The enigmatic Bart Gray led us to the far end of the barn and into a large room with white walls. On one wall hung a huge plasma television screen, on another a whiteboard filled with equations written with a blue marker. Two open windows looked out into a pasture where several horses grazed. Occasionally we could hear the squawk of a duck on the distant pond.

Holmes glanced at the whiteboard covered with blue formulae. 'Your equations baffle me,' said he. 'What kind of work do you do here, Mr Gray?'

'Let us set aside abstraction, Mr Holmes, and engage the real world,' cried Bart Gray, and he waved his hand towards the pasture. His mood was now so manic that I felt a bit uneasy.

Instantly a dragonfly swooped into the room through an open window. It circled around all of us and halted five feet from Holmes's head, hovering. On the huge television screen suddenly appeared a close-up image of Holmes's face. When the dragonfly backed away from Holmes, the image shrank slightly.

Bart Gray laughed. He wiggled a lever on the small control device in his hands . . . and the dragonfly flew away. Dizzying images swept across the television screen. The creature hovered in the open window. On the television screen appeared a green pasture and horses.

'Observe, gentlemen,' said Bart Gray, fiddling with the control device.

The dragonfly vanished.

Across the plasma screen streaked a surreal blur of trees and bushes, and then a tilting manor house appeared. The flying camera veered through an open window and into the house. I recognized the hall where Holmes and I had entered Widcombe Manor. The merry little flyer then moved in for a close-up of Holmes's Greek fisherman's cap hanging on the coat tree.

'I am working on a housefly version,' said Bart Gray. 'Imagine, gentlemen, a fly-spy who could sit all day on a terrorist's wall, transmitting images and conversation.'

Holmes's eyes were ablaze with interest. Yet he maintained his Victorian reserve. 'I find it impossible to imagine how you can make an engine so small, Mr Gray. You are to be warmly congratulated.'

'Engine? There is no engine, Mr Holmes.' Bart Gray smiled. 'It is a real dragonfly.'

'Truly?'

'With a video camera mounted on him.'

'How can you mount a camera on a beast so small!' asked Holmes.

'To tell truth, Mr Holmes, designing a camera and mounting it on *Anax imperator* was relatively easy. The greater difficulty has been to find a way of manipulating the insect by gaining direct control over its nervous system.'

'Astonishing,' said Holmes.

'The great scientific breakthroughs in this century, Mr Holmes, will not be in physics or electronics or any of the traditional hard sciences. The truly civilization-changing breakthroughs will come in the life sciences. Most people do not realize that very soon we will be able to resuscitate animals thought to be dead, using cellular manipulation techniques that allow us to regrow their original organs. Their livers, their hearts, even their brains will be regrown and restored. Astonishing though it may seem, this can be done – though most people don't believe it yet.'

'I believe it,' said Holmes. 'But I haven't decided yet whether I approve it.'

'Nobody will care whether you approve, Mr Holmes.'

'So I have learnt.'

'In addition, we will be able to create completely new animals from streams of genetic coding. Even at this moment, researchers in America are extracting the genetic code from the well-preserved remains of a woolly mammoth. Soon, Mr Holmes, we will be able to bring back into the world a creature that died out ten thousand years ago! I find such a thought inspiring.'

'Inspiring for everyone but the woolly mammoth,' said Holmes.

'Pardon me?'

'The woolly mammoth would be lonely in a world not his own,' replied my friend.

Bart Gray shook his head. 'No, no, Mr Holmes. You have no need to worry. You are confusing *resuscitation* with *creation*. I am not speaking now of resuscitation. The woolly mammoth would be created anew. He would never have seen an earlier age. He wouldn't be lonely, Mr Holmes. He would be newborn.'

'I suppose that would make a difference,' mused Holmes.

'He would have no memories of the ice age, no longing for times past.'

Holmes had fallen into a mood. 'Yes,' he murmured. 'Certainly that might make all the difference.'

The dragonfly shot back in through the window and landed on Bart Gray's wrist. 'Fly home, little courier,' he said, and he moved the control stick . . . the dragonfly lifted from his arm and darted into a large glass terrarium and vanished amidst the plants. 'He is free now,' said Bart, and he set the control device on a table.

'How long can your dragonfly live,' asked Holmes, 'with the modifications you have—?'

Just at that moment Alexis rushed into the room. 'The ambulance has arrived!' he cried. 'They are loading Grandpa.'

'I must be with him,' said Bart, and he darted away.

Holmes, Alexis and I strolled back towards the house at a more leisurely pace, past the silvery swan pond. In the great hall Professor Hugh Blake stood gazing at his collapsed birthday cake. 'An inauspicious beginning to my sixty-first year,' said he.

I gave Marianne Hideaway my card and told her to contact me if I might be of assistance to her in her research. She and the rest of the family, anxious to get to the hospital to be with Grandpa Gray, flew away like blackbirds. Holmes and I were the last to leave Widcombe Manor.

We walked out of the house and along the edge of the meadow towards my car. A light breeze blew from the west across a field. Holmes suddenly turned, left me, strode away across the grass. After fifteen yards he stopped, stooped, plucked at something, then stood up holding a handful of tiny violets. He gazed across the pond and shouted, 'Your game is up, at last!'

He turned and came striding back towards me, clutching the bright blue cloud of violets as if he were choking them. He lifted the flowers to his face and breathed deeply, closing his eyes. Then he climbed into the car and slammed the door. I drove down the tree-lined drive, turned toward the London road.

Holmes gazed at his violets, frowning.

A minute later he opened the window and tossed them on to the roadway.

SIX

A Devilish Passage in Paganini

Three days later, Detective Chief Inspector Lestrade of Scotland Yard strode into our flat on his weekly visit. Because of his grandfather's famous association with Sherlock Holmes many years ago, Lestrade had been assigned to keep tabs on Holmes's progress and to help him adapt to the twenty-first century. He shook Holmes by the hand, patted his arm. 'How are you feeling this morning?'

'Quite excellent.'

Lestrade was a lean man about our age, not tall, with a thin face and a pleasant but reserved manner. 'You look good, very good indeed. Dr Coleman's grand gamble appears to have been successful.'

'Evidently,' said Holmes.

'Any problems?'

'Occasionally something happens and I seem to be in a past time.'

'Have you told Dr Coleman?'

'I will. But first I want to do some experiments.'

'Experiments?' Lestrade looked at him doubtfully, seemed about to speak, then veered into another track. 'Well, I am particularly thankful this morning for Coleman's efforts, for I have a little problem, Holmes. I am hoping you might be willing to help me with it.'

'Of course!' Holmes rubbed his hands together, in anticipation.

'Perhaps you can give me a fresh point of view on the matter.

But before I forget . . .' Lestrade opened his case and pulled out a bound manuscript. 'I hope this is the one you wanted.'

'Excellent!' cried Holmes, taking it. His face shone like a child's who is getting a birthday gift.

'As you said, it was in the storage box of material Dr Watson rescued from your Sussex cottage.'

Holmes gazed at the bound manuscript. 'Last time I saw this was 1910. How perfectly amazing to see it here.'

I looked over his shoulder and read the title of the typescript: THE PLAYS OF SHAKESPEARE AND THE BACON DELUSION. *By S. Holmes.*

'By the by,' said Lestrade, 'when will Dr Coleman's account of your resuscitation appear in *The Lancet*?'

'I'm hoping never.'

'Hope what you will, Holmes; but be realistic. You must know his article *will* appear. Do face up to that fact. It will make headlines around the world; you will become famous once more. And you will become *infamous* amongst the crowd who believe that if men were meant to fly they would have wings, that life should not be tampered with, and that the dead should stay dead. When Coleman's article appears I am afraid you will simply have to face the music – and look as cheerful as you can.'

'I'll manage,' said Holmes.

'I am sure you will. Oh, by the way, I found this in the storage box under the manuscript – thought you might like to have it.' He handed Holmes a large black fountain pen.

Holmes gazed at it, a faint smile on his lips. 'I'd forgotten about this. I wonder if it still works.'

'Why not?' said Lestrade. 'Dried ink can usually be loosened with a solvent.'

Holmes began twisting the small top end that, in most fountain pens of that type, lowers and raises the piston to suck ink from a bottle. He kept twisting and twisting.

'Here, now!' said Lestrade. 'You'll break it if you keep twisting.'

'Not at all,' said Holmes. 'This is a Krueger pen.'

'Never heard of it,' said Lestrade.

'Let us see, gentlemen, how well-made the Krueger pen is, and how it has survived its long sleep.' Holmes unscrewed the cap. 'If you will move to the side just a little bit, Wilson . . . thank you.'

Holmes gripped the fat pen firmly, pointed it towards the wall, pressed the top . . . and his hand jerked.

A silvery dart thudded into the woodwork eight feet away.

'My god,' said Lestrade, walking towards the tiny metal dart.

'Don't touch it!' cried Holmes.

Lestrade backed away.

Holmes sprang to his feet. 'My brother dipped the point in curare. I have no idea whether the poison is still potent.' Holmes with difficulty removed the steel dart from the wall. I could see it was razor sharp. He carefully placed it back in the pen casing.

'That would go through a man's neck,' I said.

Holmes closed the pen and slipped it into his shirt pocket. 'A Krueger pen can be deadly at close range, even without the poison. Now, my dear Lestrade, you mentioned a problem?'

Lestrade sat down very lightly on a chair, crossed his leg on his knee. His mouth smiled pleasantly, but there was worry about his eyes. 'Last evening I had a terribly frightened man in my office, Holmes. I listened to his story, decided that his fears were groundless, reassured him, and sent him home. But after he had gone away I began to have doubts. I scarcely slept last night, worrying about the matter.'

'Pray, give me the details,' said Holmes, leaning forward with an intent expression on his face.

'I suppose you are aware of what happened four nights ago at the Capinelli violin concert?'

'I know only what the newspapers printed,' said Holmes. 'A loud popping sound, or bang, was heard, and two audience members were carried from the hall by medics.'

'Yes, and they were both music critics,' said Lestrade.

'That is very suggestive,' said Holmes.

'The worried man in my office yesterday was Maurice Pilkington, music critic for the *Guardian*. He was scheduled to cover the Capinelli concert but at the last moment he was unable to attend. He fears that someone intends to do him serious injury, just as was done to his colleagues. I assured him he had nothing to worry about. But last night I lay awake an hour thinking about the matter, and I began to wonder if I had made a mistake. This morning it occurred to me that since my grandfather occasionally sought your assistance, I should not be too proud to do so also.'

'I am only too glad to be of assistance,' said Holmes.

'Frankly, one of your intuitive leaps of logic might give me a new perspective on the situation, and set my mind at ease.'

Holmes leant backwards in his chair, took a deep breath. 'What further facts can you furnish me?'

'Only a few. Our investigation reveals that the victims were injured not by a pellet gun, as we had originally thought, but by miniature bombs that somehow had been placed on their bodies. We believe that tiny bombs were placed in their pens, and this theory is borne out by the nature of the wounds. Mr Wilkins had his pen in his shirt pocket, and he suffered injuries to the chest and stomach. Mr Bledsoe had his pen tucked behind his ear, and he suffered head injuries. We may learn more about the nature of these bombs after our laboratory has finished examining the evidence.'

Holmes laid his index finger across his thin lips, and he stared vacantly for a few seconds. 'Has it occurred to you, my dear Lestrade, that this incident might be connected with several other disturbances that occurred recently in London – specifically, the exploding lute during the performance of *A Midsummer Night's Dream*, and the exploding electric guitar in the Green Park pedestrian subway?'

Lestrade shook his head. 'I cannot discern any connection between those incidents and this one, Holmes – beyond the superficial one that all three cases involved musical performances.'

'And explosions,' said Holmes.

'I blush to say that we really don't know that all three incidents involved explosive devices. Between ourselves, the Green Park pedestrian subway incident was not properly investigated. It was a busker in a subway, and, well . . . it was an easy one to let slip through the cracks. Naturally, we have investigated the incident at the play, but so far we have been unable to determine what damaged the lute, or what caused the actor to fall. Was it a small explosion from a planted device that damaged the lute? Or did Titania's fairy inadvertently fire his popgun just as the scenery collapsed from some other cause, and crush the lute by falling on it? Both seem possibilities. One would suppose the cause should be obvious, but so far it isn't. Our lab has the remains of the lute and is working on it. I can tell you this, it was a very small explosion, if explosion it was at all.'

'That is the most curious feature of all these events,' said Holmes.

'What is?'

'The smallness of the explosions.'

'Do you think so?'

'Several months ago,' said Holmes, 'I came across a paper by a military analyst who argued that the greatest terrorist threat to mankind is not nuclear bombs that can blow up cities, but mini-bombs and microbombs that can damage individuals. He argued that microbombs, if spread widely throughout the population, would cause enormous psychological terror. They would affect individuals directly, in their own homes. No one would feel safe.'

Lestrade shrugged. 'The idea that terrorists would be able to spread microbombs throughout a population is fantastical. I can't really imagine it.'

'Most people can't imagine it,' mused Holmes. 'And therein lies the danger . . . tell me, Lestrade, did any music critic other than Wilkins and Bledsoe attend the concert?'

'No.'

Holmes tilted his head back and gazed at the ceiling a long while. Motionless. Then he began to shake his head, very faintly. Suddenly he sprang to his feet. 'I fear your Mr Pilkington may be in serious danger.'

Lestrade stood up. 'Really?'

'I fear the worst, Lestrade. You must contact Pilkington immediately. Warn him not to listen to any music.'

'What!' said Lestrade.

'It is absolutely crucial that he not listen to any music what-ever,' said Holmes. 'He must stay away from radios, concert halls, CD players. Tell him not to even whistle.'

Lestrade looked bewildered. 'If you say so, Holmes . . . but what—'

'Then you must bring him here. He must wear exactly the same clothes he was planning to wear the night of the concert. Also, he must have on his person all the items he would have taken to the concert – glasses, watch, pen, breath mints, pad of paper, and so on.'

'I have a busy day, Holmes . . . but if you think it important . . .'

'Crucial. Would two o'clock suit you?'

Lestrade nodded. 'I will be here at two o'clock with Maurice Pilkington.' He grabbed his case.

When he had gone, Holmes looked exceedingly cheerful. 'I'm off to perambulate in the park and ponder the curious case of the missing Shakespeare letter,' said he. 'Then I must return and practise my violin for several hours. I hope you won't mind, Wilson.'

'Fiddle to your heart's content,' I replied. 'I have a luncheon appointment.'

It was a little after eleven in the morning when I stepped into a little wine bar off Fleet Street to meet Freddy Dunne. He sat at our usual corner table. He was one of my old newspaper colleagues, originally from Chicago. I had been thinking about my visit to Widcombe Manor, and I asked Freddy if he knew anything about a writer called Alexis Gray.

'I know that he writes the "Delphi Diary" column in *Arts Weekly,* under the pseudonym Bif Carcanson,' said Freddy. 'His column is often provocative, sometimes wicked, occasionally wise. I understand he has a new book coming out. I can't recall what it is about . . . some sort of literary history, I think. I've never met the chap.'

After lunch I headed back to the flat. As I navigated through London towards Baker Street, yesterday's strange experiences at Widcombe Manor were much on my mind. I wondered if Holmes had gleaned any promising clues during our visit. I certainly had not. I had seen nothing that suggested anyone at Widcombe Manor had either the temperament or style to steal so much as a book of matches. What a strange group they were! There was Alexis holding forth grandly as if he were on stage, Grandpa Gray blowing off shots from an elephant gun or talking nonsense about India, Sir Hugh puffing on his pipe until it was shot out of his mouth, and Bart, the young mad scientist of the family, obsessed with tiny creatures and miniature cameras. Not to mention, of course, Lotte Linger floating like an ageing angel above the whole surreal scene. Only the lovely young Marianne Hideaway had seemed to me a normal person, a part of the real world. Amidst the quirks and turmoil she was a breath of sanity and sweetness.

I arrived back at the flat and had just taken my coat off when Lestrade arrived. With him was Maurice Pilkington, a portly, balding, slightly self-important, genial soul of fifty or so, with a rounded nose, merry eyes, jouncing jowls. He wore a pinstriped blue suit, vest, white shirt, pink tie, shiny black patent leather shoes. We four took seats by the window overlooking the green square.

'Your instincts are impeccable, Mr Pilkington,' said Holmes. 'You suspected you may be in serious danger, and you are – even at this moment.'

Pilkington heaved his big body forward on his chair. He pulled a large white handkerchief from his hip pocket. He mopped his shining brow, then fell heavily back against the chair as if he'd just been struck. 'You unsettle me, Mr Holmes.'

'I have learnt,' said Holmes, 'that you and your two injured colleagues reviewed Mr Capinelli's London concert last year, in March of 2008.'

'True,' said Pilkington.

'All three reviews struck me as quite negative when I read them on the Web.'

'Fair to say,' said Pilkington. 'They *were* negative, mostly.'

'All three took particular exception to the way Capinelli played Paganini's caprice number thirteen in B-flat minor.'

'Very true,' said Pilkington, nodding assent as he peered over the handkerchief drooping from his pudgy hand.

Holmes drew a folded paper from his inner jacket pocket. 'Here are a few lines from your review: *Few violinists could play this caprice so quickly as Mr Capinelli played it, and even fewer would care to. His blistering tempo transformed the music into a nearly unrecognizable blur. The prime virtue of this excessive speed was that the audience had to suffer only briefly.*'

Pilkington laughed good-naturedly, then admonished Holmes with a half-raised finger. 'A critic must be kind when he can, sir, but honest always. I feel obliged to warn the public about fiddlers who debase music for cheap effects that bring down the house.'

'Of course,' said Holmes.

'Surely, Holmes,' said Lestrade, 'you are not suggesting that Capinelli was so outraged that he tried to kill his critics with minibombs?'

'That doesn't seem likely. But let us pursue this matter a little further.' Holmes sprang to his feet and disappeared into his bedroom. A moment later he reappeared and walked towards us holding his violin.

Pilkington's face registered shock and dismay, and he swept

his chubby hand through the air – the one that held the hand-kerchief – as if to wave Holmes away. 'Oh, please, Mr Holmes, spare us, spare us. I never critique an amateur.'

'I wouldn't expect you to,' said Holmes.

'I'm very glad of that, because . . . my heavens!' Pilkington's eyes bulged. 'Is that a Stradivarius?'

'Quick eyes you have, Mr Pilkington. I bought this violin in a shop in Tottenham Court Road for fifty-five shillings. I considered it a bargain.'

'You jest!'

'Not at all. Of course, that was some years ago. Now, if you don't mind, I shall play it for you.'

Pilkington shrugged, held up his hands. 'Carry on. What will you play?'

'But first, you must take off all your clothes.'

Pilkington touched his right ear, tilting his head slightly. 'My heavens! I have seldom had such a thrilling offer.' He shuddered.

Chief Inspector Lestrade's imperturbable calm was shattered. A strange light crept into his dark eyes. 'What in God's name are you saying, Holmes! Are you feeling well?'

'Quite well,' said Holmes. 'You will pardon me if I get straight to the point, which is this: I believe Mr Pilkington is in deadly danger. A little experiment will prove whether I am right. If I am mistaken, I will offer my apologies. Stand up, sir, and disrobe! Wilson, would you be good enough to lend Mr Pilkington your dressing gown?'

Holmes's manner was so severe, so self-assured, and so unbending that we all simply did as he told us to do. Pilkington removed his jacket, tie, shirt, trousers, and laid them on a chair. He removed everything but his undershorts and stockings. Holmes bid me to take his clothing, plus his brief case, wrist-watch and glasses, and to pile it all on the hardwood floor in the middle of the dining area. Pilkington wrapped my dressing gown around him. It did not quite meet in the front, but it served to restore a little of his dignity. He sat uncomfortably on a wooden chair with his hands on his knees.

'The hearing aide,' said Holmes. 'You must remove it, please.'

Pilkington removed it. 'Be very careful with that,' he said. 'It is expensive.'

I put the hearing aide in his suit coat pocket, in the heap of clothing. Then Holmes put the violin to his chin and, with

something of the air of a showman, he proclaimed, 'Gentleman,
I shall now attempt Paganini's caprice in A minor, opus one,
number twenty-four – the identical piece that Antoine Capinelli
was playing two days ago when his performance was so shock-
ingly interrupted by groans that startled the audience.'

'You haven't played a note and already you have startled *us*,
Holmes,' said Lestrade.

'Yes,' nodded Pilkington, his jowls jiggling. 'Consider us very
definitely startled, Mr Holmes. I feel as if I am acting in a comic
opera – the madhouse scene, presumably.'

Holmes ignored this nervous commentary. He lifted the violin
to his left shoulder, raised his chin, positioned his horsehair wand
. . . and attacked the caprice. Notes leapt in wild profusion from
his violin, batted this way and that by his darting bow. I had not
imagined he could play so well. The Paganini caprices are devil-
ishly difficult.

He had not proceeded very far, however, when a loud BANG
made us all lurch in our chairs. The heap of clothes and personal
effects in the middle of the dining room floor had given a little
heave upward.

'My God!' cried Pilkington.

The clothes began to smoulder.

Lestrade darted into the dining room and grabbed a pitcher
of water from the table, and he doused Pilkington's smouldering
belongings.

Holmes calmly laid his Strad on the mantle, then knelt by the
heap of clothes and began to sort through them in gingerly
fashion. At last he held up a piece of melted plastic. 'Had you
gone to the concert two nights ago, Mr Pilkington, you might
now have been deaf – or worse. The microbomb appears to have
been planted in your hearing aide.'

'What did you say?' asked Pilkington, leaning toward him.

Holmes repeated his statement.

'How is that possible!' gasped Pilkington.

'A very good question,' said Holmes.

'I will interview Mr Antoine Capinelli immediately,' said
Lestrade.

'I cannot believe you will learn anything from him,' said Holmes.
'No artist has sufficient energy, time or resources to bomb his
critics in such a manner, even if he had sufficient anger.' Holmes
stalked across the room and flung himself into a chair, then threw

back his head and closed his eyes. 'Today we have learnt that someone is creating tiny explosive devices that are triggered by an audio signature. The targets so far have been a street busker, an actor, and three critics at a violin concert. Some very devious plot is afoot, Lestrade!'

'I do not follow you,' said Lestrade. He shook his head wearily. 'I am not convinced. I do not see the connection between those three incidents.'

'Music,' said Holmes.

'What!' Lestrade raised an eyebrow. 'We are looking for a man who doesn't like music? That would narrow the field considerably.'

'That would eliminate the field completely,' said Pilkington, as he buttoned his damp shirt. 'Have you ever met a person who doesn't like music?'

'*Beware*,' said Holmes, '*the man that hath not music in himself, Nor is not moved with concord of sweet sounds, Is fit for treasons, stratagems, and spoils!*'

'You surprise me again, Holmes,' murmured Lestrade. 'You produce the music of Paganini and the music of Shakespeare with equal ease.'

'*I have a reasonable good ear in music*,' said Holmes. '*Let's have the tongs and the bones.*'

Pilkington laughed. 'Let us have, rather, the A minor caprice on the Stradivarius. Would you be good enough to humour me, my dear Mr Holmes? You played the first bars so exquisitely that I crave the rest.'

SEVEN

Inspiration Atop the London Eye

For two weeks Holmes made little progress on either of the two cases in which he had become involved. The case of the Shakespeare letter languished. The mystery of the musical explosions did likewise. He grew more and more despondent. One morning he brought into our flat a box filled with sundry laboratory equipment, including a Bunsen burner, flasks, phials, beakers, glass tubes, and so on, and in his large bedroom he set up a laboratory. Thereafter he spent most of his days in his room, from which curious and offensive odours often wafted. Every afternoon at about three o'clock he emerged, hands stained with chemicals, and hurried out of the flat with scarcely a word. When I asked him what he was working on he always deflected my question, saying he would explain when he was more certain he would succeed.

One evening I returned from the city and walked directly from Baker Street station to Regent's Park for a bit of fresh air. I was surprised to see, afar off, the familiar gaunt figure of Sherlock Holmes strolling along one of the paths. He was moving in slow motion, with his head thrown back, breathing deeply, as if immersed in some sort of yogic meditation. Every ten or fifteen yards he would halt, pull a small notebook from his pocket, enter something in it with a pen, then continue strolling and breathing deep. Suddenly he lurched to the side of the walkway, sat down on a park bench, and began writing furiously in the green notebook. As I drew near he greeted me without even looking up, saying, 'My dear Wilson, you are smelling very *Roger et Gallet* – are you meeting a lady friend?'

'No such luck,' said I. 'Are you telling me I am too fragrant?'

Holmes closed the green notebook, waved it gently in the air. 'This notebook contains my own system.'

'System?' I said. 'For what?'

'I shall perfect it first, my dear Wilson, and then reveal it to you.'

Again the terrible thought struck me that Dr Coleman's resuscitation might have been only partially successful – and that Holmes, realizing he was sliding backwards and losing his mental faculties, had set about trying to find a way to halt the slide. It was typical of him that he would trust his own innovative abilities and chemical experiments rather than the institutions of modern medicine. I knew he was brilliant, yet his behaviour worried me. One morning he had invited me into his room to hand me a book, and on his dresser I had noticed, amidst the test tubes and flasks, a bottle labelled *Strychnine*. I feared he was taking great risks.

He now acquired a new habit: late-night walks. These nocturnal excursions began always on the stroke of midnight. I offered to keep him company on several occasions, but always he politely refused. One night he emerged from his chemical-reeking bedroom in a peculiarly cheerful mood.

'What's up, Holmes?' I ventured, looking up from a volume of Catullus.

'I think I may have discovered the effect I have been seeking,' he answered.

Before I could ask what effect that might be, he vanished out the front door.

Ordinarily I would never spy on a friend. But at that moment my angst got the better of my delicacy. Perhaps this was because I had just been reading the famous poem by Catullus describing how he visited his brother's lonely grave and said goodbye to him forever, the poem ending with the words *ave atque vale*, "hail and farewell". That phrase added to my fearful mood. I set down my book and, determined to learn the purpose of Holmes's late-night excursions, I descended our apartment staircase and hurried after him through the dark streets. He moved at so brisk a pace that I had to look sharp to keep up. He darted into Regent's Park, hurried along one of the shadowy paths. I followed, scarcely attempting to conceal myself, so anxious was I to keep him in range.

But despite all my efforts he suddenly vanished . . . like a fairy melting in moonlight. He was gone in the space of a single shadow.

I paused in the moon-shadow of a tree and gazed across the surreal moonlit scene. I looked out of the corners of my eyes, hoping to see more in this way. And yes, by and by I did see something. It was moving in the grass. I thought it must be a lost dog. Then I realized it was Holmes. He was crawling on his hands and knees. I could scarcely believe my eyes. Could he be hurt? But no, he was moving too quickly and with too much purpose. For four or five minutes I watched Sherlock Holmes crawling with astonishing swiftness across the grass, his face to the ground, moving this way and that, sometimes making little circles, gravitating slowly towards the line of bushes. He vanished. A slight shaking of the shrubbery was the last I knew of him.

For a long while I stood frozen, trying to decide what to do. Finally I turned and walked home, pondering. In the morning I rang up Dr Coleman and told him about Holmes's bizarre behaviour. I asked point blank, 'Could he be sliding backwards, his brain degenerating?'

'His behaviour is certainly bizarre,' mused Dr Coleman. 'But then, he has always been a strange individual – is that not so? I recall that when Watson first met Holmes, Holmes had recently been beating corpses with a stick to learn how much bruising could be caused after death. I also recall that Holmes once remarked to Watson, in a bragging vein, "I dabble with poisons a good deal." No doubt he is pursuing research on some arcane topic, just as he always did. I appreciate your call, Mr Wilson. But Holmes has an appointment with me in a week, and at that time I will evaluate him completely. I suspect that, far from indicating that something is amiss with him, his recent behaviour suggests that he is his old self. Let us hope so, anyway.'

I was not satisfied with this response, but I could do nothing.

One morning at breakfast, Holmes, to my surprise, suggested that we take an early morning walk in order to discuss the mystery of the missing Shakespeare letter. An hour later we were walking through Hyde Park and discussing the crime in all its aspects.

'You are an excellent sounding board,' said Holmes.

'Thank you,' I replied.

'Your conventional views often inspire me to greater mental effort.'

'Indeed?' I said. His supercilious attitude often nettled me. But I let the insult pass.

Holmes strode upright and briskly, one hand in his jacket pocket as if fumbling for a pipe. We paused on the banks of the Serpentine and silently watched the to-and-fro of ducks on the winking water. The quiet air was punctuated with their little *quacks*. But Holmes was not one for lingering long in one place, and soon we were striding along the cinder track of Rotten Row.

'Some small thing is missing, Wilson – an intimation, a hint, an imperceptible thread of colour to make the tapestry complete. Unless I can find that thread, I fear that William Shakespeare's letter may be lost.'

'Perhaps Rachel Random will remember something more, now that she has had time to recollect herself in calmness,' I said.

'Excellent!' he cried. 'Brilliant!'

He was in one of those extreme moods of his, suddenly flying higher than the tower of Westminster. But I knew that in a moment he might plunge into the depths of the Thames. 'No time like the present!' said I, and I slipped out my mobile and rang the office of Lashings and Bedrock. A woman's voice informed me that Rachel Random had taken the day off, and when I asked for Paul Primrose, she said that he also was off for the day. I then requested Rachel Random's mobile number, and the woman – to my surprise – gave it to me.

By this time Holmes and I were striding down Constitution Hill towards St James's Park. I rang Rachel's number and she answered with surprise in her voice. 'Hello?'

'Rachel,' said I, 'this is James Wilson, your uncle's old friend . . .'

'Oh, I know your voice, of course!' said she. 'Hello, James Wilson!'

I told her that Holmes wished to talk to her. She said she was just buying her ticket for the London Eye, and she asked where we were. I told her that, as luck would have it, we were very near to her, just passing Buckingham Palace. She sounded very happy to hear from me. But I realized that the joyous note in her voice must simply arise because she was happy at the prospect of seeing Holmes, for she was desperately hoping he could undo her terrible mistake. She said she would wait for us at the base of the great wheel.

Ahead I could see the London Eye high above the trees, the biggest Ferris wheel in Europe glittering like a pretty toy against the gauzy blue sky. As we crossed Westminster Bridge I spotted Rachel, her red hair and upright figure. Holmes and I met her, bought our own tickets, and soon we three were in a passenger capsule containing only ourselves and a group of elderly ladies from Blackheath.

'Ms Random,' said Holmes. 'Have you noticed anything strange or different in your daily life since the letter was stolen?'

'My whole life seems strange and different since then, Mr Holmes.'

'You've suffered a shock,' I said, solicitously.

'I suppose I appear calm and controlled,' she said, 'but that is only because I am good at faking. Since the robbery I have felt quite floatingly.'

'Have you noticed anything different in your colleagues, Ms Random? Any change in their behaviour or attitudes?' asked Holmes.

'I think I may say that Mr Lashings and Mr Bedrock have

been unusually considerate and understanding. I didn't expect this of them. As to the rest, Mr Gaston has been his usual aloof and grumpy self. Paul is the ebullient same. Over noon hour last Friday he and I went shopping for clothes for me, just as we always have done. He has a wonderful eye for the "just right" thing. His wife is very understanding – at first I thought she might object to Paul buying clothes for a redhead.' She laughed.

The London Eye had lifted us till now we looked down from quite a height at the river to the east. I gazed with pleasure at the shining new Hungerford Bridge, so ship-like and nautical with all its bright spars. A silvery train – looking like a toy – slid across the bridge towards the gleaming new Charing Cross Station. I tried to remember what the smoky old Victorian station had looked like, but already I had trouble picturing it. How quickly, I thought, the past slips away!

'Since the theft,' said Holmes, 'has anything occurred in your life that strikes you as unusual?'

'Unusual, Mr Holmes?'

'I don't know exactly what I mean,' said Holmes. 'I was hoping you would know.'

'Just the *usual* unusual things, I guess I could say. It is unusual to lose something, but I'm always losing things. So it's not *that* unusual.'

'What did you lose this time?'

'My sunglasses. I'm beginning to think I am a careless person. I get very upset over even trivial losses. You can imagine what losing Shakespeare's letter has done to me.'

'Never mind,' said I. 'It is normal to be upset. Holmes was very upset when he lost his pipe the other day.'

'I had owned that pipe a very long time,' said Holmes. 'I could hardly avoid being upset.'

Rachel laughed. 'Well, it is even worse with me, Mr Holmes. I had owned my sunglasses only an hour when I lost them – of course, it was the day after the letter was stolen, so I was flustered already and maybe that explains it. I had just purchased the sunglasses, so I was very conscious of them, and I was trying so hard *not* to lose them. And I know perfectly well that just before I stepped into the restaurant I had carefully put them into my coat pocket, safe in their metallic case. I remember making sure they were deep in the pocket before I hung my coat. I felt them. After I had eaten lunch I put on my coat and walked into

the street, and when I reached into my pocket the glasses were
gone. I fretted over that puzzle the rest of the day. The other
upsetting thing was that my grocery list went missing from the
other pocket. They'd stolen that also. I suppose they'd just rifled
through the pockets and grabbed everything. So I had to write
out my grocery list all over again.'

'Oh, look,' cried one of the elderly ladies from Blackheath.
'Can you imagine seeing Parliament from so high? It looks quite
different, doesn't it?'

Holmes seemed to have frozen. He stared out the window as
we slowly rose higher and higher. He put his finger tips together
and raised his prayer-like hands to his lips, and he continued to
gaze out over the vast and unfolding city. He had vanished,
momentarily, into another realm.

'Your uncle Percy is very much taken with you,' I said to
Rachel. 'When I met him in Wales a few months ago, your name
was on his lips before we had spoken ten minutes.'

'He has always doted on me,' she said. 'I love my Uncle
Percy. If he weren't my uncle, I think I'd marry him.' She touched
my sleeve and laughed softly as she spoke. She was one of those
people who just naturally reach out to touch others. 'He always
speaks very highly of you – telling me how he knew you first
at Eton and then at Oxford. He has told me tales of your prowess
as an oarsman, your bravery in battle and your brilliance in
reporting. He sometimes becomes really quite tedious on the
subject of James Wilson.'

'Heavens,' I said, 'the man is deluded by old friendship.'

'I wonder,' she said.

'Tell me,' said Holmes, turning towards her suddenly, 'what
was the restaurant?'

'Restaurant?'

'Where you lost your glasses.'

'Farnham's Bar and Fish Emporium. I eat there every Friday
with my girlfriend, Jill.'

'And what coat was it?'

'The one I'm wearing.'

Holmes looked her up and down. 'Very lovely. Rather well
made.'

'Paul helped me choose it. He has plans to design his own
women's clothing line – that's his dream. Meanwhile, he gives
himself pleasure and makes a bit of money by doing alterations.'

'Did this coat require alterations?'

'Not really,' she said, laughing. 'But Paul felt the coat was not quite perfect, and he has a wonderful eye. So I trusted him. He shortened the sleeves and the hem, just ever so little. I could scarcely tell the difference afterwards.'

'The coat looks very new,' said Holmes.

'I bought it only a fortnight before I met you, Mr Holmes.'

'May I ask where you bought it?'

'At a little place in Regent Street.' She opened her purse and looked in. 'Here, here's their card.' She produced it and gave it to him. 'They only had a few of these coats left, but if you need a gift for a lady, it is quite a nice shop.'

I could see a glitter in Holmes's eyes. And then, as the wheel slowly lowered us towards the Thames, Holmes sighed a little. At last he turned to Rachel and said, 'I'm afraid I must soon shock you.'

'Concerning the stolen letter?'

'Yes,' he replied.

Disappointment fell over her face like a veil. 'Is the letter lost forever!'

'On the contrary,' said Holmes. 'There is every chance of finding it. For I now know who stole it.'

'Really!' she said.

'There can be little doubt,' he said. 'But we must hurry. Look, look.' He waved his hand at the vast city laid out below us like a tourist map, all shining in sun and swept with shadow. 'There is the city where William Shakespeare worked, and below us is the same broad river that he crossed many a time, and I have no doubt that the rabble of humans below us have the same obsessions as the rabble that Will Shakespeare bumped against so long ago in crowded London streets, and put into his crowded plays. And his letter is out there somewhere if I can but find it! It has taken me too long. What a fool I've been! If I fail in this, I shall never forgive myself!'

This speech he delivered with great urgency, and with a passion worthy of a fine actor. He delivered it with such flare and gesture that Rachel looked a little shocked, and the elderly ladies in our car were, for a moment, stilled . . . until one murmured, 'He does carry on, doesn't he?'

'Can you inform us who it is, Holmes?' I asked. 'We are most interested.'

He didn't seem to hear me. He was on another channel. 'We must act quickly, Watson – Wilson. The criminal hardly matters. The letter we must, at all costs, recapture. How slowly this wheel turns!'

'Like Fortune,' said I.

'Call someone on your mobile, Wilson. Ask them to speed it up.' He flung his fingers at me imperiously.

'There is no way to speed it up, Holmes,' I said. 'And you can't jump. So you had best have patience – I know patience is not your strong suit.'

'I suppose not.' He laughed nervously.

He was quivering. I realized that as soon as he stepped off the wheel he would dart away like a rabbit, and I – and even the bold-striding Rachel Random – would have trouble keeping pace with him.

EIGHT
Secret Alterations

Our taxi glided through a wasteland of bleak brick apartment buildings. A few sooty trees along the pavements looked as if they had given up and would grow no more. Somebody's washing hung from a third-storey window. Then I saw the police van parked outside Paul Primrose's apartment. Chief Inspector Lestrade answered our knock and ushered us into a ground floor flat, which was grim but tidy. A tiny vase of daffodils graced the coffee table. A print of Renoir's *On The Terrace* hung above the easy chair.

Paul Primrose sat on an old black sofa next to his wife. Dorothy Primrose was a slim woman of thirty who looked old. Her straight brown hair fell to her shoulders. Her lips smiled politely. But her brown eyes were frightened, her thin hands nervous. Paul Primrose, who had seemed so shining and ebullient in the office in New Bond Street, suddenly looked so old that for an instant I was not sure I recognized him. A little girl sat sober-faced on the couch between them, big-eyed, with ringlets of dark hair falling to her cheeks. She held a doll. Lestrade introduced the

other police officer, Sergeant O'Malley. O'Malley was a big man
with red tufts of hair around his big ears.

'We only just arrived ourselves,' said Lestrade.

'In that case,' said Holmes, 'perhaps the best thing would be
for me to tell you how the letter was stolen, and then –' looking
at Paul – 'you may correct me, sir, if I am wrong.'

Paul made a gesture of acquiescence, shrugging his shoulders
and opening both his hands.

'You see, Lestrade,' said Holmes, 'Mr Primrose somehow
managed to learn that a particular letter, thought to have been
written by William Shakespeare, was going to be brought to
Rachel Random for examination. Mr Primrose then devised a
subtle plan for stealing the letter when it arrived. It happened
that he had recently helped Ms Random buy a long mauve coat
of lamb's wool from a shop in Regent Street – this in his role
as her fashion consultant. To prepare his plot to steal the letter,
he hurried back to the shop in Regent Street and purchased a
second coat, identical to the first. Then he suggested to Ms
Random that her new coat might be made to fit just slightly
better if the sleeves and hem were altered, and she agreed. Mr
Primrose brought the coat here to his home where he made the
promised alterations, no doubt using that sewing machine in the
corner of this very room. But he also made one large alteration
that he had not promised: he cut a hidden pocket into the side
lining – perhaps a zippered pocket – a pocket which could be
reached only from the inside of the coat. An expert seamstress,
which this gentleman most definitely is, might create a zippered
pocket so subtly obscured by the surrounding fabric that even
the owner would be unlikely to notice it. He then returned the
coat to Ms Random. She did not notice much change in the fit,
but was pleased.

'Mr Primrose knew that the Shakespeare letter would be brought
in by Sir Hugh Blake, the famous Shakespeare scholar, but he
did not know when. He simply had to wait. Sir Hugh called for
an appointment ten days ago, and that same day he arrived at
Lashings and Bedrock. He had a conference with Ms Random
in her office and, leaving the letter with her, he departed at a
little after five o'clock. Uncharacteristically, Mr Primrose stayed
after hours and busied himself with filing duties. Mr Gaston
always worked in the evening until five forty-five, then left, and
so he was in the office when the theft occurred.

'Not many minutes had passed before Paul Primrose, looking straight down the hallway from his desk, saw Ms Random step out of her office and into the WC. Here was his brief window of opportunity. He hurried down the hall to her office and on the desk he spotted the envelope containing the Shakespeare letter. Doubtless he slipped the letter out of the envelope to make sure it was what he assumed it to be. He then hurried to the coat rack that stands just inside Ms Random's office door. Her coat was hanging there. He slipped the envelope into the secret pocket he had created in the lining of the coat. Then he ran down the hallway to the emergency exit stairwell. As he ran down the emergency staircase, which makes two turnings before reaching the emergency door at street level, he hollered, "Stop!" He then pushed open the emergency door, setting off the alarm.'

As Holmes talked, Paul Primrose sat on the couch looking as if struck. Lifeless. Without saying a word he had already admitted his guilt. The woman was looking down at the child, and she touched the little girl's hair. The child was clutching the doll. All three looked fearful.

'And what, Mr Holmes,' said O'Malley, 'was the particular point of this elaborate charade?'

'Simply to explain why the letter was suddenly missing,' said Holmes. 'Suddenly it appeared that a thief had taken it. The thief and the letter would be sought for in the streets of London, though both were still on the premises of Lashings and Bedrock.'

'A pretty pass for the police!' muttered O'Malley. 'Then Will Shakespeare's letter was right in the car with us, and was with us at the station all the time we were questioning the poor lass, and she all white with worry, for she wore that very coat.'

'Exactly,' said Holmes. 'Is it not so, Primrose?'

Primrose stared at Holmes without expression. 'Quite so, Mr Holmes. And I wish to God I hadn't had to do it.'

The woman, still looking downward, touched his arm.

'And now we come to the part of the scheme where the error was made,' said Holmes. 'The instant I learnt Ms Random had lost her new sunglasses, I suspected what had happened. When I learnt she had also lost her shopping list, my suspicion became almost a certainty. I realized that Mr Primrose, as Ms Random's supposedly good friend—'

'I *am* her good friend!' said Primrose in a strangled voice.

'However that may be,' said Holmes, severely, 'the theft

occurred on a Thursday, and you were aware that on Fridays
Rachel Random always had lunch with a friend at Farnham's
Bar and Fish Emporium. I presume – judging by the expression
on your wife's face at this moment – that at this point you
involved your wife in the plot. I presume your wife wore the
second mauve coat to Farnham's that day, and hung it on the
coat rack near Ms Random's coat. Meanwhile, Ms Random and
her friend were just round the corner eating in the dining room.
Perhaps your wife went into the bar for a quick drink, to make
it all look natural. Then, as she left the restaurant, she made
certain to take Ms Random's coat and leave the other identical
one. Later she must have noticed the sunglasses and shopping
list in the pockets, but by then it was too late to go back and
set things right. She therefore proceeded home.'

Dorothy Primrose looked up. 'You are quite wrong, Mr Holmes.
I had *two* drinks at the bar. One was not nearly enough. But after
the second I felt perfectly courageous. And I took the other coat
and walked out into the hum of London traffic feeling quite elated,
quite normal, and quite victorious!'

'Where is the letter?' said Holmes.

'Gone,' said Paul Primrose. 'Taken.'

'By whom?'

'By the man who crippled me. He had a faint accent. German,
I think. Or Swedish.'

'He paid us five thousand pounds,' said Dorothy Primrose. She
went to a cabinet and brought out a fat envelope. 'It is all in here.'
She handed the money to Lestrade. 'This has been a nightmare.
It has been awful. We didn't dare spend it or deposit it.'

'Did he give you a name?' asked Holmes.

'He said his name was Sigvard and that he worked for clients
in Egypt,' said Paul Primrose.

'Not bloody likely,' said Sergeant O'Malley.

'He first came here on a Saturday afternoon,' said Primrose.
'Dorothy was working, I was here with the child, and there came
a knock at the door. He was a nice looking man, older, blond.
Dressed in expensive leisure clothes and carrying a small
umbrella. He said he was in the fashion industry, had heard about
me, and had a business proposition. He asked if he might come
in. I invited him into the sitting room. He told me directly that
he wanted me to steal a letter from Lashings and Bedrock. He
said he would pay five thousand pounds for my trouble. I could

hardly believe what I was hearing. I laughed at him outright, said I was not a criminal. He didn't argue, Mr Holmes. He said not a word. The umbrella was actually a short iron truncheon. He smashed my leg with it, and I went down. The child saw.'

'He hit Daddy!' said the little girl, raising her doll high over her head. Not smiling.

'I can tell you, Mr Holmes, the pain was excruciating, and seemed to make his next words burn in me. He said that I had a choice between five thousand pounds in cash or a broken back, a dead child and a dead wife. He told me he would soon stop by my office with the first one thousand pounds, and that if any police were alerted I would return home to find my family dead. He said it in such a way that I believed him.'

'Can you describe the man?' asked Lestrade.

'About six feet, late fifties, blond hair stylishly cut, very blue eyes, wearing a blue Turnbull and Asser shirt, Gucci grey suede jacket, Moreschi Davide shoes. He had wonderful taste in clothes, which somehow made his explosion of violence all the more . . .' Paul Primrose shook his head in anguish and for a moment couldn't go on. He finally took a deep breath and said, 'Terrible! Talking to him was like . . . like standing next to a bomb and wondering when it would go off.'

'And did he come round to your office as promised?' asked Holmes.

'One day he just appeared, handed me an envelope. It contained one thousand pounds and a note informing me that a certain Professor Hugh Blake would deliver the letter soon. He was right. On Thursday that week Hugh Blake called, made an appointment for four thirty that afternoon. By then I had already made my plans for stealing the letter – it was all just chance, really. Rachel and I had just bought the coat in Regent Street, so the plan occurred to me rather naturally. Almost without effort. These were the most terrifying two weeks of my life. I don't know if you can quite understand. This man made it sound as though he had armies behind him, multitudes of shadowy characters who could eliminate me in the winking of an eye. I felt impotent. I wanted done with it. The bone in my lower leg was crushed and the doctor had told me I might never completely recover. The pain reminded me every day why I had to steal the letter.'

Holmes looked at Lestrade. 'There is a security camera in the

ground floor lobby of Lashings and Bedrock. Can it provide a
picture of this man who calls himself Sigvard?'

Lestrade nodded. 'If Mr Primrose can tell us the time of his
visit, the task will be easier.'

'I can tell you exactly,' said Primrose. 'It was on the second
of March at four thirty p.m.'

'Then we will get the picture,' said Lestrade. 'And after you'd
stolen the letter, how did you hand it over to Sigvard?'

'He came by here one morning when Paul was at work,' said
Dorothy Primrose. 'He checked the Shakespeare letter only
briefly, then slipped it into the inner pocket of his sport coat.
He handed me an envelope containing four thousand pounds in
hundred-pound notes. He said, "Now you just forget about this
whole affair and spend your money, madam." And he walked
away down the street.'

'Did either of you look at the letter while it was in your possession?' asked Holmes.

'No,' said Paul.

'I couldn't have looked at it, for it made me sick,' the woman
said. 'It was a nightmare, the whole thing.'

When Holmes and I left, Lestrade was still talking to Primrose
and his wife. I wondered how the eyes of the law would view
them, and what would happen to them.

That evening I drove up to Hampstead Heath to visit my old
friend Percy Ffoulkes at his home. I wanted to report on the
progress of Sherlock Holmes's investigation. Rachel Random
was there and she enthusiastically whipped us up a delicious
meal which we ate as light faded over the heath. They were
astonished when I explained how Paul had engineered the theft.

'Poor man!' said Rachel. 'What will happen to him?'

'I wondered the same thing,' I said. 'I am sure he has legal
problems.'

'My main concern,' said Percy, 'is what has happened to the
Shakespeare letter.'

'Holmes seems to think that some member of Professor Blake's
own family holds the clue to the letter's whereabouts, for – other
than you, Percy – they were the only ones who knew about the
letter. And I suppose you have told no one?'

'No one at all,' he said. 'Only Rachel.'

'My understanding,' said Rachel, 'was that Professor Blake
had told only his wife and Uncle Percy, and no one else.'

'It appears that Lotte told all her children,' I said.

'Oh, of course she did,' said Percy. 'Lotte never knew the meaning of a secret. All the world to her is a blue sky.'

'But I was surprised how much her indiscretion upset Sir Hugh,' I said.

'Oh, it would. He is not quite able to cope with the complications he finds surrounding him. He has thrown himself amidst a very complicated family – it was certainly too complicated for me . . .'

'For you?'

Rachel laughed. 'Uncle Percy dated Lotte for a while.'

'I am astonished,' I said.

'Yes,' said Percy. 'For a few years after Lotte had divorced her second husband – that utter cad Eldon Hideaway – she and I used to see a good bit of each other. She was often here to the house.'

'She was a very elegant woman, and she took great notice of me,' said Rachel. 'Which won me over, of course. She sometimes brought her little girl with her, Marianne.'

'So you know Marianne Hideaway!' I said, in surprise.

'Oh, certainly,' said Percy. 'A lovely child. She's at Oxford now, you know. Working on her own projects and also, I understand, doing research for Hugh.'

'Quite beautiful and quite brainy,' said Rachel.

'Lotte,' said Percy, leaning back in his chair, 'is a woman who is gracious and blunt, thoughtful and thoughtless, careful and careless. She has a great talent for changing, for feeling a hundred emotions a minute. I found her to be always exciting and often exhausting. It was I who introduced her to Hugh.'

'I didn't know that,' I said.

'I thought he had the temperament required – which I certainly didn't. To be with Lotte, my dear James, one needs to be as calm as the sea, and not mind tidal waves. It was all just a little too difficult. My energy and hers added up to too much. And the other thing was that Bart, for some reason, didn't like me. I could never think why. Slim and skulking young Bart seemed to be always lurking about and scowling, ever disapproving of something. I could not, for the life of me, tell what displeased him. Lord knows, I tried to win him over. Perhaps I was too civil. Now, James, if it had been *you*, I suppose you would have taken the young man out behind the barn, lifted him up against the boards with one arm, and given him such a thrashing with the other hand that he would never have skulked again. And you would have asked him what ailed him, and you would have met his objections squarely, and all would have been well. But I just wasn't up to it, I'm afraid.'

Rachel looked at me, and her red hair fell to her shoulder as she tilted her head. Her eyes were very green, and her skin was strangely perfect in the last light of day slanting through the dining room windows. 'Are you the sort of person, James, who thrashes people?' she asked me, coyly.

'Oh, heavens!' cried Percy, rising to his feet and walking to the sideboard, and picking up a new bottle of wine. 'You should have seen him at Eton, my dear Rachel. Wilson looks very civilized and proper in polite company, but at Eton we knew him as the heroic sort he really is – captain of the rowing team, envy of all the younger boys, always walking about looking rather splendid and invincible.'

'I had no idea anyone viewed me in *that* way,' I said.

'No, you wouldn't,' said Percy. 'You were too unselfconscious, which is part of the reason you always seemed so graceful and impressive. Remember Eric Eagle?'

'Oh, yes,' I said.

Percy laughed, and looked earnestly at his niece. 'Eagle was a very big boy who had a very rich father. Wasn't the old man in shipping or something, Wilson? Anyway, young Eagle imagined he could push around whomever he wished at Eton. He was a bully and for some reason he had it in for me. I remember one day Eagle almost had me crying in the quad, but Wilson happened along and warned Eagle to leave the younger boys alone. Eagle went away, but with a sneer on his face meant to prove he wasn't afraid of Wilson. As soon as he had the chance, of course, he was back to his bullying. For a long while Eric Eagle was a great dark threat floating on my landscape, blotting all my joys. And then came that day by the river, the day of reckoning for Eric Eagle . . . do you remember, Wilson?'

I was amused to see Percy so animated, and I was rather looking forward to hearing the story again, to refresh my memory.

Percy took a sip of wine, and set down the glass, magisterially, and as he told the tale he looked mostly at Rachel, who seemed terribly amused at just about everything her uncle said.

'One day I was walking with two friends through the fields by the Thames, at one of the bends above Eton Bridge, when Eagle caught up to me and began asking me about some girl he'd seen me talking to. He grabbed my shoulders and spun me around and kicked me in the rear. I fell face forward on to the earth. Then Eric Eagle stomped on me. As I got to my hands and knees I was hurting badly. I can see it as if it were happening even now: my hands on the grass, Eagle's legs, the blurry river in the distance. And the smell of green grass and mud. I staggered to my feet, and then I heard a distant shout, "To the bank, Grimsby!" – and dimly I realized that the voice was James Wilson's. I looked, and there he was out on the river, rowing amidst a crew, and Grimsby was the coxswain. My heavens, what a sight. That racing shell veered and came straight towards the shore, with all those boys rowing it furiously, like slaves rowing a Roman galley or something. What I remember most of all is how Wilson looked as he sprang towards the bank – that picture has been etched in my memory, indelibly. Like a ballet dancer, he was. Or a pirate. In my superheated imagination he seemed almost like a god as he landed lightly on the bank and came bounding up through the grass behind Eagle, and he said, "Eagle, I've had enough of you!" and he grabbed Eagle by the shoulder and spun him. Then, using just his left arm, he hit Eagle hard in the chest with the flat of his palm. I remember Eagle's head sort of jarring forward on to his chest, as if maybe it wasn't fastened on tight. And then Wilson smacked him again, and again, *bam bam*, knocking him back another pace each time. And I must say, James, you looked rather splendid – your muscular arms, your white shirt – a nice contrast to Eagle and I who were, of course, in our school uniforms. And then, my dear Rachel, Wilson gave his memorable little speech: *Eagle, if I ever find you bullying Ffoulkes again, or making a joke of his name, I will rearrange your face so you won't recognize yourself in the morning mirror. Oh, do not smile, foolish fellow! For I never make a threat or a promise that I won't carry out. You are no eagle, but a worm, and if you cross my path again, or so much as cross me with a look, I mean to make you meat for robins.*

'For a moment Eagle's face twisted in anger, and his lips screwed up to say something. But there was horror in his eyes. He turned and hunkered off across the field, and the boys nearby began to shout and jeer at him.'

I sipped the claret and smiled. Percy was very animated when he talked.

'And the next day,' said Percy, 'a group of us boys went down to London to see *Macbeth*. Afterwards I remember thinking that not a speech in Shakespeare's play could touch James's magnificent extempore speech on the banks of the Thames.'

'By the way,' said Rachel, 'there is a new production of *Macbeth* in London. Would you two like to go.'

'Of course!' cried Percy. 'Wilson?'

'Certainly,' said I.

'Then let us set a date,' said Rachel. 'And I shall get the tickets, and we shall all go together.'

NINE
Lars Lindblad Appears

Holmes placed his soft-boiled egg in the egg cup and knocked off the top with a knife. He applied salt and pepper, then deftly dipped the tip of his spoon into the blurry mass for the first bite.

I looked back at my morning newspaper and laughed. 'I swear, Holmes, we English must be the world's most eccentric race. Every day I find news of some character who behaves outrageously. Yesterday it was a man in Fulham who had been pronounced dead two days, then had the bad taste to sit up at his own wake and demand a ham sandwich – causing two visitors who had come to view his body to faint, and a third to have a heart attack.'

'A similar thing happened in Naples in 1897,' said Holmes.

'You always deflate me with your compendious knowledge,' I said.

'I don't mean to, my dear Wilson.'

'And here's today's bit of London *exotica*, on page four. Last evening an architect was, let me see . . . *was walking across Westminster Bridge when the large portfolio case he was carrying suddenly burst into flame. According to witnesses, he flung the case into the Thames, staggered across the sidewalk, tumbled into the roadway, and was struck dead by a bus.*'

Holmes's hand froze over his egg cup. He looked at me with that alert and hawk-like stare so characteristic of him in tense moments. 'Would you mind reading that again, Wilson?'

I read it again.

'What time did this occur?' Holmes asked.

'Midnight, exactly.'

He pondered . . . 'Midnight.'

'Exactly.'

'Then I will tell you the name of the architect involved.'

'If you can do that, Holmes, you are a wizard, for there must be ten thousand architects in London.'

'Believe me, Wilson, I hope I am wrong. Otherwise this is yet another incident in a crime spree that seems to be accelerating – first the busker in the Green Park subway, then the exploding lute in Shakespeare's play, next the violin concert explosions . . . is the man's name Ian Fiero?'

I crushed the paper together and laid it aside, and took up my muffin. 'Why do I bother to doubt you any more? Carry on, Holmes! The explanation is due. Who is Ian Fiero?'

'Have you not heard the name?'

'It is vaguely familiar,' I replied.

'You probably will remember that he is the fellow who recently tried to wrap Parliament in red tape . . .'

'Ah, yes.'

'. . . but he was arrested before he could get his ladders in place, and the police confiscated his spools of tape. It has always been a matter of debate amongst the *cognoscenti* whether Fiero is an "urban landscape artist" of the *avant-garde* variety, as he claims to be, or is a genuine architect, or whether he is merely a self-promoter who bluffs people into giving him prizes for his work. He designed what he called a "cubescent cathedral" in Spain, which won a prize but offended everyone. He designed an arts centre in Newcastle which lasted only a season before heavy rains collapsed the roof. But Fiero gained notoriety mainly for artistic schemes which he proposed but never completed, such as the Parliament red tape fiasco. Or such as burying the Wellington Monument half in sand and renaming it "Ozymandias". Or such as dyeing the Thames red and dumping in a hundred thousand biodegradable dummies to represent Iraqis killed by Tony Blair's warmongering policies. Several weeks ago he proposed – in honor of Britain's subservience to the US – painting the clock faces of Westminster blue, painting the tower white, and installing red fluorescent lights on the clock hands. This outrageous proposal occasioned an article about him on the Internet, which I happened to read.'

'I am astounded by the number of curious facts you pick up, Holmes.'

'My *modus operandi* depends upon doing so, and is simplicity itself: gather a chaos of facts, use intuition to extract the relevant ones, and use imagination to form them into a theory.'

'You make it sound almost automatic.'

'Hardly. It is, in fact, tedious. But Imagination cannot create out of Void, only out of Chaos. That is why the first step must be to gather a mass of fact through careful observation. Out of the chaotic mass usually only a few facts are required to create a brilliant solution – but noticing those few and putting them in the proper order often requires both imagination and logic. You told me an architect was walking on Westminster Bridge when his portfolio exploded. You also said it happened at midnight, whereupon I deduced that the chimes of Big Ben were then sounding. Recent explosions in London have been touched off by musical sounds and have been designed to injure an artist's body, his audience, or his performance. Ian Fiero planned an artistic endeavour involving the Big Ben clock tower. Ergo, when the bell of that clock tower rang and an architect's portfolio exploded, the victim was very likely Ian Fiero.'

'You make it sound as certain as Euclid.'

'Hardly,' said Holmes. 'It is a matter of probabilities, which is to say a matter of educated guesswork.'

'I am beginning to think that your intuition, Holmes, is the equal of your logic.'

'Intuition is a version of logic that overleaps certain steps in order to reach a conclusion quickly.' He shrugged. 'Of course, only someone who thoroughly understands the nature of logical steps can sense when it is safe to overleap them.'

'You have acquired a penchant recently, Holmes, for speaking in paradoxes.'

'True intuition is almost the diametrical opposite of leaping to conclusions, which is mankind's common fault.'

'You are sounding very *Zen* today, Holmes.'

'Intuition is the mode of one who knows. Leaping to

conclusions is the mode of one who gambles.' He popped out of his chair and clasped his hands behind his back, and he walked nervously to the window. 'I begin to think that I have been following the wrong scent.'

His mind darted like a swallow at dusk. I had no idea what he was talking about. 'In what respect?'

'At first, music seemed to be the unifying motif in these explosions. Now the motif has expanded to Art in general. But even that cannot be right, Wilson – I have been on the wrong scent! Art is superficially involved, but the matter is deeper than that. It must be! Consider the miniature high-tech devices involved. Developing them costs money, time, resources. Consider the planning required to target this artist or that, the manpower required to plant this bomb or that. Consider the risk involved! Who would do all this simply to punish an artist for supposed ineptitude, or a critic for supposed wrong views? No one, surely! Unless he were a madman.'

'A madman with huge financial resources,' I said.

'You excel yourself, Wilson.'

'Thank you,' I said.

He paced the length of the room and back to the window. 'So there must be another reason. But what could it be? I need more facts.'

'While you await the appearance of facts,' said I, rising to take my coat out of the closet, 'I must be off to meet my banker in the City. I find that in these gloomy economic days I need to do something different with what small assets I have left.'

'Linger, Wilson!' he cried, suddenly rapping hard on the window pane. 'For here comes Chief Inspector Lestrade!'

Holmes rapped on the window again, and waved down at the street.

A minute later Lestrade was in our flat. He appeared energized, concerned, bewildered. 'Have a look, Holmes,' he said, producing a photo. 'This is the man who visited Paul Primrose. The images on the lobby security camera were far from clear, but we identified him with certainty. His name is Lars Lindblad.'

'I am not familiar with the name,' said Holmes.

'You wouldn't be,' said Lestrade. 'He wasn't around in 1914, and he hasn't been in the news for several years. He is Swedish, an international criminal who began his career forty years ago by robbing a French provincial bank and making off with five million francs. French police captured him in one of the last *pissoirs* in Paris and he was subsequently convicted after a long trial in which he proved himself adept at showmanship and a master of the *bon mot,* which made him something of a darling with the public. He escaped from Clairvaux prison within the year, and he further endeared himself to the public by handing fifty thousand francs to a cleaning lady at a small hotel in Marseilles on his way out of the country. For a few years thereafter the public followed his adventures in Algiers, Cairo and Istanbul, viewing him as a sort of European Robin Hood who could amuse the world with his deeds of derring-do. He turned up back in Europe in the seventies. Interpol was after him relentlessly, but to no avail. In the eighties he was observed several times in South America – usually on his way out of a bank. One of his more brilliant exploits was when he knocked over the casino at Monte Carlo and got away with sums never disclosed. The affair was hushed up by the government of Monaco, for obvious reasons. But people knew about it anyway. And such is this man's charm that the whole European public was again amused when he quipped to the press, "It was just luck – and for once the casino lost." I suppose the refreshing thing about Lars Lindblad is that he is an old-fashioned criminal who is in the game for the money and who, so far as we know, has never murdered anyone. Yet there is a dark side. It is believed that he was involved with the kidnapping of the Swiss banker Eric Knockel, who was kept in a trunk in a mountain hut for three days until his bank – though this was never admitted – paid out fifty million Swiss francs in cash. And there is some evidence that he began running weapons to Pakistan. No one is sure whether he has a connection with Al Qaeda, but we hope he doesn't. He has denied any connection, but denied it with an ambiguous quip sent via email to a Berlin newspaper, in which he paraphrased a remark attributed to Voltaire: *Both East and West imagine that God favours them, but I have noticed that God is always on the side of the heaviest battalions.'*

'Then he is a cultured man?' said Holmes. 'Perhaps not a man who would put at risk a letter by William Shakespeare?'

'He is certainly cultured,' replied Lestrade. 'He is fluent in five languages, including Turkish, and as a student at Heidelberg he wrote a monograph on the poetry of Heinrich Heine. He studied piano at the Paris Conservatory for a year, but quit when he realized the difficulties in attaining a concert career. He then took a degree at Heidelberg in biology, preparing to be a physician. But he dropped that also. He is a pilot, balloonist and glider pilot, and he is terribly interested in mechanical gadgets of all kinds. He is also one of the world's great collectors of Greek, Minoan and Cycladic art, particularly statues. Where he keeps his extensive art collection we have no idea, though we suspect it is somewhere in Sweden. Recently an exquisite statue of Apollo was stolen from a museum in France, and the theft had all the hallmarks of a classic Lindblad heist. Oh, yes, he is certainly a cultured man, and in the broadest sense of that term. He is a cryptographer of some note, and we think he at one time worked for the Russians in this capacity. He also loves theatre. He saw the Peter Brook production of *A Midsummer Night's Dream* three times in 1971, and he declared it the most brilliant production of that play ever put on the stage.'

'He is right,' I said. 'I saw that production myself. Twice.'

'The third time he attended we thought we had him,' said Lestrade. 'We had four detectives sitting in the theatre. But he knew we were looking for him and he outsmarted us. Lindblad hired a poor London actor and disguised him to look like Lindblad would look if he were in a *mediocre* disguise. We tumbled for it. We arrested the decoy, certain that we had Lindblad. We had the man in the police car and were halfway to Scotland Yard before we began to guess the awful truth: Lindblad had been in the audience, all right – but he had been in a *brilliant* disguise, a disguise so good that we never spotted him . . . particularly as we were drawn off by the hired actor. That, Holmes, is the kind of man you are up against.'

'In describing his career until now, you have mentioned no violence,' mused Holmes. 'Yet he smashed Paul Primrose with an iron truncheon.'

'Maybe age has changed him,' said Lestrade. 'One might read his biography as that of a man who has always been on the edge of violence, but who has always been able to avoid it. I would not count on his charitable instincts when money is involved – and the Shakespeare letter, if it is real, is surely worth millions.'

'And yet,' I suggested, 'a man so obviously intoxicated with Shakespeare as Lindblad is, might simply want the letter for himself, simply to *have*. Perhaps he doesn't need more money. Perhaps he prefers to acquire objects of cultural importance at this point in his life.'

'It is possible,' mused Lestrade. 'We know he collects art and we know he has great wealth. One gets the feeling that he floats about Europe, often in disguise, picking off targets as much for amusement as for money. He will be sixty this year. Very fit. Reportedly runs five miles every day, at eight minutes to the mile. For a while we thought that his running habit might be his undoing. But, alas, many people run. We also hoped his predilection for beautiful women might lead us to him, one way or another, but . . .'

'That also is a predilection many of us share,' I said.

Lestrade shrugged. 'Anyway, though love of running and love of women have not proved his downfall, let us hope that love of Shakespeare will. Here, Holmes, take the photo. I will leave the matter, for the moment, in your capable hands. But do keep in contact.'

Holmes took the photo, curiously. 'A handsome fellow.'

'Very.'

Holmes slipped the photograph into his coat pocket.

'Tea, Lestrade?' I asked. 'A biscuit?'

'Thank you, Wilson, but I must be off.'

He clapped Holmes on the shoulder, shook my hand, and a moment later he was gone.

'How very odd,' mused Holmes.

'What's odd?' I asked.

'That a man like Lars Lindblad, who has always engaged in such colossal schemes, would interest himself in so small a theft. I doubt that the letter is worth a million pounds, as Lestrade imagines. And even if it were, that is a piddling sum for a man like Lindblad. Yours is the only theory that makes much sense, Wilson – that he simply wants the letter for a keepsake. And yet even that is not convincing. For one thing, how would he have learnt of the letter except through one of Lotte Linger's family members? For another, even if he somehow learnt of it, how could he have had any confidence that the letter was genuine? So why would he risk time and effort on so slight a hope?'

'For fun?'

'Thin, Wilson, very thin! We are thin on motive here – just

as we are in this other case of exploding microbombs. So little meets the eye in each of these cases, that in each instance one feels there must be a huge realm of motive and meaning as yet utterly obscure.'

'Will you start looking for Lindblad?'

'It seems unlikely that I could succeed where Interpol and Scotland Yard have, for forty years, failed.'

'But you underestimate yourself,' said I. 'You, my good fellow, are to crime detection what Shakespeare is to poetry.'

'That is pitching it rather high, Wilson!' he said, with a nervous laugh. 'Far *too* high.'

'Perhaps,' I agreed.

'I am a very proud fellow, and jealous of my own powers, as old Watson often observed. But there are limits, Wilson, there are limits!'

'Still, you are not ordinary.'

'Perhaps not, perhaps not,' said he, caressing his own cheek with his thin hand. He turned away, and looked into the wall mirror, and gazed at himself briefly, in a pose of pondering. 'A fresh view of things, an unorthodox view, such as mine, coming as it does from another century, another age . . .'

'Precisely, Holmes!' I cried.

He paced to the window. 'I think the path to a solution leads through the family of Lotte Linger, and that is the route I will pursue first. I should like to talk to your friend Percy Ffoulkes, for he knows the family and may have insights into their minds and habits.'

'If you want insight into the mind of Alexis Gray, you might try looking at the "Delphi Diary" columns he writes for *Arts Weekly*.'

'I didn't know about them.'

'I forgot to mention them to you. Here's the most recent copy. He writes them under the pen name Bif Carcanson.'

Holmes opened the magazine, turned to the column. He was about to set the magazine aside but then he looked back at it and squinted. 'What an exceedingly odd name, Bif Carcanson.'

'I thought it might be French,' I said.

'Perhaps,' said Holmes. 'But the curious thing, Wilson, is that it is an anagram for Francis Bacon.'

TEN
Sharp Words and Small Explosions

Scarcely had I set off to meet my banker than Marianne Hideaway rang my mobile and asked if she might query me further about journalism and literature. Several hours later we met. She came bounding towards me down the steps of the British Museum, her blonde hair dancing in the light breeze. For a moment I felt as if I were viewing the climactic scene of a romantic film. She gave me the perfunctory 'hug of friends' and said she was in London for a week – and we hurried up the museum steps. We ended by spending a very pleasant day together. But we became so involved in our discussions of art, Oxford, George Orwell, my experiences in the Afghan war, styles of cookery in India, and a hundred other topics, that I altogether forgot that I had intended to elicit from her some information about her family – information that might help Holmes to find the missing letter. It was late by the time we were sipping our last drink together at her hotel in Montague Street, and very late by the time I opened the door of my flat near Baker Street.

I turned on the table lamp and was just feeling in my pocket for a handkerchief when Holmes emerged from his bedroom in slippers and robe. He looked more like a ghost than a man. 'Good evening, Wilson,' said he, as he glided towards me in the dim light, his hands in his pockets. 'I perceive you have spent the day with Marianne Hideaway.'

'Holmes, Holmes, please don't do this!' said I.

But he, of course, could not desist. 'I perceive she wore blue, and that you took her to supper at an Indian restaurant in Marchmont Street, and afterwards you had a Scotch whisky at her hotel in Montague Street and then, as it was getting late, you took a taxi home; and that is all I can deduce in this dim light.'

I sat down, exhausted, in the chair by the lamp. Holmes faded into darkness by the window, looking out as he did so often. 'And what makes you think so, Holmes?'

'Perfume,' came his voice, sounding very far away. 'Her perfume is distinctive, delicate. French. Chanel Number Nineteen . . .'

'Yes, yes.'

'I sometimes despair, Wilson, that my "Grand Resuscitation" so strangely increased the powers of the olfactory lobe of my prosencephalon. I feel nowadays almost like a bloodhound. It is sometimes overwhelming – not so much the smells, as the memories they evoke. Memory comes upon me like a mad dream. I sometimes lose myself.'

'Her perfume, then. Yes. I was with her.'

'And the blue bit of fuzz on your sweater tells me she wore blue – I remember she wore blue at Widcombe Manor, too; the colour suits her.'

'Precisely.'

'And on your sleeve is a spot of brown, as in *curry brown*. And it smells of curry. And I know all your favourite London restaurants.'

'Precisely,' I said.

'You have the smell of Scotch on your breath, and in a pub you always have beer, but in a hotel bar you are inclined to Scotch, so I think you drank at her hotel. It is in Montague Street because she told me at Widcombe Manor that she always stays in a hotel next to the British Museum. And it was so late when you came home that the underground was no longer operating, so you must have taken a taxi.'

'Precisely.'

'And to clinch the case,' he laughed, 'you have, Wilson, the slightly giddy look of an older man who has been gallivanting about with a very young and beautiful woman.'

'Holmes, please! I was assisting her, nothing more. She is half my age.'

'More like a third,' said he, 'if my calculation is correct.'

'Precisely.'

'Pray, tell me, Wilson – did you learn anything that might be of help to the legacy of William Shakespeare?'

'Not a thing. I forgot.'

He laughed. 'Understandable.'

Sitting in the chair, under dim lamplight, exhausted, I cast my mind back to our day of conversation, trying to locate something that might be useful to Holmes 'Well, there was one comment that Marianne dropped that might be helpful,' said I. 'She invited us to a soirée at the flat of her brother Alexis, who lives just on the north side of Regent's Park. Attending may give you opportunity to question them further. The whole family will be there. Sir Hugh and Lotte are driving down with Grandpa Gray, who is recovering nicely from his broken collar bone. Bart may be a little late for he is returning from a business trip to Brussels.'

'Nicely done, Wilson! All of them together. Excellent! Nothing could be better. A chance to probe these people is just what I need. I am convinced that one of them must know something about what happened to the Shakespeare letter.'

'And how did you spend the day?' I asked.

'In the library researching some small matters of importance in the Shakespeare case. Also, making copies of the Bif Carcanson column in the last two years of *Arts Weekly*.'

'Have you read any of those columns?'

'That is on my agenda for tomorrow morning.'

'Goodnight, Holmes.'

He turned and shuffled away, and vanished. His *goodnight* was punctuated by the closing of his bedroom door.

I sat long in the chair by the little table, musing. I did not believe that Marianne had any knowledge whatever of the Shakespeare letter, or any part in its disappearance. I suddenly thought – strangely enough – of my ex-wife, who had run off to Connecticut with a computer expert, and who had always said she did not want children. I had never wanted them either, particularly. But somehow as I sat there alone, remembering the day that had passed, I thought for the first time in my life how nice it would have been to have had a daughter.

The following morning I arose at my usual time but Holmes had long been at work. He was sitting by the window intently reading the sheaf of photocopies he had made yesterday at the library, the Bif Carcanson columns from *Arts Weekly*. It was impossible to break through the wall of his concentration when he was in one of these states, so I made breakfast for myself, ate it, cleared away the dishes, and sat down to read the paper. From time to time, as Holmes busily burrowed through the pile of columns I heard him chuckle softly. Once he murmured 'By Jove!' – an exclamation that surely went out of fashion at least a century ago. Yet, oddly enough, as soon as someone says something, it tends to sound quite normal. And it sounded quite normal to me in our quiet flat that Thursday morning.

Holmes began to fidget. I felt the intensity of his attention increase. He was making notes in margins with a pencil, writing rapidly. By and by he laid aside the sheaf of papers and let his pencil drop to the floor. He sat back in his chair as if perplexed. 'It can't be so,' he said.

'What is it, Holmes?'

'A moment, a moment . . .' He sprang to his feet and went to his desk and sat down. For five silent minutes his pen scratched. At last he slowly rose and turned to face me. 'I have found a strange connection.'

'Between what?' I said.

'It may be an illusion.'

'I'm a jaded ex-reporter. I see through illusions. Try me.'

'When Alexis Gray criticizes someone in his column, within a few weeks that person is likely to explode.'

'Coincidence,' I said.

'In January he wrote, *Street musicians come in two varieties, the Appropriately Pathetic Player and the Assault Artist. A singer on a street corner is always pathetic, and because she offers only brief snatches of song she is often pleasing, appropriate, and worth a penny. By contrast, the electrically amplified Assault Artist in a pedestrian subway causes anxiety and actual pain, and makes me more inclined to kill the man than to give him a coin. Yesterday in the pedestrian subway that links the Victoria and Piccadilly lines at Green Park I was assailed by waves of battering sound from just such a vicious performer. He left me limp, exhausted and angry.'*

Holmes looked at me.

'And then the Green Park Assault Artist's guitar exploded,' I said.

'Precisely two weeks later.'

'It must be coincidence.'

'Perhaps,' said Holmes. 'I am sure you are right. Yet here is another coincidence. In late February Bif Carcanson wrote this: *The current production of* A Midsummer Night's Dream *perverts Shakespeare's glorious fairy vision into a fiery calamity with all the charm of an* auto-da-fé. *Every detail is designed by the relentless director to accuse, abuse and confuse the helpless victims in his audience. The first of Shakespeare's sweet songs, for instance, is sung in a pugnacious style by a fairy who carries a popgun and who evidently cannot tell a lute from a tommy gun.'*

'Heavens!' I said. 'And I presume that was the selfsame fairy who fell from his perch and disrupted the play?'

'Precisely so, just sixteen days after this column was published.'

'I don't know, Holmes. Coincidence is an omnipresent force.'

'Coincidences happen all the time,' said Holmes. 'As evidence, here is another. Alexis Gray, in his guise as Bif Carcanson, wrote this recently: *The brilliant violinist Antoine Capinelli was ambushed by moralists posing as music critics at his London concert last year. Apparently Capinelli's technique was too brilliant (Bledsoe), his interpretation too sensitive (Wilkins), and his tempo too fast (Pilkington). We hope that these three critics stay away from the Capinelli concert, since it is apparent that their artistic judgements have been subverted by their animadversions. It is regrettably true that Antoine Capinelli has denied the holocaust, has praised the political acuity of George W. Bush, has claimed Charles Darwin was a fraud, and has pronounced that women have primitive intellects. But Art is its own world, unrelated to the flaws of its practitioners. It is to be judged by its own standard. A critic who cannot hear that Capinelli is in the first rank of violinists, or who carps at trivialities, is a critic unworthy of his craft.'*

'I'm beginning to wonder,' said I.

'One can hardly help but wonder,' said Holmes. 'Shortly after that column was published, Bledsoe and Wilkins were injured by minibombs.'

'And poor old Pilkington had his hearing aide melted.'

Holmes lifted another sheet and carried it to the light of the window. 'Some days ago Bif Carcanson criticized the art and architecture of Ian Fiero. *Fiero,* he wrote, *is one of the few artists living who could best beautify the earth and exalt the soul of man by destroying all traces of his work. Instead of wrapping Parliament in tape, let him wrap his entire oeuvre in Night, and silently steal away.'*

A shiver fled over my skin. 'And he blew up. In the night.'

Holmes paced the length of the room and back. 'Since January of this year, every single person who has been severely criticized by Bif Carcanson has met with a minibomb. In his column Alexis Gray deals with many ideas, mentions many artists and works of art – most of them favourably, or indifferently, or with amusement. Only these few that I have mentioned has he severely criticized.'

'Surely,' I said, 'having had his revenge in print, he couldn't be mad enough to want to attack his victims in the real world!'

'One wouldn't think so,' said Holmes. 'And it would take a very bold or very foolish man to publish the names of his victims in advance.'

'The idea is absurd,' I said. 'Apart from everything else, can we seriously contemplate the notion that the Gray family could be involved in *both* of the criminal cases in which you have become interested? The notion, I repeat, seems absurd.'

'You may be right,' he said, and he sat down again in his chair by the window. He felt in his breast pocket for the pipe that wasn't there, drew out instead the photograph of Lars Lindblad. 'Handsome man,' he mused. He slipped the photo back into his pocket, grabbed a magazine from the side table, brandished it lightly in the air. 'Here, Wilson, is the current issue of *Arts Weekly*. This week Mr Alexis Gray takes to task a Swedish artist by the name of Solveig Nordstrand. What I cannot help but wonder is whether his criticism is sufficient to make us fear for Ms Nordstrand's safety . . . presuming, of course, that my tentative theory is correct – which, as you point out, it may not be.'

'Read on, Holmes. What exactly does he say?'

'I quote: *An exhibit of Ms Solveig Nordstrand's paintings opens at the Atria Gallery next week. One had hoped that this time around she would spare us her usual nonsensical art criticism, and simply let us enjoy her excellent pictures. Alas, it appears that such is not to be. In a television interview last week Ms Nordstrand yet again informed us that her oeuvre demonstrates "the inversion of negative space and the conversion of Time into Colour". The lovely Swede has been repeating this meaningless mantra – a quotation from her own autobiography – for five years. Insofar as it means anything at all, it means that she is as inept with a pen as she is brilliant with a brush. Let us hope she does not, during the exhibition, torch her own work by repeating such blather.'*

'It seems a much milder criticism than the others,' I said.

'Yes,' he mused. 'He praises her work. And yet that last sentence, about the torch, seems almost a warning.'

'It might be read that way,' I admitted. 'I suppose you are worrying whether you ought to warn her.'

'It is all so tenuous, so vague. Mere guesswork. Her exhibition opened yesterday. Nothing has happened – and very likely nothing will. And yet there does seem to be a pattern . . .'

'If you are worried, Holmes, why not go down to the gallery

and look around? Get a feel for things. Make your decision then whether or not to warn her.'

'Dash it! Let us go!' He leapt to his feet and grabbed his hat and topcoat. 'You are a sensible fellow, Wilson!'

As we emerged on to the street in front of our apartment, further apprehensions seemed to assail him, and he said, 'I only hope we are not too late.'

Hurrying to match his swift stride, I cried, 'Heavens, Holmes! The chance that Alexis Gray's columns cause explosions is small, and the chance that his mild criticism of Solveig Nordstrand will cause one is even smaller. He criticized only her palaver, not her painting.'

He kept walking fast towards the Baker Street station and then suddenly he spotted a taxi and cried, 'Come, Wilson – let's take a cab!' And he was running and waving. A moment later we were sitting in the sombre silence of a London cab and sliding south along Baker Street. Spring was in full flower: the trees were wearing more leaves, the women fewer clothes. Sunlight darted off vehicles, and throngs flowed like a river along Oxford Street. Suddenly we were in silent small streets as the cabby threaded his way to avoid traffic. In a black shadow we slid through the silent, compact and opulent centre of the great city.

When we turned into Dover Street I could see commotion ahead, evidently a traffic problem. Our cabby slowed, made the final turn ... and then we saw the fire engine. Black smoke poured out of the lower windows of the building. A crowd of onlookers had gathered. Holmes leapt out and hurried along the pavements.

ELEVEN
Katrinka Pushkin Startles Lestrade

Solveig Nordstrand was tall, voluptuous, blonde, sleek, stylish, posh, self-assured and probably about fifty. Her gallery was filled with people despite the reek of smoke. The fire truck had departed, the police officers had vanished. Most of the smoke had been blown out of the shop by a fan in the front doorway. As we approached, Solveig Nordstrand turned to us pleasantly. She waved a gentle hand towards the milling crowd, and smiled. 'Maybe,' she said, 'we ought to burn a painting every day, if it brings in such crowds.'

I nodded towards the scorch on the wall. 'Even that scorch might be modern art, if you called it so.'

'Hello,' said my companion. 'I'm Sherlock Holmes, and this is my friend, James Wilson. May I ask you a few questions?'

'You are . . . Sherlock Holmes?' she said, smiling – a bit uncertainly now. 'Are you a journalist, or . . .?'

'I am working with the police,' said Holmes.

'I know you are not Sherlock Holmes . . . but are you a police?'

'Unofficially.'

'Then I don't know if it is right for me to speak with you, if you are not a police officer.'

'Perhaps you may speak *unofficially*,' suggested Holmes.

'Well . . .'

Holmes pointed towards a picture on the wall. 'By the way, I very much like your painting of Mount Everest.'

'Everest!' I said, staring at the asymmetrical blotch of colour and dark.

'Thank you, Mr Holmes,' she said, warming to him. 'Few people recognize it.'

'I didn't recognize it,' I said, 'and I've been there.'

'Mount Everest from directly overhead,' said Holmes, 'and at sunset, when the colours change and shadows distort.'

'You have a keen eye, sir!' She broke into charming laughter. 'Are you an art critic?'

'Merely one who observes the world.'

'You observe it carefully,' she said.

'I always take into account the point of view, and the light. Together they are everything.'

She laughed. 'I like unofficial policemen, Mr Holmes. What do you wish to know? I have no secrets.'

'Please tell me what happened,' said Holmes.

She moved a step towards him, and her large earrings swayed. She stood very close to us as she spoke. 'This morning we opened the gallery, and a few people came through, signing the book, you know, and then browsing. By and by one lady looked puzzled, so I walked to her and introduced myself. She asked about the painting called *Massacre of the Innocents*, which was a paraphrase of a Bruegel painting. I told her a little about it, and as we were talking, POOF, my *Massacre of the Innocents* burst into flame. I know it does not sound possible.' She shrugged. 'But that is how it was.'

'Can you recall what you were talking about when the painting burst into flame?'

'I was just explaining to the lady my theory of painting, how I conceive of what I am doing.'

'Would you remember the words you spoke?' asked Holmes.

'I said that my work is based upon the inversion of negative space, and the conversion of Time into Colour. Just at that moment –' she shrugged again, and smiled – 'POP.'

'Who has handled that painting?' asked Holmes.

'The gallery owner has handled it, and I have. No one else.'

'How many people visited the shop yesterday?' he asked.

'A few in the morning, a few in the afternoon, and many invited guests at the evening party.'

'Do you remember any of the people who visited the gallery yesterday, before the evening party?'

'A few,' she replied. 'The first were two elderly ladies from Sussex. They signed my visitors register. Next was, let me see . . . yes, the Swedish gentleman and his lady.'

'Swedish?' said Holmes quickly.

'Well, yes. He spoke with me in Swedish.'

'Is this the man?' asked Holmes, and he slipped the photo of Lars Lindblad out of his pocket and showed it to her.

'That is him . . . he did not sign my guest register.'

'Now, Ms Nordstrand, did this man spend much time near the painting that burned this morning.'

'He did, yes!' she said, as if remembering in surprise. 'He stood very close to it, he and his lady friend. For a long while they stood there. I had begun to think they would buy it.'

'And the lady friend,' said Holmes. 'What did she look like?'

'I remember quite well. Medium height, dark hair, brown eyes, very nice skin. She wore a gold necklace chain with an Egyptian ankh on it, and matching gold earrings. Nice against her black dress. She was foreign. She spoke but little. She had an accent. Russian, I think.'

'Is there a security camera on the premises that might have recorded her picture?'

'I can draw for you . . .'

'Excellent,' said Holmes.

Solveig Nordstrand took up a sketch pad and a pencil. She thought a moment. Then her hand flew over the blank sheet, darting, jotting, filling in. And in a very few minutes a picture appeared. The woman's face was quite beautiful. I didn't say so, but that little sketch seemed to me the best art in the gallery.

'There, that is pretty close,' she said.

'Thank you very much, madam,' said Holmes.

She half closed her eyes and shook her head. She touched his lapel with her strangely large and beautiful hand. 'I hope you can find the ones who did this. Such things are not pleasant.'

'We will do our best.'

She laughed, tilting her head slightly. 'You know, you even look like Sherlock Holmes – I imagine him to be like you.'

Holmes smiled faintly and said, 'I didn't know I was *that* good looking!'

They both laughed.

Seldom had I seen Holmes in such a sociable and genial mood.

She turned to me and said. 'I should like to paint you, Mr James Wilson. You have a most interesting face.'

'You are very kind,' I said.

'It is an offer,' she said. 'I am sincere.' Then she turned away and wished Holmes well in his investigation.

Solveig Nordstrand seemed a nicely matured version of those buxom beautiful Swedish movie stars seen in old James Bond films. But her effect on Holmes had worn off by the time we reached Scotland Yard. By then he was again fidgety, nervous, hyperactive. Lestrade immediately summoned us up to his office. His secretary waved us through, and as we passed by her desk I heard her cancel an appointment to make time for us.

Lestrade, seemingly so sober and thoughtful, so reserved and remote, was, in truth, a warm and generous soul beneath it all – just as was his more famous Victorian grandfather. This modern Lestrade, who had kindly undertaken to supervise Holmes's recovery after 'the great resuscitation,' took his responsibility not only seriously but with almost religious devotion. I suppose that ever in the back of Lestrade's mind was the remembrance that Holmes had given great assistance to his grandfather on crime cases in the old days, and that he thus had helped him to rise in the force, and later had even helped him to find a wife

– so perhaps Lestrade felt that he owed not only his own job, but his very life to Sherlock Holmes.

Holmes told Lestrade how we had hurried to the gallery this morning, but had arrived too late.

'How did you know, Holmes, that Solveig Nordstrand might be in danger?'

'I was guessing.'

'Yes, yes, yes – but what made you guess as you did?'

'I must ponder that,' said Holmes. 'But you will be interested to know that Lars Lindblad was in the gallery yesterday, showing great interest in the very painting that this morning exploded and burned.'

'What!'

'Solveig Nordstrand identified him.'

'Lars Lindblad again! But how does this fit with the theft of the Shakespeare letter?'

'I haven't any idea,' said Holmes.

Lestrade rose and walked around his desk, rubbing his chin. 'But it must be connected – don't you think?'

'I cannot see the connection as yet,' said Holmes.

And now it was Lestrade who showed signs of nervous energy. His hands gestured as he said, 'Lars Lindblad, Lars Lindblad! His *modus operandi* has always been to work on one big and profitable thing. He has never piddled with small matters. He doesn't rob a chemist's shop one day, Holmes, and set a fire the next. He has always, for forty years, operated on a grand scale. He has never, to anyone's knowledge, committed a crime for vengeance, for amusement, for political beliefs or for social justice. He has committed crimes only to make very large sums of money. You may count on it, Holmes: that is his motivation here. Stealing the Shakespeare letter fits that profile. Burning somebody's more-or-less worthless painting does not.'

'But he was in the shop,' said Holmes.

'I understand that.'

'And this lady was with him,' said Holmes, handing him Solveig Nordstrand's sketch of the dark beauty.

Lestrade stared at the sketch with amazement. 'I recognize her, Holmes!'

'Yes?'

Lestrade rubbed the back of his neck. 'This woman is Katrinka Pushkin – that is *one* of her names, at any rate. She is forty years old and looks much younger. She is an operative for Al Qaeda. It is believed she travelled with Osama bin Laden in the days right after 9/11, those days when the US Army was busying itself with the invasion of Iraq. Her name is Russian but her nationality is Egyptian, born in Cairo in 1969 to a Russian father and Egyptian mother. She attended Yale University, then the London School of Economics. She was radicalized in 1999 by a boyfriend named Jalil Akbari, an Iranian she met in London when he worked here as a physician. They both returned to Iran in 2001, and . . .' Lestrade shrugged. 'My heavens, it is most unfortunate if Lars Lindblad has associated himself with Al Qaeda.'

'And what does Ms Pushkin do for Al Qaeda?' asked Holmes.

'To the best of our knowledge, she makes purchases, and then routes what she buys through intermediaries in other countries. We also believe she may be a contact for industrial spies in this country. We wish we knew exactly what she does – most of this I have gotten from a friend in MI5.'

'It sounds very fresh in your mind,' said Holmes.

'We were discussing her recently. We suspect she is doing something that we don't much like, but we don't know what it is. There is little point in picking her up for questioning until we have at least a faint clue what we are looking for. And now I learn she may be hooked up with a master criminal who has evaded every police force in the world for forty years.'

'His luck may be running out,' said Holmes.

'Yes, yes, I could well believe it, Holmes – now that you have been taken out of the deep freeze and set back in action. Maybe he will now meet his nemesis. I take it you are on his track – and, true to your old form, not telling old Lestrade everything you know!'

'I'll make a suggestion, however,' said Holmes, reaching for the pipe that wasn't there.

'What happened to your pipe?' asked Lestrade. 'That is the second time you have groped for it. You look quite lost without it.'

'I stepped on it,' said Holmes. 'I have a new one coming.'

'Ah. Well. You were saying . . .?'

'You might like to take a look at the Bif Carcanson columns that have been published in *Arts Weekly* magazine since January of this year. They were written by professor Hugh Blake's stepson and are suggestive. Yet I cannot make out what, if anything, they really mean. Perhaps you are a cleverer man than I am.'

'Since you put it that way, I must certainly read them,' said Lestrade, with a rueful smile. 'For a hundred years my family have been trying to prove themselves your equal in cleverness – with little success. Since you offer me one more inning, I must not let the home team down by refusing it.' He laughed, and touched Holmes on the shoulder, as was his habit. And winked at me as we departed.

Holmes and I walked towards home through Green Park.

'For a while there,' said I, 'I was under the impression that you were making great progress. Now, suddenly, I feel rather at a loss. What do you have, Holmes, but a sketch of a woman, a photo of a man, a missing letter, and a series of apparently nonsensical small crimes based on critical attacks in an art magazine?'

'You have summed it up admirably, Wilson. Perhaps Alexis Gray's soirée will provide further clues. You said all the family will be there?'

'Yes.'

'Excellent! I am more certain than ever that amongst the Gray-Linger-Hideaway-Blake family we may find hints towards a solution to both of our mysteries. For a start, one of that clan must surely know where the Shakespeare letter is located, or know who does know – of that I am convinced.'

'But wait, then you are saying that one of them is in league with Lars Lindblad?'

'That seems a sensible hypothesis,' said Holmes. 'One or more of them.'

'But Holmes! Are we not then led to the damning conclusion – to the almost preposterous conclusion – that one of that clan is working with Al Qaeda!'

'Stranger things have happened. But that conclusion is, I think, premature. Much of this case is dark, Wilson. Very dark. We are walking at night along a gloomy road with only a glimmer of moon to show our way.'

We hailed a cab and soon we were back at the apartment.

'Perhaps you should tell me, Holmes, what you would like me to do when we get to Alexis's soirée. We have only four hours. I really have no idea how to go about querying these people. Surely it can do no good to ask them directly whether they know the whereabouts of the stolen letter, or whether they know Lars Lindblad?'

'That would not be wise.'

'I am at your service, my friend. What is the plan?'

'Our plan, my dear Wilson, is to be genial and let them talk. *C'est tout*. Tiny glimmers of their lives will spill out in their conversation. We will note these. You have read Freud, I presume?'

'A little.'

'In *The Case of Dora*, Freud said something that strikes me as perfectly true . . . I believe I can quote it . . .'

'Sherry?' I asked, holding out a glass.

'Yes, thanks very much.' Holmes sat down and leant back. His long, thin left arm drooped over the chair arm, his feet were outstretched, his right hand held the sherry glass, half-lifted: '*He that has eyes to see and ears to hear may convince himself that no man can keep a secret. If his lips are silent, he chatters with his finger-tips; betrayal oozes out of him at every pore.*'

I laughed. 'Believe me, Holmes, I shall watch carefully for the little droplets of betrayal. Cheers . . .'

'Cheers . . . by the by, is this a formal event?'

'Marianne said that a coat and tie will suffice.'

TWELVE

Holmes Plays Soirée Games

Colonel McKenzie, late of the Indian Army, was, in the publishing industry of modern London, something of a throwback to an earlier time – not a throwback clear to the nineteenth century, perhaps, but back to the nineteen-thirties or so, to that era when books were still read by editors, not marketing committees, and when publishing companies were family affairs and not divisions of creativity-crushing conglomerates. Colonel McKenzie, ninety-two years old, slim, rose at the far end of Alexis Gray's sitting room, lifted his long arms, and attempted – amidst the tinkle of glasses and twitter of voices – to gain the attention of the lovely women with glasses in their hands who were drooped over furniture about the room, and the attention of the intense men in their dark suits who were earnestly informing each other of things surely not fully appreciated by the hoi polloi. On the two terraces overlooking Regent's Park could be seen snatches of colourful dresses amidst the sober navy and grey of pant legs. Colonel McKenzie genially persisted. Someone now began tapping the rim of a wine glass with a dessert fork, trying to assist Colonel McKenzie in attracting the general attention to the front of the room. Slowly, people pushed in from the terraces. Some of the young men looked very flushed.

From the moment of my arrival in this penthouse overlooking Regent's Park, I had been surprised by one thing after another. First, by the fact that the purpose of this soirée was to announce the publication of a new book by Alexis Gray. Second, that so many people had been invited to what I had imagined would be a small family affair. Third, that nearly every woman in view was enticing (I later learnt the rather curious reason for this). Fourth, that Holmes fit very well into the group in his dark blue suit with a faint stripe, and his white shirt, and burgundy-and-blue tie. His distinctive profile – his slenderness, his blade nose, his rigid posture – might have been remarked at certain moments by some people, but on the whole Holmes looked like any bookish Londoner who might be at a book-announcement gathering.

'I am very proud to announce,' said Colonel McKenzie, 'that on Monday next our firm will publish a new and ground-breaking book by our own Mr Alexis Gray.'

The crowd clapped, and someone shouted, 'Hear, hear!'

'The book,' cried the Colonel, holding up a copy, 'is a brilliant piece of literary criticism entitled *The End of the Shakespeare Dream*. It demonstrates that the Shakespearean plays were written not by Shakespeare but by Francis Bacon, and that is why we expect it to cause not merely a stir, but an explosion of outrage and interest.'

'The more stir, the more sales,' said a gentleman standing near me.

'The more outrage the more publicity,' said another.

'What is most unusual for a literary essay such as this,' pronounced Colonel McKenzie, grandly, 'is that film rights have already been sold to Hollywood . . .'

'Bravo!'

'Apparently,' said Colonel McKenzie, looking suddenly a bit

bewildered and bemused, 'they are turning it into fiction, a James Bond sort of thing.'

'I thought it *was* fiction!' cried a voice, and this comment elicited a burst of laughter from the crowd.

'Come, Tommy!' said Alexis Gray, pointing at the speaker. 'The greatest fiction ever foisted on the world was William Shakespeare – other than God, of course.' Alexis looked rather splendid in his dark coat and dazzling shirt, and with his blond hair shining in the light of the fireplace mirror behind him.

'Alexis – be a good boy,' called one of the women near me, a blonde with ringlets at her cheek.

'Why should he be,' said a gorgeous brunette, 'when he gets so famous by being a bad one?'

'He is a very superficial person,' said the blonde.

'That is his charm,' said the brunette.

'I suppose you are right,' sighed the blonde. 'But we've heard all these tired arguments before. I can't really imagine his book amounts to much.'

'It doesn't need to,' said the other. 'They sell better when they don't.'

Lotte Linger appeared, slipping lightly through a gap in the crowd. 'Oh, it is all quite silly, this argument about authorship. I tell Alexis that the plays of Shakespeare were not written by Shakespeare but by another man of the same name, and this makes him furious.' She laughed. She looked lovelier than either of the other two women, though she was sixty and they were in their late twenties.

'Then you believe in Shakespeare?' asked the brunette.

'I might as well believe in Shakespeare as in a phantom – and all the rest are but phantoms. And, after all, the plays are the plays, whether written by William or a phantom.'

The two women laughed: Lotte had brought them both into the fold, and the three women now shared a vision.

'Where is Bart?' I asked.

'One never knows about him,' said Lotte. 'Brussels, I think. He is supposed to turn up. I hope soon. Grandpa is becoming sleepy and grumpy, and Bart is his keeper.'

She glanced towards Grandpa Gray and it seemed to me she shuddered, almost imperceptibly. He was sitting in a corner, a bunched figure wearing a tuxedo, holding a . . .

'What is he holding?' I asked.

'I do hope it isn't loaded,' said Lotte. 'You have heard of angry old men with shotguns, haven't you, Mr Wilson?'

'I'm not sure I have,' I said. 'But what is the poor old fellow angry about?'

'It has been my experience,' she replied, 'that anger needs no reason. Why was Iago angry? Why was Richard?'

'Because he had a humpback?' said the brunette. 'Do you know, Ms Linger, you were in the first Shakespearean play I ever saw. You were wonderful! Our school group went to see *Anthony and Cleopatra*. That was almost two decades ago. I was nine, and so impressed.'

'Thank you, my dear. A half a compliment is better than none,' said Lotte, and she laughed.

'Oh!' said the brunette, putting her hand over her mouth.

Four young men had formed a scrum around Marianne, and when finally I located her I could not easily get to her. By and by, however, she broke out of the huddle of admirers, spotted me across the room, and sought me out. She touched my sleeve most fetchingly. For a moment I imagined she really preferred my company to that of all the glitterati and literati and younger people in the room. But scarcely had we greeted each other when Alexis came over, looking splendid, with a drink in his hand and a redhead on his arm. The redhead looked very Irish and ripe, and reticently gentle.

Alexis looked at Marianne and me. 'Well, you two look very much a couple,' said he.

'I think so too,' said Marianne.

One of the young men who had huddled around Marianne now pressed his way into our group. He had a handsome head, a big smile, a muscular body. He looked like an athlete who had been stuffed into a £1,000 suit. He wore a grey ascot. 'I notice there are no ugly women here, Alexis,' said he. 'Is that by design?'

'No, it is by nature,' replied Alexis. 'In nature there are no ugly women, or men. If you think you see an ugly person, tell me, and in a while I will find out her beauties, or his. What the world calls a true beauty is merely someone who is beautiful from more angles than most of us are. I will find beauty in a fat girl, a crippled army sergeant, or a starving dog. Every creature on this earth is beautiful from some angle – though sometimes, admittedly, patience is required to find the angle.' He paused, smiled. 'And I am very impatient. I confess, my guest list is based on my impatience.'

By eleven o'clock many of the guests had left. I chatted for a while with Sir Hugh, and asked him what he thought about his stepson's thesis that Francis Bacon had written the plays of Shakespeare. He leant towards me. 'Utter nonsense. I often wonder, Wilson, what is it in human nature that makes men conjure up conspiracy theories that cast doubt on obvious truths? *That* is the puzzle I should like answered.'

'I have often thought,' said I, 'that in the case of Shakespeare some people just don't want to believe that a country boy could be so smart.'

'Could be, could be.'

'Others, perhaps, don't dare believe that a man could write so magnificently in apparently so offhand a manner, without puffing up his achievement – not even worrying, apparently, about whether his plays were published. To the generality of mankind, who take themselves and their tiny achievements so very seriously, such an attitude seems almost incomprehensible.'

'It does, it does,' agreed Sir Hugh.

'But I believe that the very fact that Shakespeare did not take his work so terribly seriously may be one of the reasons he pulled it off so brilliantly. It is generally true, is it not, that the most graceful of people are those who think least about themselves?'

'I think you have something there, Wilson.'

Alexis lifted a bottle. 'May I pour you another drink?'

I held out my glass.

'Who is your friend, really,' asked Alexis.

'You mean Sherlock Holmes?' I said.

'Come now, Mr Wilson. Surely you don't expect us to believe he is *the* Mr Sherlock Holmes – that would be the story of the century if it were true.'

'That is precisely why the story is so easily kept secret,' said I. 'The truth is never believed. The result is that Holmes's anonymity is preserved – as he prefers. But I fear when Dr Coleman publishes his articles, detailing how he resuscitated my friend, it will be quite impossible to keep the story quiet. I understand Coleman is preparing papers for *The Journal of the American Medical Association,* and *The Lancet.*'

Alexis Gray looked bemused.

At that moment Marianne took my arm and drew me out on to the terrace. She and I discussed a number of topics, including a café we both knew on the Rue de Bac, while gazing out over the soft dark of Regent's Park. But by and by the murmur in the room behind us changed tone, and we saw that Bart had arrived. He looked rumpled in brown corduroys and blue wool sweater and hiking shoes. His necklace of blue stones peeked out from under his white shirt collar.

'Welcome back from Brussels,' said Alexis. 'How was the journey?'

'Long,' said Bart. His shoulders were slightly rounded, and his darting glance leapt about the room. A smile played about his lips, uncertainly, as he shook his brother's hand and congratulated him. 'I hope you sell a million copies, Alexis,' he said, as he pulled a mint from his pocket, popped it into his mouth. Then he turned and greeted his mother, and kissed her on the cheek, and hugged her. He gave Marianne only the barest nod. He offered a perfunctory *Hello, Sir Hugh* to his stepfather, then hurried towards Grandpa Gray and knelt down beside the old man, patted his hand with true affection, took the shotgun away from him, and spoke to him softly.

Marianne led me back out on to the terrace and there we were joined, a few moments later, by the lovely Lotte Linger, who proved to be the perfect conversationalist. Whatever topic a person served up, Lotte would volley it like a happy tennis player, and if you switched balls on her, she would go with the new one – her roles in Shakespeare, the weather in the Channel Islands, the food in northern Italy, the quintessence of Ibsenism. Lightly and deftly she would volley and patiently await your return, and sometimes put a little spin on it to make things interesting. But despite her vast experience of the world, and her fame, she never tried to put you down with a slam. I tried to elicit information from her that might help Holmes in his quest for the letter, but I had little success.

We three strolled back into the main sitting room and there was Holmes standing next to the fireplace conversing with Bart Gray. As we entered the room I heard Holmes say, 'Logic is the lowest form of thought.'

Bart looked startled. 'You, who claim to be Sherlock Holmes, would say *that*? Whoever you may be, you are quite wrong to call the nature of logic in any way *low*.'

'It is merely straight-line thinking,' said Holmes. 'It lacks the imaginative curves of higher thought.'

'I don't understand you,' said Bart.

'A small logical problem may demonstrate my point,' said Holmes. 'Have you seven five-pound notes?'

'I think I do.' Bart slipped out a wallet and brought out some bills. 'Sorry, only five.'

'That will do,' said Holmes. 'Lay them face up on the table. That's right. Now, the problem is to place four of these notes so that each touches every other, but touches only at one point.'

Bart quickly laid three notes flat on the table to form a triangle, corners touching. He then took the fourth, bent it in the middle so it stood on edge, and placed it in the middle of the triangle with one corner touching the meeting point of two of the flat notes, and the other corner touching the middle of the third. 'Nothing difficult in that problem,' he said.

'Your solution is logically infallible, but imaginatively flawed,' said Holmes. 'You have limited yourself to straight-line thinking, and failed to imagine what your solution might lead to.'

'I don't follow.'

'My meaning will dawn on you eventually,' said Holmes, and he quickly leant and plucked something from Bart Gray's sweater. He held the *something* up to the light. 'One seldom finds heather in Brussels,' he said.

A shadow of doubt floated across Bart Gray's face.

Sir Hugh Blake pushed forward towards Holmes, his face piled with smiles. 'Mr Holmes, I almost forgot. Your briar pipe arrived at Widcombe Manor this morning, a beautiful piece made by the incomparable Mr Sedley of Hexham. I forgot to bring it along, but I shall send it to you in a few days.'

'Thank you, Sir Hugh,' said Holmes. 'It is a gift I shall cherish.'

Holmes extended a hand to Alexis and congratulated him once more on the forthcoming book, and thanked him for the evening.

I did the same.

Marianne hurried up to me. 'Can we meet for lunch next Thursday? I'm staying in London till the end of the week.'

'Delighted,' I said.

A moment later Holmes and I were out in the dark, walking briskly towards home.

THIRTEEN
Mr Holmes and Mr Hyde

'Well, Holmes,' said I, 'you were looking for a motive. Now you surely have one.'

He strode in silence through the soft London dark, hands clasped behind his back, deep in thought. 'A motive?' he said.

'Alexis Gray! A genuine Shakespeare letter could undercut sales of his book, abort his Hollywood film deal, and make his thesis that Bacon wrote Shakespeare not merely doubtful but ridiculous.'

'Possibly,' said Holmes.

'Assuredly,' said I. 'Every newspaper in the world would be proclaiming news about Shakespeare the poet; Alexis alone would be trying to prove that such a poet never existed. In an instant, his years of labour writing the book, and his beliefs of a lifetime, would be turned to dust. I'd call that a motive.'

'But there are problems, Wilson. Why didn't he steal the letter in his mother's house, where it would have been easier to steal?'

'Because then it would have been obvious that an insider stole it,' I said.

'Excellent, Wilson. But to hire Lars Lindblad for the job is like hiring a bulldozer to dig up a bed of daisies. Lindblad is an international criminal who deals in huge crimes and huge sums. Why would he steal a Shakespeare letter for whatever pittance Gray could pay?'

'Maybe Lindblad is a personal friend of Alexis – or a fanatical believer in the cult of Bacon. Or both.'

'Anything is possible,' said Holmes.

'And also remember,' said I, 'that whomever Alexis criticizes in his column gets attacked – by Lars Lindblad.'

'Again you have put your finger precisely on the problem, Wilson!'

'I have?'

'The motivation problem.'

'I thought I just solved it.'

'I don't mean Alexis Gray's motivation. That is obvious. But Lars Lindblad's is far less clear. Why would such a man get involved? That is the question. He has never in his life been motivated by anything but huge sums of money, far more money than Alexis Gray is able to supply. *That* is the problem, my dear Wilson. We might assume, and it might be true, that Alexis would do extreme things to protect his book and his reputation. He might be a thoroughgoing psychotic and not only wish to criticize in print the artists of whom he disapproves, but to maim or kill them. All this is possible – barely. But why would Lars Lindblad trouble himself with killing an architect, injuring a music critic, blowing up a street musician's electric guitar, or popping a lute in a bad production of *A Midsummer Night's Dream*?'

'I see your point.'

'And when we learn that Katrinka Pushkin, an operative of Al Qaeda, is apparently involved in helping Lindblad set fire to a painting at an exhibition – the matter becomes even more bewildering.'

'Maybe Katrinka Pushkin has nothing to do with anything. Maybe she is just his girl friend who happened along for the fun of it.'

'Maybe,' said Holmes. 'But I hope not. Often it is the odd and unexpected element in a problem that leads to its solution. She is odd, she is unexpected. I shall concentrate my mind on her for a while – oh, look . . .' He pointed across the dark street, and then he darted away. A moment later his tall, angular figure passed through the lit doorway of an Indian grocery store. He stood at the counter behind a Filipino girl whose hair was pulled back in a jaunty ponytail. The girl emerged and melted into street shadows. Holmes lay something on the counter . . . he darted out of the shop, crossed the street, and was beside me once more.

'*Arts Weekly*,' said he, folding the magazine and slipping it into his coat pocket. 'Just delivered for tomorrow morning.'

'I shall be interested to see what artist Bif Carcanson has marked for execution,' I said.

'But you know, Wilson, this whole business has nothing to do with art.'

'It certainly seems to have something to do with it.'

'Superficially only. No. As I said before, I fear the art element has been leading me astray.'

'What, then?'

He walked some steps in silence. 'It is a family affair. We will find the genesis of all these crimes somewhere amidst the secrets of the Gray-Linger-Hideaway-Blake family. I thought it slightly odd that when Bart came in the door he hugged Alexis, kissed him on two cheeks in the French manner, and said, "Congratulations, *frère*. This day makes me think of when we were young and truly happy." The statement struck me as touching, but excessive.'

'Bart is strange,' I agreed.

'Second,' said Holmes, 'I found it curious that Bart so dislikes his sister.'

'I noticed that also.'

'Third,' said Holmes, 'I found it suggestive that Bart is a liar who apparently has everyone in the family fooled – everyone except perhaps his mother. Lotte Linger has the air of a woman who knows what is going on at all times, and just pretends she doesn't notice.'

'I think you are quite right about Lotte,' I said. 'Her charm and grace are a mask for her deeper thoughts. She keeps people at a distance while making them feel close to her. But why do you call Bart a liar?'

'He pretended he had just arrived from Brussels, but in fact he had just arrived from Scotland.'

'Scotland! What makes you think so?'

'Mint, heather and Robert Burns.'

'I am mystified.'

'When Bart Gray came in the door I noticed he was finishing off a packet of mints from Buchanan's of Greenock – mints available elsewhere but most common in Scotland. Second, I noticed that two heather leaves were stuck to his sweater. These initial observations prompted me to induce him to lay his bank notes on the table. Four of the five were Scottish bank notes, not English – three of them from the Clydesdale Bank featuring the likeness of Robert Burns. The likelihood of having a pocketful of Scottish bank notes without having been recently to Scotland is not great.'

'So *that* was your ploy!' I said. 'I wondered what you were up to, propounding so simple a puzzle.'

A few steps later we had reached our building.

Holmes proclaimed that he would think no more tonight of the mystery surrounding the Shakespeare letter, or the mystery of the exploding art events. He intended to have a bath, go to bed, and fall asleep reading a new book about which he was very enthusiastic, *Black Holes and Body Heat* by E. C. Drubbing. 'You ought to read it, Wilson,' said he. 'It argues that animate and inanimate forms in the universe are evolving together, and in the end will merge.'

'I'll borrow it from you when you finish. Meanwhile, may I borrow *Arts Weekly*? I'm curious to see who, if anyone, is on Alexis Gray's hit list for the coming weeks.'

'Let's hope no one.'

Twenty minutes later I was comfortably propped up in bed, a glass of water beside me, the lamplight streaming over my magazine. Feeling nicely drowsy, I intended to let the ramblings of Bif Carcanson lull me to sleep. Instead, his third paragraph slapped me wide awake. This is what it said:

> We learnt of a new ploy by the law enforcement fraternity last week when a detective pretending to be none other than Sherlock Holmes appeared with his trusty companion and set about pretending to solve various crimes in both London and Gloucestershire. Whether this man is a true detective we do not know. We suspect he is a member of the actor's guild – the latest attempt by the Metropolitan Police to frighten credulous criminals into finding honest work. Whatever or whoever he is, we consider his masquerade an insult to admirers of the real Holmes, an insult to literary tradition, and an insult to the history of crime in England. It is our considered view that actors ought to strut their stuff on stage, where they can be amusing, not ply their craft in the streets of the city, where they can only be offensive.

I would not have guessed that our visit to Gloucestershire had so upset Alexis Gray. Or perhaps it was his habit to pretend to various injuries and strong opinions in order to fatten his column. Whatever the case may have been, it struck me that now Holmes and I might very likely be targets, just like Pilkington, Fiero, Nordstrand and all the others. For a moment I thought I had best go tell Holmes immediately. On second thought I decided not to disturb him. Eventually I turned off my light and fell into a dream-filled sleep, and much of the night I spent running through fields of heather in search of a red-headed girl, trying to elude a man in a cape who said he had some letters to sell me, and trying to find the right tunnel through which I could walk to Belgium – but people were streaming out of scores of tunnels, and I couldn't read the signs, so finally I asked directions of a tall thin man with a hard face who wore a captain's cap and a false beard, and he told me to take the train on track B.

In the morning I told Holmes of Alexis Gray's comments in *Arts Weekly*. Holmes grabbed the magazine but only laughed as he read the passage. He seemed not in the least disturbed. 'Excellent, Wilson. Perhaps this will bring the criminals to me, and save me the trouble of going after them. It may prove a blessing in disguise. Bravo for Bif! Let us be as patient as we can until when you meet Marianne Hideaway and I meet Lotte Linger. Perhaps the ladies, when we speak with each of them alone, will offer us the information we require.'

Holmes had learnt that Lotte was coming to town in a few weeks to meet with a theatrical agent. She would be staying at Brown's Hotel and Holmes had arranged to meet her there, primarily to show her the pictures of Lars Lindblad and Katrinka Pushkin and learn if she had ever seen them. 'The case is going nowhere, Wilson,' he said. 'So the time has come to tip our cards. If we tip them to the wrong person, well, maybe something will come of that, as well. I wish I had shown the pictures to Lotte at the party.'

'I cannot believe,' said I, 'that Lotte Linger is involved in crime.'

'Nor can I,' said he. 'But I rule out no possibility.'

'And what is it, precisely, that I am to ask Marianne?'

'I hope you will find opportunity to ask her how her family has gotten along together, how she has gotten along with her brothers, what they all feel about each other, that sort of thing. I am not quite yet at the level of logic, Wilson. But I, like everyone, occasionally have uneasy feelings that prompt me to probe in certain directions. Something in that family seems to me very strange. And I cannot help but feel that it is from this strangeness – whatever it is – that all these crimes might have arisen. But I don't mind telling you, Wilson, this realm of mere feeling is very uncomfortable for me. It is a wild stream, and I refuse to abandon myself to it.'

'I will do my best, Holmes, to dredge up whatever is hidden in the Gray clan's past. Marianne was but a child when her brothers were at university. Yet she has lived with the family for twenty-three years, so I suppose she must know a good deal.'

'By the way, Wilson, something most strange occurred last night after the soirée. Remember that Filipino girl in the Indian grocer's shop . . . where I bought the magazine?'

'Oh, yes.'

'She had recently purchased shoes in Antigua, had had her hair done in Brittany, and had visited an Italian spa – hardly what one would expect of a girl who asked the grocery man to put a packet of gum on the tab. What unexpected lives people live, Wilson!'

I did not ask him how he knew. There are limits to my curiosity.

During the following four days there were no developments in the Shakespeare case, and Holmes, to my dismay, directed his attention once again to his chemical experiments. He disappeared each morning into his den of test tubes and chemicals, and emerged about supper time reeking of strange smells. Late at night he disappeared into his room for a while, presumably administering some concoction to himself, and then he ventured forth on his nocturnal walk. I dared not follow him on these walks, and preferred not to imagine what he might be doing. The tale of Dr Jekyll and Mr Hyde crowded into my head again and again. Could my friend, while struggling to stop his own disintegration, actually be enhancing it? Could he be turning himself into a primitive form of life while struggling to remain a man? None of this made much sense, when considered in the clear light of day. Yet at night, when I saw the wild and nervous look in his eyes as he set out for another nocturnal walk, even my wildest imaginings seemed plausible. I feared he might suddenly fall back into his own time frame, might shudder and shrink, and collapse into a loathsome and wrinkled creature.

About that time an incident occurred that startled me considerably. Mrs Cleary, who lived in the ground floor flat below us, each morning appeared in the garden to give her two small dogs a walk. 'Those poodles give me an idea,' said Holmes one day. He gazed down at them from our window. To my surprise he then grabbed his hat and hurried downstairs and followed Mrs Cleary and her two poodles into the street. A little later, I was returning from my morning outing to buy the newspaper when I saw Holmes still sauntering behind Mrs Cleary and her two dogs. One of the dogs stopped to sniff a patch of ground near a flower bed. Mrs Cleary dragged the little creature away from the spot, and no sooner had she done so than Holmes – to my utter astonishment – fell to his knees at the selfsame spot and put his face to the ground. There he remained a while, apparently sniffing. He paid no mind to the people walking along the street – and, to their credit, they paid no attention to him. Finally he got to his feet. I hung back awhile and caught up with Holmes only as he reached the apartment house. I felt the impulse to ask him about this incident, but as the question rose to my lips I found I preferred to say nothing.

Holmes had always been a rather strange individual, as Dr Coleman had recently argued; and eccentricity has its charms. But what disturbed me deeply, and haunted me on many a night, were those moments when Holmes appeared not so much eccentric as utterly mad – when he howled into the darkness 'Look out! It's coming!' Or when, while choking a bouquet of violets, he howled at no one, 'Your game is up, at last!'

From the beginning that first cry, *Look out! It's coming!*, had seemed vaguely familiar. On the day of the incident with Mrs Cleary's dogs it occurred to me that perhaps I had not heard those words but *read* them – perhaps in Watson's chronicles. The *it* was suggestive, and brought to my mind that phantom from Hell described in *The Hound of the Baskervilles*. I pulled down a volume of Dr Watson's life of Sherlock Holmes and opened it to that famous narrative about the unfortunate Baskerville family on Dartmoor. In a twinkling I had located the relevant passage. It described how Holmes and Watson and Lestrade had sought the hell-hound amidst rolling fog in the moonlit darkness of Dartmoor, and how Holmes had cocked his pistol and cried, 'Look out! It's coming!' Shortly thereafter he emptied five shots into the beast as it pounced upon Sir Henry Baskerville. I made another discovery: brandy was a part of that ancient scene. Lestrade twice had given the fallen Sir Henry a sip of brandy from his flask, to revive him. And later, at Holmes's urging, Lestrade had also given the unfortunate Mrs Stapleton a shot of brandy.

That evening I indulged in a sip of Percy's exquisite old brandy – or perhaps two sips. Holmes was sitting in his favourite chair, reading. I said, 'I say, Holmes, may I intrude for a moment on *Black Holes and Body Heat* to ask you a question?'

'Of course,' he said, laying his book aside.

'I have a theory, and I wonder if you would be good enough to tell me if it is correct.'

'I am all ears,' said Holmes.

'The night Percy Ffoulkes came to see us he brought me a bottle of rare brandy that he had purchased at auction. It was more than a hundred years old. I recall you sniffed it repeatedly, and a little later you scared me by staring out the window and crying, "Look out! It's coming!" Could it have been the identical brandy that Lestrade had in his flask all those years ago on Dartmoor – I mean, the time when you were tracking the hound of the Baskervilles? In short, did the smell of that brandy carry you back to that moment?'

'Exactly right,' he replied. 'When I first sniffed that old brandy, my whole body suffered a shock. The smell wafted me back to an earlier time with hallucinatory clarity. Suddenly I was on Dartmoor, reliving the incident.'

'And has this sort of olfactory flashback occurred again?'

'Yes.'

'The violets at Widcombe Manor?'

'Yes.' He shuddered a little, though on his face was a look of amusement.

'I don't have a theory what that might have been about,' I said.

'Oh, you couldn't have guessed that whole business,' he said. 'Watson never mentioned it, for it was an inconsequential thing, one of the million incidents of life that flee by us unnoticed every day. You may recall that when Watson and I were involved in the Moriarty affair, he and I went to Switzerland and stayed one night at the Englischer Hof inn in the village of Meiringen. The next morning we set off for the hamlet of Rosenlaui. As we walked towards the Reichenbach Falls we passed a field of flowers. I remember Watson stopped and plucked a handful of violets, and smelled them, and he handed them to me, saying, 'The scent is wonderful, don't you think?' I smelled them and they did smell exquisite. They lifted my spirits on that dismal day, for I knew Moriarty was close on my track. When I smelled those same flowers at Widcombe Manor, I was first intoxicated by their subtle scent, then entranced, then carried away – and suddenly I had Moriarty by the throat, and I cried out the words that, without the scent of those violets, I would never have remembered I'd said – "Your game is up, at last!" And a moment later I let go of Moriarty's throat, blocked his lunge at me, and toppled him over the precipice and into the terrible chasm of Reichenbach.'

FOURTEEN
Marianne Hideaway Tells a Tale

At seven in the morning of a fresh April day I met Rachel Random for breakfast. Percy was supposed to be with her but did not turn up. Rachel and I had a lively conversation and then she was forced to hurry away to work in New Bond Street. At ten o'clock I met Marianne Hideaway on the steps of the British Museum. She wore white slacks, a form-fitting blue top, a ribbon that held her blonde hair in a pony tail. She leant up quickly and hugged me as we greeted each other, and then we walked through the old gloomy columns and into the astonishingly modern spaces of the largest covered square in Europe.

We spoke, as we walked, of her research paper. I gave her more of my views on journalism and poetry, and I suggested other writers whom she might consult. But on this occasion I also remembered the mission Holmes had entrusted me with, and soon I directed our conversation to her life growing up – a topic that interested me for its own sake.

'The first days I remember were in Scotland,' she said. 'We spent summers there, at Castle Mornay. What a lovely place it was! My first memory was of falling on a hillside of heather, and getting lost, and being terribly frightened. I can see my two brothers coming towards me, tall as towers, and they rescued me. It was a lovely time, my childhood. I *had* brothers then, though they were but half-brothers. I knew they loved me. I was too small and too innocent for either of them to despise me. Only later did the troubles begin. The castle was one that Lord Gray had purchased in the glory days when Lotte was young and famous, and he was wealthy. Of course, I never knew him. He died a few years before I was born. Then Lotte married my father, and I never knew him either, for I wasn't even a year old when he made his exit. He was a scoundrel, I am told. Well, better a scoundrel gone than a scoundrel hanging about. I am fourteen years younger than Bart and eighteen years younger than Alexis, so they might have been my father figures, but as it turned out they weren't. Alexis was far off in London by the time I was ten, making his career and getting married twice. Bart was a bit closer to me, at first. But then, well, I might as well tell you, because really there is no reason not to. When I was sixteen he began to be interested in me as a woman. One summer when we were on holiday in Scotland he became very pressing, and I realized he wanted to seduce me. He tried to do this, in his awkward way. And then one day he became violent. Till then I had thought of him kindly. After that I couldn't. He was handsome enough, but he was thirty, far too old for me – even if we hadn't been half-siblings. I just had no interest. The day the terrible thing happened we were down by the loch looking along the shore and he was picking up small flowers and showing them to me, and picking up very tiny pebbles, and trying to explain what minerals they were made of, and just all of a sudden he began to caress the palm of my hand – and before I could even understand what was happening he grabbed me and pushed me down into the grass. I was confused and at first I thought he was playing, and then I realized what was happening. I became frightened and struck him with a rock, and scooted to my feet, and ran back to the castle. When Bart came home Lotte asked him what had happened to his head – it was all purple with a lump. Bart told her he had fallen. I did not contradict him. After that Bart was angry at me. I suddenly realized, as I had never realized before, that he was a strange person. When you grow up with strangeness, you don't notice it. But then suddenly something happens and all at once you see things differently. That's what happened to me. And ever since that time Bart has . . . hated me, really, I think. I don't feel comfortable in his company. Nor, I think, does he feel comfortable in mine. It has been a bit of a trial for me, living at home with Lotte and Hugh, for Bart often comes back from Cambridge to work in his barn lab. But we stay clear of each other, which is easy enough. He is more like a shadow than a real person in the manor. He has his room, spends most of the time in the lab. It works out. But I hope to get a flat in Oxford after this term. That will be more convenient.

'When Lotte married Hugh Blake I was quite pleased. I always liked Hugh. He is like a long-lost grandfather who one fine day suddenly stepped into my life. He has been a wonderful help to me, not only in my research at Oxford but in my home life. I think Alexis was more or less indifferent whether Lotte married Hugh, so long as he pleased her – which obviously he did. But Bart was incensed when he learnt his mother was going to marry Professor Hugh Blake. I remember one afternoon at Widcombe Manor we were waiting for Hugh to arrive, for he was to be our supper guest, and Bart was almost shouting that her marriage was a betrayal of all Lord Gray had stood for – by which he meant, mainly, I think, that Sir Hugh Blake was a Shakespeare scholar. Actually, Bart was rather charmingly funny that day, in a scary sort of way. He was shouting, "Mother, for heaven's sake, you could marry a butcher, a baker, or a candlestick maker, but to marry that silly ass of a Shakespeare faker is a disgrace."

'Now, you may wonder what he meant, James. What he meant was simply that Sir Hugh Blake believed that Shakespeare wrote Shakespeare. I know it must seem astonishing that any family could get so embroiled and angry and alienated over so fine an intellectual point. But such is my family. Lord Gray had devoted much of his life to proving that Francis Bacon wrote the so-called plays of Shakespeare. His two boys admired their father greatly, and he died when they were at the age when boys still need to believe in their father, need to believe that the world he bequeathed them is right and true. Bart was twelve or thirteen, I think. And they have both taken up his belief in Francis Bacon almost as other children take up their parents' belief in a partic-ular god. Lotte floats above it all, of course, in that wonderful way of hers. How many times have I heard her say, in all seeming innocence, "Oh, *la*! Of course Shakespeare wrote Shakespeare – unless it was another gentleman of the same name." She knows perfectly well how that statement unsettles both Alexis and Bart, for it suggests that their entire argument is frivolous. My mother is not willing to take any nonsense from anyone, and won't – but at the same time she doesn't wish to waste her energy in silly discussions, and won't. Nor does she wish to be in the least impolite, and never is. But she gets her way and has her say and is gone before anyone knows quite what has happened. The boys love her but don't quite approve of her.'

Marianne and I were entering the restaurant now, for an early lunch, and I turned the conversation to Holmes. I wished to see what she thought of him, to see whether she had heard any rumours, and to learn whether she believed them. She told me, yes, she had read of Dr Coleman's experiments with reviving mice who had been in cold storage for five years. She had a vague notion that reviving a man could be possible, providing he had been well frozen and that his internal organs were not too damaged. She brought up the fact that just a few months earlier she had read how some Americans had recovered the full genome of a woolly mammoth, and were estimating that soon, for a cost as little as five million pounds, they would be able to bring a member of that extinct species back into the world. She said she understood that this was not quite the same thing that Dr Coleman was doing, but she said it made her realize that modern DNA techniques opened up possibilities beyond the imaginations of most people. But she said – as she fingered her glass of wine – that, after all, if Holmes were not Holmes, he was merely another gentleman of the same name.

I laughed and told her she was as gracious and winning as her mother, and then we toasted Mr Sherlock Holmes – whoever he might be – and wished him a speedy solution of the case of the missing Shakespeare letter. At that moment our waiter set our pasta before us, and it struck me what a lucky life I had, being here in London at this moment in time, involved simultaneously in the worlds of the colourfully young and the curiously old.

As the meal went on, Marianne drifted back to speaking of her family life, as if she had come to trust me, having found in me a sympathetic ear and soul. 'You know, James, I really find Alexis quite appealing, though he is such an intellectual sort that one feels his feet were never firmly on the ground. Whenever I come to town I bring him groceries, fearing he won't have anything in the house to eat. He is drifting in some other world, imagining himself communing with Oscar Wilde, with Epictetus, with Plato. He is a warm soul, but his warmth is diffused in a thousand cosmic directions, and never at a real person. A person like me. Bart, by contrast, is perfectly practical, and perfectly cold. I always feel he is up to something. Perhaps this is just because his work is secret work, government work. He often flies off to Belgium to meet people. He leads a secret life. He has few friends, and those few are odd. A couple of months ago he introduced me to one of his friends. A man named Filbert Abernetty. About Bart's age. Apparently Bart had known him for some years, in a business connection. Supposedly Filbert

Abernetty had seen me somewhere, and was keen to meet me. What was most strange was that Bart should put himself out to introduce us. They drove up together from Bath, where Abernetty has his business, and we three had lunch at a place in Oxford. Bart was more genial than I had seen him in years. He spoke glowingly of my accomplishments, and of Filbert's, and when it appeared we both liked the same sort of music, Bart hastily – in his clumsy way – offered to buy us tickets to a concert at the Royal Festival Hall the next day. I didn't wish to be rude, but managed to decline. Filbert Abernetty was a thin man, with thinning hair, thin fingers, a thin voice, and a quietness about him that might have been modesty, might have been reticence, might have been – and this is what struck me most, and seemed most appropriate since he was Bart's friend – secrecy. Several times I have gotten calls from Filbert Abernetty, asking if I might be free to go here or there. I have politely evaded him. I told him I was still dating George Bingly. A couple of weeks ago Bart cornered me at Widcombe Manor and demanded to know why I had been so rude to his friend Abernetty. He was really quite . . . *threatening* is I guess the word. But I'm not in the least afraid of Bart . . .'

'Maybe you should be,' I said. For I was getting a little fed up with Bart, just hearing about him.

'Oh, I'm not one to be afraid of much,' she said with a laugh. 'Anyway, I told him that I had men friends of my own, didn't need another, and that he might do his Filbert a favour by gently suggesting to him that he was wasting his time in phoning me. And Bart smirked, and said something vaguely offensive, and, frankly, I haven't spoken with him since.'

'Is he unstable?' I asked.

She nodded. Laid down her fork. 'I think he is, really. And do you know when I realized it, James? I mean, you'd think that I'd have realized many years ago that Bart was not quite normal – but it was only within the past year or so that that fact struck me with force. It was the day Lotte's new lawyer came out to the manor and brought us the news that her investments had been carelessly handled and that very likely both the property in Scotland and the one in Gloucestershire would need to be sold within the next year. We were in the large hall when he said this. Bart sat hunched in his chair, as he always sits. By and by the lawyer left. Bart was still sitting there. I had come to clear away the tea cups when I noticed he was shaking. Then I saw he was crying, tears streaming down his cheeks. 'Not Scotland and here both,' he said to me – not quite realizing, in his surprising grief, that he was speaking to one whom he despised. I hurried out of the room to leave him in solitude, which I knew he preferred. I was sorry that he knew I had seen him crying.

'I was surprised, really. For the castle in Scotland had been closed up and the servants had been let go, and no one had been up there, so far as I knew, for five years. So it seemed to me that not much would change in any of our lives if the castle were sold. And Lotte and Hugh had been talking for several years about selling Widcombe Manor, so that should have come as no surprise. They loved the place but were struggling with the upkeep, and wanted a change, perhaps a small condominium somewhere, Oxford or London.

'It was the only time in my life that I had seen Bart crying. I remember Lotte remarking that even as a child he never cried. So, seeing him shaking and sobbing in his chair quite startled me. Since then I have tried to explain his behaviour to myself. I could only imagine that he felt bad because the sale of the castle and the manor would be like the sale of his childhood. He had spent many splendid summers at Castle Mornay, and he had grown up at Widcombe Manor, and he must have remembered many happy days in each place. Now, suddenly, a new lawyer appeared and told him his childhood was about to vanish forever. But my explanation to myself never satisfied me completely. I think, James, that yours is closer to the mark: Bart has always been unbalanced, and in this moment something in him broke. I have always thought him secretive, and dangerous, and cold, and cruel. But perhaps he wouldn't be so if he had been made of sterner stuff.'

'That is possible,' I said.

'I pity him, really,' she said.

'Pity him if you will,' said I. 'But beware of him. Weakness is a dangerous thing.'

'Don't worry about me,' she laughed.

And then, as the waiter brought the mousse, we spoke again of poets and pamphleteers, and she said she thought, as the weather grew warmer, she might like to take a drive to Scotland, to see the castle of her childhood. She asked if such an outing might suit my fancy. I said to her, 'I have always loved Scotland. Perhaps you and Holmes and I could go.'

'Or just you and I, if he can't,' she said.

I reached home that evening feeling quite good, optimistic, the sort of feeling that often fills a man on a fine spring day.

Holmes, too, seemed to be in fine fettle. He had evidently sucked the marrow from *Black Holes and Body Heat*, for as I entered our sitting room he waved the book in the air and said, 'An amazing performance, Wilson – this book by E.C. Drubbing is truly an astonishing performance.'

'It has certainly occupied your mind for longer than I thought it would,' I said.

'It is true that some of Drubbing's concepts are so large as to nearly vanish,' said Holmes. 'He says, for example –' Holmes opened the book and read from it – '*Resurrection Day will come not because a god intervenes but because Time will come full circle and knowledge will be complete.*'

Snapping the book closed, he stood up suddenly and strode to the window and looked out. 'The problem, Wilson, is the mental life.'

'The mental life?' said I.

'Let us say we could extend the physical life to the end of time, and that we became wiser and wiser the longer we lived. But that is precisely the problem. As our knowledge became more and more complete, would we not become more and more bored? It is the excitement of the new, the unknown, that makes life worth living. Paris, as you once observed, is exciting the first time you go, for it is new, unknown, thrilling, even slightly dangerous, and there is much to discover. The second time it is also pleasing. But by the twentieth time it is merely commonplace, and is in danger of becoming a bore. Drubbing speaks as if knowledge is what we are after, but . . .'

'Well, *aren't* you?' I said.

'Only enough knowledge to solve the present conundrum, not all conundrums. It is not knowledge that makes life a joy, but the *lack* of knowledge. For that is what makes a mystery. Could a life without problems, without mystery, be worth living? A life without mysteries to plumb and problems to solve would be a desert of boredom. I should go mad.'

I poured myself a glass of sherry. 'I met Marianne today, Holmes—'

'Yes, yes, I am most interested.'

'She told me quite a tale.'

'Ah!' he cried, and he sat down in a chair by the window, and faced me. 'Spare me no details, Wilson.'

So I told him all she had said – or most of it – as concisely as I could. He listened intently. Occasionally he asked for a point of clarification. I skipped much of the story, of course, for I could not reproduce a day's worth of conversation. And I nearly omitted the episode about Bart's friend Abernetty. But because Abernetty irritated her so, and therefore irritated me, I was led into repeating what she had said about him . . . and scarcely had I done so than Holmes held up his hand and said, 'What, pray, was the man's Christian name? Not Filbert, I suppose?'

'Yes. Filbert. How did you know?'

Holmes's head lifted and he looked amazed. He cried, 'Where was he from, Wilson? Did you learn where he was from?'

'Bath,' I said. 'Evidently he has a business there. You are familiar with the name?'

'I knew a family named Abernetty, years ago. Yet, surely, it cannot be the same!' He rubbed his hand over his brow. 'And yet, they also were from Bath.'

'When did you know them, Holmes?' I asked.

He didn't seem to hear the question. 'The plot grows darker and darker, Wilson,' he cried. 'And yet . . . it may be some other family, after all.'

He was frowning. I didn't press him further. He would tell me in due course, if there was anything to tell. He had gone into one of his trances. Once I had felt that this trance he so often displayed was mostly an affectation, a dramatic performance to impress others and convince them that he was concentrating with supernatural intensity. But by now I had learnt that it was just Holmes, the way he could not help being. It was as if a problem seized him and lifted him with huge hands and refused to let him move. He sat frozen in his chair.

I took a book from the shelf and retired to my bedroom to read. But as I closed the door, I was thinking that I had heard that name, *Abernetty*, before. Or read it. Yes, perhaps in Watson's chronicles of Holmes's earlier career. I couldn't shake the thought, and finally I drew down a volume of the Watson chronicles, and almost as if Fate were guiding my hand I fanned through a few pages and came to what Watson had called *The Adventure of the Six Napoleons*. I turned another page – and there, buried in a paragraph towards the bottom, was what I was looking for: *You will remember, Watson, how the dreadful business of the Abernetty family was first brought to my notice by the depth which the parsley had sunk into the butter upon a hot day.*

It did not seem likely that the same family who were operating a hundred years ago would be operating today. I wondered, however, what the Abernetty family's 'dreadful business' could have been, that the mere mention of *Filbert Abernetty* could startle Holmes so violently.

FIFTEEN
Illogical Doubts About the Bard

Solveig Nordstrand rang me and said she had painted my portrait from memory. She asked if I would like to see it. How could I refuse? As I stepped into her studio in Clarges Street she came towards me smiling, and her eyes were very blue. I complimented her silk blouse and necklace.

'You should see me when I paint – I am in jeans and an old shirt.'

'Do you wear a beret?' I asked.

At that moment I stumbled over a canvas leaning against a post, and she laughed and took my hand and led me behind her easel, and she held out her other hand. 'That is my vision of you, Mr Wilson,' she said.

'What a strong and bold painting,' I said. 'But I fear it flatters me. I seldom feel so glowing as I look on your canvas.'

'You always seem very glowing and robust, to me. You seem the sort who was a rugby man at school.'

'I was, in fact. But I am quite amazed you could remember my face so well – having seen me only so briefly.'

'I am an artist, Mr Wilson – and you interest me.'

Her English was tinged with a Swedish accent, and when she looked up at me and said "you interest me", she reminded me a little of the meltingly feminine Ingrid Bergman looking up at Bogy in *Casablanca*.

'The painting is for you,' she said.

'What a wonderful gift!' I said. 'But perhaps you should keep it for me – until I think how to display it.'

We went to lunch at a nearby restaurant and there, over the rim of her red wine glass, she asked about Holmes's progress on her case. 'Has he found the man and woman who destroyed my painting?'

'He has learnt who they are.'

'I wonder why they set it afire?' she said, and she laughed. 'I did not think it was *so* bad.'

'Oh, it had nothing to do with your painting, my dear lady – of that I am convinced. You were a random victim.'

'But the crime must have had a purpose, Mr . . . may I call you James?'

'Of course.'

'Those people must have had a motive, James. No?'

'That is the puzzle in all this,' I replied. 'The man who burnt your painting is an international criminal, never known to have involved himself in a crime that did not net him millions of pounds. Yet suddenly he seems to be involved in little more than vandalism. Holmes believes that in recent weeks this individual has exploded an electric guitar during a street busker's performance, destroyed a lute during a performance of *A Midsummer Night's Dream*, injured two music critics during a violin recital by Capinelli, and destroyed (probably inadvertently) an environmental artist – or, to use the right term, killed him . . .'

'Killed who? Not Ian Fiero!'

'You knew him?'

'Oh, my God,' she gasped.

'I'm sorry.'

The colour faded out of her face. 'I knew Ian, yes. I knew he had died, of course. They said only he was hit by a bus. I did not know he was murdered!'

'The murder may not have been intentional. A small explosion in the portfolio he was carrying caused him to fall off the kerb. The portfolio contained – this is Holmes's theory – drawings of his scheme to alter the Big Ben clock tower.'

She put her finger to her lips and gazed at me, perplexed.

'Then this criminal seems to have a grudge against art – is it not so? He attacks instruments, art critics, an architect, a painting . . .'

'Yes,' I said, 'and also attacks a letter by a great poet – which would fit your theory. Holmes believes he recently stole a letter by Shakespeare, perhaps simply in order to destroy it – though this is not clear.'

Her eyes opened wide. 'William Shakespeare!'

'Yes.'

'To destroy a letter by Shakespeare . . . I do not understand.'

'That is one of Holmes's working theories.'

'He seems a very clever man, this Holmes.'

'He hypothesizes that there may be a fanatic on the loose who believes, with all the heat and fervour of a religious conviction, that someone other than Shakespeare wrote Shakespeare's works. Holmes suspects that this person may have arranged to have the letter stolen before it could be authenticated, since if the letter were thought to be authentic it would strengthen the case that William Shakespeare of Stratford-upon-Avon was really the author of the plays we all admire. As you may know, no genuine letters from the hand of William Shakespeare have been discovered in four hundred years. So if this letter should prove authentic, it would be quite a find.'

'I have heard of this theory that Shakespeare wasn't written by Shakespeare. It sounds quite absurd to me, James.'

'It always has seemed a rather silly argument to me, too,' I said. 'I never really understood the argument, until Holmes explained it to me.'

'What did he say?'

'Holmes says that everyone agrees that there was a man called William Shakespeare who lived in Stratford-upon-Avon. Everyone also agrees that this man went to London, became part owner of the Globe Theatre, and put on plays advertised as having been written by William Shakespeare. Contemporary documents prove all this. What Shakespeare doubters dispute is that this William Shakespeare of Stratford-upon-Avon really wrote the plays.'

'But who else would have?'

'The Shakespeare doubters argue that maybe William Shakespeare, the theatre owner, bought or stole the plays from somebody else. Or maybe Shakespeare was given the plays by the real author, a person who – for some obscure reason or other – wished to remain anonymous.'

Solveig laughed. 'But everyone at the time thought Shakespeare wrote the plays, no?'

'Yes. Many documents show this. But the doubters argue that the people of the time didn't know the truth, either.'

She laughed again, almost merrily. 'So they argue that Shakespeare was fooling everybody? That seems a very silly thing to think. How could they think it?'

'Holmes described the illogical arguments of the Shakespeare doubters very succinctly. First, because we know very little about Shakespeare's life, they conclude that his life could not have been rich enough to fill the plays with all those wonderful scenes concerning law, royalty, seamanship, soldiering, botany, hunting, far cities, historical perspectives, and so on. But of course, the fact that we know so little about his life might, with equal logic, mean exactly the reverse – that his life was filled with rich experience. Who can say he did not take the grand tour of Europe, know every king on the continent, spend hours with barristers and seaman every month of his life, and so on? Second, because there is no documentary evidence that Shakespeare ever attended school, the Shakespeare doubters conclude he didn't attend school, and they go on to argue that this means he could not have been literate enough to write the plays – ignoring the fact that Homer, Chaucer, Robert Burns and Mark Twain were not known to have had much schooling either. Third, because in his last will and testament Shakespeare mentions no library of books, they conclude that he did not read all the books which obviously the author of the plays must have read. Fourth, because Shakespeare wrote no letters claiming that he wrote the plays, they conclude he didn't write the plays – ignoring the fact that nobody else in the world ever wrote a letter claiming to have written the plays, either. It is quite incredible, the arguments of these doubters. Shakespeare never wrote a letter saying he wrote the plays, therefore they conclude he didn't write them. Francis Bacon never wrote a letter saying he wrote the plays, therefore they conclude he *did* write them.'

After lunch we walked along the bustling street towards her studio.

'You are one of the few men who walk as fast as I do. I so hate walking at a snail's pace.'

'You know,' I said, 'I often think it is human nature to love mysteries. For instance, it is plain that Shakespeare wrote his own plays, but since those plays are so magical, people find it fun to make a mystery of them, to concoct fantastical circumstantial arguments to prove that someone else might have written them.'

'Won't you come up to my studio?' She opened the door.

'Thank you, yes . . . in fact, there is not a shred of documentary evidence that the plays were written by Francis Bacon, Edward de Vere, William Stanley, Christopher Marlowe, John Fletcher, Sir Francis Drake, or any of the other candidates who have been offered up as the real author of the plays.'

'No evidence?'

'There is nothing at all. No documentary evidence. Not a shred, not a line. The so-called "proofs" that these others wrote the plays are pure fantasies, concocted by posterity. But there is one document from that time that indisputably and unambiguously names the author of the plays. It states that William Shakespeare, *of Stratford-upon-Avon*, wrote them.'

'Slip off your jacket, James. It is warm. And what is that document?'

'The First Folio of Shakespeare's plays. It was published in 1623, seven years after Shakespeare's death. It was published by Shakespeare's actor friends. Shakespeare's name is listed as author, and the plays are printed there – and two people who wrote prefaces to the book allude to the fact that the author was Shakespeare of *Stratford-upon-Avon*.'

'How interesting,' she said, looking up at me and tilting her head a little.

'In short, my dear Solveig, if we eliminate all fantasies and stick only to demonstrable facts – facts in the form of contemporaneous documents that unequivocally name someone as the author of the plays – then the score is this: William Shakespeare of Stratford-upon-Avon, one; everybody else, nothing.'

'Come to my room, James,' she said, taking my hand. 'I want to show you something.'

SIXTEEN
Alexis Gray Makes a Surprise Visit

On a dark and rainy morning in the middle of May I stood beneath the awning of the news-seller's shop and watched as old Mrs Cleary passed by carrying an umbrella and leading her two little dogs. The dogs were happy in their puddles and the old woman was talking to them fondly. When I returned to our flat I found Holmes struggling to make breakfast. 'We ought to get a dog to amuse us,' I said.

'Where is the pepper?' he replied.

I sat by the window, sipping coffee and reading the news of the day. 'My heavens, Holmes – here is an item that may have a connection with your case!'

He appeared in the doorway, spatula in hand.

'Two months ago,' I continued, 'two men riding in a fox hunt in Gloucestershire were blown out of the saddle by small explosive devices that were, according to people on the scene, apparently planted by animal rights advocates who were protesting the hunt. The explosions occurred just as the bugle blew to signal the beginning of the chase. One man hit his head on a stone when he fell, and for weeks he has been in a coma. Yesterday he died.'

Holmes stalked towards me, looking startled. 'May I see it, Wilson?' He stood by the window reading the article, then sank into his chair with an uncharacteristic sigh. He put his right hand to his forehead, as if age had really caught up with him.

'Well?' said I.

'You are quite right,' said he. 'These two men,' – tapping the newspaper – 'Frank Sweet and Harvey Barnes, fell from their horses just as Alexis Gray, in his Bif Carcanson column of some months ago, said they ought to do. The pattern is identical: someone attacked in his column is then attacked in the world. What a fool I have been, Wilson! I begin to wonder if my brain has begun to degenerate.'

'Come, now, Holmes! Don't talk rubbish.'

'I had beguiled myself into thinking Art was at the centre of this mystery. And to this moment I still hadn't quite shaken free of that notion.'

'Certainly one had reason for thinking so,' I said, 'when one considers the musical performances disrupted, the murder of that flamboyant artist named Fiero, the destruction of Solveig's painting, the stolen Shakespeare letter . . .'

'Misled, utterly misled!' cried Holmes. 'Art is only superficially involved with these crimes. As I said the other day, something deeper is going on, my friend.'

'But what? You mentioned earlier a terrorist plot.'

'Something very deep and devious. I paid little attention to Gray's comments on the fox hunt gang, for I was focusing on his criticisms of art and artists. It seemed to me that he was a little off topic in discussing fox hunting, which he said was neither art nor sport, but a cult of cruelty and cowardice. He called Sweet and Barnes "the unfit in unfair pursuit of the unfortunate," and he recommended that if they had no consideration for the beauties of the fox they might at least stop despoiling the beauty of the countryside by obscuring it with their own chubby and unhandsome figures. He recommended that if they wished to do the world a favour they might, instead of sitting in plain view on their horses, find a comfortable ditch to fall in where they couldn't be seen. The column struck me as very different from all the others, for it was not about art but sport.'

'The other attacks took place in London,' I said. 'This one took place in Gloucestershire.'

'And not far from Widcombe Manor,' he said.

'Will we be making a journey to talk to the master of the hunt?'

'Not at present. I have an appointment at St Bart's with Dr Coleman at ten, an appointment with Lotte Linger at four, and I must call Lestrade immediately to ask what he knows about the Abernetty family.'

'Come now, Holmes! Surely the criminal Abernetty family of a hundred years ago – if criminals they were – could not be the same . . .'

'Never proved, that was the problem,' said Holmes.

'It seems doubtful they could be connected with the Abernettys of today.'

'I wonder, I wonder,' he said, frowning. His mobile flickered in his palm, and he hit the button. 'Hello, Lestrade . . .?'

I put some bread in the toaster, started a new pot of coffee. When I returned, Holmes was already off the phone.

'What did you learn?' I asked.

'Lestrade must ask permission before he gives me any information on the present-day Abernettys.'

'What!' I cried. 'That means there *is* information on them in the files of Scotland Yard. I am astounded.'

'It is no more than I expected,' said Holmes. He sprang to his feet. 'Well, I must get ready for Dr Coleman, Lestrade, and Lotte Linger. A busy day!'

Someone knocked at our door. It was the resident porter with a package for Sherlock Holmes. Holmes opened the package almost with the glee of a child. 'Sir Hugh Blake has been as good as his word,' said he, and he held up a very handsome briar pipe.

'Magnificent,' I said.

'It feels fine in hand – as if made for me,' said Holmes.

'It *was* made for you,' I laughed.

'Mr Sedley of Hexham, my congratulations!' cried Holmes, brandishing the pipe in the air. He then slapped it lightly betwixt his teeth and, speaking expertly from one side of his mouth, he said, 'Professor Blake sent a very gracious note with it, Wilson. Let me read it to you:

> *My Dear Sherlock Holmes,*
>
> *The enclosed briar is a token of thanks for your efforts on my behalf. Sorry for the delay, but the pipe went missing for several days after it arrived here from the shop of the excellent Mr Sedley of Hexham, and I only found it again this morning. I fear I am getting forgetful in my old age.*
>
> *Wishing you all the very best of good fortune in your search for Shakespeare's letter, I remain,*
>
> *Ever truly yours,*
> *Hugh Blake.'*

'He sounds most appreciative, Holmes.'

Holmes gazed smiling at the pipe. 'It is certainly a wonderful piece of craftsmanship – alas that no tobacco is allowed – but 'tis a comfort just to hold it in my hand.'

The day passed quickly and most pleasurably for me, for I spent it in bookshops. I arrived back home at six, and Holmes was already there.

'I must have a full report, Holmes,' said I.

'Easily done,' said he. 'Dr Coleman was entirely pleased with my progress and sees no problems. He checked all the regrown organ tissue, believes my mental processes are normal . . .'

'I presume he meant *as normal as they ever were . . .*'

'Touché, Wilson!' he cried.

'And Lotte Linger?'

'Charming woman, most pleasant company. At our early dinner I showed her the pictures of Lars Lindblad and Katrinka Pushkin. She said she had never seen either of them.'

'And Lestrade?'

'I met him and he handed me a thick dossier on the Abernetty family, but he said I must read it only in the room where we sat, and that I must take no notes.' Holmes leant back in his chair with a satisfied look on his face. 'The case of the stolen letter is still a bit vague, Wilson, but the related case of the exploding artists is now coming into focus.'

'I am certainly interested in the Abernetty family, Holmes.'

'In short, the Abernetty family have, ever since 1605, engaged in . . .'

But he was interrupted by the ringing of the doorbell. We were startled to hear the voice of Alexis Gray come over the intercom.

'By all means, come up,' said Holmes. Instantly he had forgotten about the Abernettys. A new eagerness possessed him.

Alexis Gray stepped into our flat and for a fraction of a minute his eyes darted about almost furiously as he seemed – evidently out of habit – to appraise the decor, the *objets d'art*, the pictures on the walls.

'No, I don't much fancy that landscape painting, either,' said Holmes.

'Pardon me?' said Alexis Gray, looking away from the forest scene that hung over our entry table.

Holmes did not bother to enlighten him as to how he had read his fleeting thought, but only welcomed him.

Alexis was as handsome as ever, but a change had come over him. He was retiringly polite, almost reticent. 'Good morning, Mr Holmes, Wilson.'

Holmes waved him into a chair and sat down opposite, and I likewise took a chair.

Without further preliminaries Alexis Gray leant suddenly far forward, very earnestly, and said, 'Mr Holmes, I need your help. Something has been happening which, frankly, terrifies me – though it may be nothing, nothing at all. If you can assure me it is nothing at all, that would be wonderful. I will double your fee, in that case. But if I'm right –' He shook his head, half closed his eyes and shuddered as if unwilling to face the possibility – 'then I must know the cause. It is just inexplicable . . . and terrifying.'

'Compose yourself, Mr Gray,' said Holmes. 'Would you like some tea?'

'No, thank you. No.'

'Then tell me, what is the terrible thing to which you refer? I will certainly help you if I am able.'

'You are, in fact, a bona fide detective, are you not? I have been assured of this by several people.'

'I am,' said Holmes.

'I choose you, Mr Holmes, because I am told that you operate below the radar of the official police.'

'That is an apt characterization,' said Holmes. 'Although, of course, if I become aware of crimes . . .'

'Of course, of course,' said Mr Gray. 'That goes without saying. But the terrible thing I refer to, Mr Holmes, is related to that very point: I have begun to look like a criminal, even to myself. Yet I know perfectly well that I am not. First of all, I must tell you that I spend most of my time writing books but I supplement my income by writing a column for a weekly arts magazine, using a *nom de plume*. It is this arts column that is causing me all the trouble and consternation. Several months ago I began noticing something odd, and it was this: whenever I severely criticized anyone in that column, that person soon suffered some sort of inexplicable attack – I mean a physical attack, in the real world. The first time this happened I was certain it was a coincidence, and no serious damage was done to the person, and in fact I even laughed and said to friends, "Well, it couldn't have happened to a worse musician." But then it happened again, to someone else I had criticized, and I was a little astonished, but, you know, coincidences do happen. The same thing happened repeatedly, and as time went by the attacks became less and less trivial and more and more dangerous, until finally one was fatal. A man was killed. In short, Mr Holmes, at first I knew these things were just coincidences. Later, I *thought* they must be just uncanny coincidences. Still later, the horrible realization came upon me that they couldn't be coincidences – though still I tried to convince myself that the coincidence explanation was *possible* . . . which of course it was, since anything in this world is possible. But today, Mr Holmes, when I read about a fox hunter who died – a man named Sweet, whom I'd criticized in my column several months ago – a cold hand gripped my heart. It was almost as if I had killed him myself. I laid down the newspaper and came straight to you. I want you, Mr Holmes, to find out who is doing this.'

'Have you any idea who might be doing it, or why?'

'No!' cried Alexis Gray, regaining some of his customary energy. 'I can think of no reason whatever. That is what is so maddening and frightening. That is what prevented me for so long from seeing what has been happening – because what has been happening makes no sense whatever. There is no point to it. Nobody gains by it.'

'Perhaps someone who wants to hurt you would gain by it,' said Holmes.

'Yes, I thought of that, and it is true that there are many in this town who would like to have my guts for garters,' said Gray. 'Making enemies is my stock in trade. But for someone to maim and kill people I mention in my column, in hopes of making me a suspect, or in hopes of preventing me from daring to be critical – no, it is just too fantastic, Mr Holmes.'

'As it happens, Mr Gray, this case has already interested me. Have you ever seen this man?' Holmes handed him a photograph.

Alexis Gray shook his head. 'Never.' He handed it back.

'Or what about this woman?' asked Holmes, handing him a drawing.

'Don't know her – though perhaps I'd like to.'

'She is quite beautiful, isn't she,' said Holmes. 'But I don't think you'd want to know her, Mr Gray.'

'I will take your word for it, Mr Holmes.'

'Mr Gray, there is most definitely a motive behind this series of attacks. Someone is lavishing a great deal of money, time and resources on carrying them out. What the motive may be is still a mystery. Let me ask you this: as you have thought about the problem over the last few weeks, has any person at all popped into your mind – however quickly you discarded the thought, however ridiculous it might later have seemed – as being possibly involved?'

'Well, no,' said Alexis Gray, slowly. He touched his own cheek. 'Certainly my brother would have no reason to do something like this. And when it comes to . . .'

'Then why did you mention him?' asked Holmes.

'I . . . I don't know,' said Gray. 'I suppose because he's . . . well, he has looked up to me all his life, and believed I was right in everything I said. Even when he was a little chap he fiercely defended my opinions, even when I didn't need defending. That's why the thought occurred that he might be involved – but I quickly realized that I was foolish to think such a thing. I was just grasping for some sort of explanation.'

'Would your brother be willing, do you think, to steal the Shakespeare letter in order to prevent it from contradicting your forthcoming book?'

'That is quite out of the question. For one thing, the letter, if it were made public, might well increase sales of my book by spurring new interest in the whole subject of Shakespeare's life. The only way it would hurt sales of the book would be if it turned out to be a genuine letter written by Shakespeare in Florence, and if it turned out that in that letter he mentioned some of his own plays, mentioning them in such a way that it was unequivocally clear he was claiming to have written the plays, and was presuming his recipient shared that assumption. And for all that to be true of the missing letter, Mr Holmes, is most unlikely.'

'What makes you think it unlikely?'

'First, because I know Bacon wrote the plays. Second, because even if I am wrong, and Shakespeare wrote them, seldom is a piece of evidence so unequivocal that it is sufficient to prove a case beyond doubt.'

'I am very keen to get the letter back,' said Holmes. 'Have you seen it?'

'No,' said Gray. 'My stepfather, Sir Hugh, was very careful not to let me catch so much as a glimpse of it. I believe Marianne, my half-sister, has read it.'

'She told me she has not,' I said.

'Ah, well.' He shrugged. 'Then I guess she hasn't.'

'Let us imagine for a moment, Mr Gray,' said Holmes, 'that your brother Bart did steal the letter. Let us imagine that the letter is, at this moment, in his care and keeping. You know your brother better than I. What do you think? Would he destroy it, or hide it?'

'Well, he does like to destroy things,' mused Alexis Gray. 'But . . .'

'Why do you say that!' asked Holmes, sharply.

'I wonder myself why I say it,' said Alexis, and his blue eyes opened wide. 'He is a complicated little brother. He was always very cute, as a child, but he liked to blow up frogs with fire-crackers.' Alexis laughed. 'I can't say he had a temper, really. More a smouldering resentment. And you never quite could guess who it was he resented until his resentment exploded in some angry action.' Alexis laughed. 'Like the time he knocked Grandpa Linger – that was my mother's father – off his crutches. Little Bart just stood there, watching silently, as Grandpa Linger rolled down the embankment. Why did he do it? I can't even remember. Some small thing, no doubt. Grandpa Linger had reprimanded Bart, perhaps. Something trivial. Mostly, though, we had lovely times when we were children.'

'So he might destroy it,' said Holmes.

'Probably not, Mr Holmes. No. My guess would be that he would not destroy it, but keep it. I think he would prefer to hide it. That is his nature. Secretive as a schoolgirl.'

'And is there a particular place where he would hide it – if, for instance, he were still a child. Now that he is an adult he has the whole world in which to hide it. But *if* he were a child, was there a place he hid things – known only to you and him, perhaps?'

'How perceptive you are, Mr Holmes!'

'It is only that I and my own brother, Mycroft, had a secret hiding place when we were young. So I thought . . .'

'Yes, there is one, Mr Holmes.'

'Where?'

'It is in our castle in Scotland, Castle Mornay, where we used to spend summers when we were young. No one has been up there for years – Mother closed the place in 2004 and since then she has only had a caretaker who looks in once a week. In fact, it is unlikely he would have travelled to the Highlands to hide a letter.'

'Ah, but still. Just for the sake of thoroughness, Mr Gray, would you be good enough to give me the details of the hiding place? After all, it is a *Shakespeare* letter. We must leave no stone unturned.'

'Amazingly enough, Mr Holmes, you have guessed the spot without meaning to. The hiding place is under a particular stone, a stone in the Great Hall of the castle. Let me think a bit about how best to describe the precise spot for you. Why don't I draw a diagram, and type out some instructions, and send them to you in the morning?'

'Excellent,' said Holmes, rising from his chair. 'If that is all, Mr Gray, I will be in touch with you soon.'

Gray rose also, but held up his hand. 'That is not quite *all*, I fear, Mr Holmes.' He wiped his forehead with the middle three fingers of his right hand, took a deep breath. 'I must tell you something, Mr Holmes, that bothers me greatly. In my last column in *Arts Weekly* I wrote a snide comment about you and your friend Wilson. A criticism, frankly. It was quite an unfair criticism, I now realize. But it's done. As a result, I worry that you may be in danger. I am terribly sorry and, frankly, I am not only chagrined at my unkindness, but frightened for your safety.'

'Not to worry,' said Holmes.

'But I do worry,' said Gray.

Holmes took the handsome new briar pipe out of his mouth, and gestured with it. 'I'll try to make very certain, Mr Gray, that no one slips me a microbomb.'

SEVENTEEN
An 1882 Manet View

The following day Solveig Nordstrand rang up early and asked if she might buy lunch for Holmes and me, saying she wished to thank the great detective for his help. To my surprise, Holmes immediately accepted her invitation. Later that morning we stopped by Solveig's gallery in a taxi to collect her, and soon we three were slipping happily through London streets, hermetically sealed in a black shadow. Solveig said,

'Perhaps we should eat at that little restaurant by Covent Garden, James, where we had lunch last week.'

'I should very much like to take lunch at the Savoy,' said Holmes.

He said it in such a way that brooked no argument. I again was surprised. I wondered why he had such a strong preference.

We were fortunate to get a table at the Savoy, and we had a very nice conversation over lunch. Afterwards Solveig suggested we look in at the Courtauld Gallery, since we were so near. Holmes was amenable, so was I, and that is what we did. We walked straightaway to the most famous painting in the gallery, Manet's *The Bar at the Folies-Bergère*. We stood in silence gazing at the beautiful and passive bar maid who gazed in our direction without really making eye contact. She leant ever so slightly on the marble edge of the bar, with her white wrists turned towards us. By her right arm were unopened bottles of Bass Pale Ale and champagne. By her left arm was a bowl of fruit. Behind her in the mirror were reflected her derrière and a number of bottles on the bar. Also reflected were the multitude of people and objects that she gazed out upon in the grand room, including chandeliers and even the feet of a performer on a trapeze.

'It was painted in 1882, Holmes. Did you ever meet Manet?' I asked.

'I never had the honour,' he replied.

Solveig laughed at what she imagined to be my joke about Holmes's age, and she said, 'I love this painting because at first look it seems realistic, but then you look again and realize it is hallucinatory, contradictory. You see?'

Holmes moved himself in front of the painting. 'I am sorry to disagree,' said he. 'But you have got it exactly reversed. The fascinating thing about this painting is that although at first it looks contradictory, it is perfectly realistic.'

Solveig, tall and beautiful, with a lovely complexion even at fifty, laughed gently and said, with feminine surprise and grace, 'Surely you cannot think so! Do you not see the contradictions?'

'But there are none,' said Holmes. 'The reason you think you see contradictions is that you do not have the right point of view. But I have deduced the proper point of view.'

Modesty and tact were never Holmes's conspicuous virtues.

'Possibly, possibly,' she said, obviously unwilling to argue.

'I am afraid I agree with Solveig,' said I. 'There is much in the painting that simply doesn't match reality. That is its charm.'

Holmes shook his head impatiently. 'You two fail to understand where the painter placed himself when he painted this picture – I confess it took me almost thirty seconds to deduce the truth, myself.'

'Do tell us,' she said, smiling and touching his arm. And then, with a touch of irony, 'Set us straight, Mr Holmes.'

'Yes, Holmes,' said I. 'I had not realized you were so versed in the history of art. Where did Manet place himself to paint it?'

'There is only one place where he *could* have been when he painted it.'

'You don't say,' said I, for I was becoming a little irritated by his condescending tone. 'One supposes he was standing or sitting right where I am, in front of the bar and facing the girl.'

'But one would be wrong to suppose that,' said Holmes. 'If you assume that that was his viewpoint, then you will notice all the contradictions that you have already mentioned. Those bottles on the bar are not the same ones reflected in the mirror. And the girl herself, if you were standing in front of her, obviously would not be reflected in the glass at all, for she would block her own reflection, no? Yet in the painting we see the reflection of her *derrière* well off to the right of her face and figure, which would make no sense at all if you assume you are standing right in front of her.'

'Exactly,' I shot back. 'That is precisely why Solveig calls the painting hallucinatory. The bottle of Bass Ale and other bottles do not match the bottles behind them in the glass.'

'But,' said Holmes, 'if you assume yourself to be in the position of that looming man in the mirror on our far right, the man in the top hat approaching the bar – if you imagine yourself to be in his exact position, so that your reflection is his reflection – then every object and reflection in the painting is perfectly matched, and all makes sense.'

Solveig moved over to her right. 'Yes,' she said slowly. 'That is true!'

'Ah,' I said uncertainly, trying to grasp the truth that, even now, nearly eluded me. 'I see what you mean.'

'So *there*, my dear Wilson, on the far right of the scene is where Manet set up his easel to paint this picture. Indeed, I shouldn't wonder if he painted a version of himself there, just at the edge, looking at the girl and the bar – we see the gentleman only in the mirror, as Manet saw himself, though I think the face is not precisely his. He painted the figure where his own figure appeared in the mirror, and then he erased the easel from the scene, and . . . *voila!*'

'You should have been an art critic,' I said.

'Clarity depends on point of view,' said Holmes, a bit sententiously. 'Finding the proper one is my métier. It saves a world of trouble.'

'You have explained the mystery of this painting to me, Mr Holmes,' said Solveig, and she was obviously much impressed. 'I am now ever so sure you will find the person who attacked my work.'

'I infer, Holmes,' said I, 'that you are drawing a comparison between viewing a painting and viewing a crime scene.'

'Precisely so,' said Holmes. 'We have been puzzling over two little mysteries, you and I, mysteries that now seem to be merging into one. We have before us a multitude of facts, just as in Manet's painting we have before us a multitude of images. Yet our facts, like the bottles on the bar and bottles in the mirror of Manet's painting, don't seem to match. They cannot, at first glance, be reconciled. Our facts, too – like Manet's bottles and their reflections, like his bar girl and her reflection – seem misplaced, confusing, and impossible. But if only we can find the proper point of view, Wilson, the proper *angle* from which to view them, then suddenly – or such is my hope – all the details will cohere, will fit, will create a single startling and perfectly comprehensible scene.'

'You see – you will surely solve it!' said Solveig. Her smile was as bright as the sun, and her silvery blonde hair glowed warmly in the muted atmosphere of the gallery. She was, it occurred to me, much more lovely than the girl at the bar of the Folies-Bergère.

'And have you found such an angle?' I asked.

Holmes shrugged. 'Perhaps the viewpoint of a child would clarify our scene – a child who is family-centred to a fault, easily angered, and demands that the world of his happy childhood must never change.'

'That is not an adult person, who thinks that way,' said Solveig.

'Perhaps not,' said Holmes.

'No!' she said. 'We must take the innocence of childhood and bring it into our ageing world, to keep us fresh. That is all. A person who thinks the way you say is mad, really. I think I am right.'

'I think you are perfectly right,' said Holmes.

At Solveig's gallery she stepped out of the taxi and then leant back in to me and said, 'James, you left your umbrella here – I will get it.'

'Oh, let me,' I said, and I hurried out of the taxi after her. In the gallery she handed me the umbrella, and gave me a parting friendly hug. 'We must go together to the Tate Modern, sometime,' she said. 'Would you like that?'

'Absolutely,' I said. 'We must count on it.'

'Ring me, then?'

'I will,' I said, and I hurried out to the taxi.

When we reached our flat I took a shower, shaved again, dressed in light grey wool trousers, a splendid new shirt and a navy blue blazer. Holmes was in one of his agitated and moody states, flitting hither and thither almost annoyingly.

'Why don't you find a place to perch, Holmes, and give yourself a rest.'

'I wish I could. There is something very . . . I wonder, my dear Wilson, would you be good enough to ask your Marianne if she . . .'

'*My* Marianne! Really, Holmes, you surprise me!'

'I only meant that you see her rather a lot, nothing . . .'

'And very pleasant company she is, too!'

'Would you be good enough to ask her for precise directions to the family property in Scotland?'

'I will ask her. I know it is somewhere north of Inverness.'

'And please ask her to alert you the moment Bart Gray leaves on his next journey to Brussels.'

'I am quite sure she can do that,' I said. 'I know that she returned home to Widcombe Manor yesterday, for she called me from there. She will be there for some time, and so will be able to keep an eye on Bart. And I'm certain she will be glad to do what you ask. I will ring her right away.'

I called Marianne and she provided directions to Castle Mornay in excruciating detail. I wrote them all down. Then she told me something rather odd. She said that her vitamin pills had exploded.

'What did you say, Marianne – I don't think I heard you correctly.'

You heard me correctly. It's true, James: my vitamin pills exploded. Or at least some of them did. The bottle blew apart. I was sitting ten feet away, playing the piano. Pills were scattered all over.

'Perhaps the bottle was sitting on a radiator or . . .'

No.

'Or the cat knocked it.'

Nothing like that, James. No. And something similar happened before. A few weeks ago I had just dropped a pill into a glass, and I was about to go to the sink and get some water, when something popped. The glass cut my hand. I decided there must have been a crack in the glass, and that I must have squeezed it, and that it popped and broke. So I forgot about it – though I could not account for the loudness of the popping noise.

'So this is the second time?'

Yes.

'The same pills?'

Yes.

'Are they in capsule form?' I knew Holmes would want all details.

Yes. Large capsules.

'Is Bart there at the moment?'

Out in his barn lab, as usual.

'I'll call you back,' I said.

I quickly hung up and told Holmes what Marianne had said. He looked alarmed, and after a moment he declared that she must not eat any pills, nor eat anything else at Widcombe Manor. 'Tell her to go out to a restaurant to eat,' he said, and there was concern in his voice.

I made the call. I knew that she would be reluctant to take Holmes's advice, and such was the case. She told me that she had just made lunch for Lotte and Hugh, who in an hour were leaving to spend a few days in France, so that she could not possibly refuse to eat the food she herself had just prepared.

'But no pills,' I said.

No pills, she agreed. And we said goodbye.

That evening I expected to meet Rachel and Percy for dinner before our theatre engagement, but Percy had been forced to cancel. And there was Rachel, waiting alone in front of the restaurant, her red hair shining in the evening sun, looking quite splendid in a bright green blouse and dark green slacks. Something had come up just yesterday, Rachel said, to prevent Percy from coming to the play. He sent his regrets. 'We must see *Macbeth* on our own! Hope you don't mind.'

I didn't mind at all. But I said, 'This is the second time Percy has failed to meet us when he said he would. How odd!'

'Yes,' she said, 'isn't it!'

The dinner was excellent, the play was fine, and afterwards we went out for drinks and a snack. She insisted that I need not take her home to her flat in Chelsea, for it was a long way out of my way. But when I insisted I would like to do that, she quickly agreed. When we reached her place it was quite late, and we spent another hour sipping wine and going through a photo album of her recent road trip through Germany. 'Where I really want to go is Florence,' she said. 'Maybe next year.'

'Florence is a place I've always wanted to visit, too,' I said.

EIGHTEEN
The Dreadful Business of 1890

It was quite late before I returned home. I did not sleep well, for my mind was besieged by phantom feelings and half-formed fears that soared over the walls of sleep and stirred up frightening dreams. I never quite awoke but often I was aware that I was tossing and feeling miserable. At last the dial of my watch showed six o'clock. I could struggle no longer. I sat up and it was then I realized my mobile had been switched off ever since I had been at the theatre with Rachel. I switched it on and was delighted to realize I had a message from Marianne. But I listened to it with growing concern:

Sorry I missed you, James. I will try to phone you later. I'm afraid I may not be able to stay here to keep an eye on Bart. I have seen several people going out to Bart's lab in the barn, and I think one of them was Filbert Abernetty. So I'm not comfortable here, really. Bart has been acting strangely. I think I'd rather stay at my friend's flat in Oxford for the next few days until Lotte and Hugh get back from Paris. So I plan to leave

*tomorrow early. I hope nothing prevents me. I packed my bag,
intending to leave this evening, but my car wouldn't start. I can't
understand this . . . I mean, it's a new car! So, it's a mystery . . .
got to go!*

I went into the sitting room and tried to call her, to see if she
was already on the road to Oxford. No answer. I made coffee,
then tried her number again. Still no answer. Not long afterwards
Holmes appeared, looking cadaverous and calm in his bathrobe
and slippers. I handed him the phone and he listened to her last
message.

'What do you think?' I asked.

'I think something very odd is occurring at Widcombe Manor,'
he replied. 'I am speaking from mere intuition, Wilson, but I
can tell you that whatever is happening there, I don't like. Be a
good fellow and call her again.'

I dialled her number. Still no answer.

We prepared a big breakfast. I cooked the baked beans on
toast, the fried tomato, and the fried eggs; Holmes cooked the
kipper. We ate this feast and complimented our own cookery,
and when we had finished I dialled Marianne's number again.
'She was probably in the shower,' I said.

But again she didn't answer.

'What do you think, Holmes?'

'I think there is not a moment to lose.'

'To Widcombe Manor?'

'Immediately.'

'Could she be in danger?'

'Very great danger, I fear,' said he.

We finished our meal.

'I filled up with petrol yesterday,' I said. 'We're ready to go.'

'You had best pack a bag,' he said. 'Include some outdoor
clothes, and boots. I'm not sure where this journey may take
us.'

An hour later we were on our way out of London on the M40.

'Filbert Abernetty,' mused Holmes. 'How strange to hear that
name again. She saw him going into Bart's barn?'

'Evidently,' I said. 'Why would Bart be trying to hook her
up with Filbert Abernetty, if he is so jealous? And Abernetty
certainly does not sound like a man to her taste. I wonder whether
he is any relation to the Abernettys from Bath that you knew
in 1910.'

'Not 1910, Wilson. It was 1889, or '90 – '90, I think. Yes, I'm quite sure it was 1890 . . . strange how one forgets.' He sounded puzzled. 'But I strongly suspect that the Abernetty family I once knew is somehow connected with the Filbert Abernetty that your good friend Marianne Hideaway so loathes and fears. If I am right, she may have very good reason to fear him.'

'You certainly know how to frighten a man, Holmes.'

'Sorry. But I thought you should know.'

'I suppose I should,' I said. 'Then tell me the awful truth.'

'My encounter with the family was brief, but memorable,' he replied, turning himself in his seat to half face me as he told his tale. 'In July of 1890 one of our minor aristocracy, a baron from the West Country, had business in London with a member of parliament. The Baron asked me never to reveal his name, so I won't, although revealing it now, after he and several succeeding generations of his family are dead, could hardly matter. This man was under the strong impression that anarchists were threatening his life. Scotland Yard did not take the threat entirely seriously, and perhaps that was why Lestrade asked me to look into the matter. At the time I was impecunious, impetuous, and impatient for work, and so I agreed to take the case – which, in fact, offered some features not altogether without interest. The Baron and his wife said that they had, on the first Monday of every month for the preceding three months, received a package containing body parts. The April package contained two severed feet. The May package contained part of an arm and an ear. And the June package contained a pile of human flesh and bone. Each of these packages was addressed to the Baron, and each contained a card with this message: *You too will soon be bits and pieces*. The Baron, however, had discarded these packages and their grisly contents without notifying authorities, and only at the time of his London journey did he bring up the horrible tale of how he had received body parts by post – which explains, perhaps, why Scotland Yard had doubts as to the man's veracity. By the time I was called in on the case, no real evidence existed any longer – if it ever had – so I was forced to await fresh facts, and to hope those facts did not come in the form of a dead baron.

'My client arrived at Paddington Station in early evening and came by hansom directly to my digs in Baker Street. Dr Watson, who was present, afterwards agreed with my impression that the Baron showed signs of mental breakdown. At all events, he was

staying at the newly built Savoy Hotel in the Strand and was
having lunch there with his MP the next day. He wanted me to
assure his safety by examining the dining room of the hotel
before he arrived to eat. He disclosed that he had, some months
earlier, given a speech on human rights in Belfast, and that this
had caused certain political extremists – anarchists, he called
them – to issue his death warrant. His story did not seem probable, but, as you may imagine, I resolved to make sure that the
man stayed safe. The next day I booked a table at the Savoy that
was very close to the table reserved for the Baron and his guest.
I arrived a quarter hour before they were due to arrive, ordered
my meal, and soon the waiter brought me a plate of bread and
a dish of butter. The butter was nicely moulded in the shape of
a seashell, and was garnished with two sprigs of parsley.

'It was a terribly hot July day, and the dining room of the
Savoy was full. And I must remind you, Wilson, that this was an
era long before air conditioning – and also long before standards
of dress had vanished so completely as they have today. The men
were sweating in their white shirts and dark suits, and the women,
in their corsets and flowing dresses, were likewise sweating, and
occasionally dabbing their brows with handkerchiefs. Everyone
was uncomfortable and suffering, but behaving precisely as if
they were perfectly comfortable and having a fine time. It was
an age, Wilson, when even simple actions like eating lunch on a
hot day demanded a certain level of elegance, forbearance, style,
and concern for one's fellow diners – by which I mean, one
didn't drag down the general cheer by acting as if one were
anything but cheerful. And I must say that people today might
learn . . . but I digress. I don't wish to sound like a curmudg-
eonly old man.'

'Different ages, different customs, Holmes,' said I.

'As I awaited the arrival of the Baron, I began to worry about
the small table-for-two that separated my table from his. On that
table the bread had been set down, and the dish of butter likewise, and a crumpled napkin had been laid on one of the two
chairs. But there was no sign of the diner. It struck me as odd
that the napkin had been laid – against all etiquette and good
sense – on the chair rather than on the table. I leant over and
plucked the napkin from the chair and, as I had suspected, I
found that it hid something. What it hid was a package about
the size of a very large book. The package was wrapped in paper

and tied with string, and it was addressed to *Ignis Fatuus, Life's End Cottage, Bexleyheath, Kent* – as if about to be posted. I waved to the waiter and said, "Was the gentleman at this table in room 205?"

'"No, 101, sir."

'"I believe he may have forgotten his package."

'The waiter said, "No, sir. He ordered his meal but was called away. He said he will return shortly."

'"But how long has he been gone?" I asked.

'"Oh, not long, sir, not long – he will return shortly, I'm sure," was his reply. And he hastened away to serve another table.

'The waiter was busy, of course, and when one is busy it is easy to lose track of time. What worried me was that the missing diner had obviously been gone for a good half hour. This was clear from how far the parsley had sunk into his dish of butter – I had only to compare his parsley with the parsley in my dish of butter, and the parsley on the dish of butter where the two ladies nearby had already finished their meal, to make that rough calculation.

'When a man comes down to lunch, hides a package under a napkin on a chair, tucks the chair under the table, leaves with a promise to come back shortly, and after half an hour still has not returned, it does not take great powers of deduction to conclude that something might be amiss – particularly when the package is addressed to swamp gas, and is set just next to the table of a man who has reason to fear he has been marked for death by anarchists. I saw my client just coming into the dining room with his MP. He looked nervously about, then spotted me and nodded and smiled slightly, and seemed reassured. Just as he sat down to his table, and was engaged in the usual gentlemanly banter with his guest, I quickly grabbed the package from the chair and strode out of the room. I went to the desk and asked if I might have the name of the gentleman in room 101, for I had a package to return to him. The clerk looked surprised and said, "He has just checked out, sir – but look, there he is just going out the front door. Perhaps you can catch him."

'He was a tall man, well dressed, and as he reached the top of the steps he put on his top hat. I followed him out of the Savoy and down the steps to the Embankment, and as I did so I lifted the package to my face to smell it, for I wondered if it might contain something that smell might detect – and that is when I heard it ticking. The gentleman in the top hat turned right. I kept my eye on him, ran down to the river and tossed the package into the Thames. I paused only briefly to watch it float away, half submerged, and then I hurried after the top hat. I feared I had lost him but soon I caught sight of him walking up Carting Lane towards the Strand. I followed him into Haxell's Royal Exeter Hotel. There I heard him ask at the desk for the room number of Mr Abernetty. I heard the clerk's reply, waited until the gentleman had ascended the stairs, and soon I was standing quietly outside the room of Mr Filbert Abernetty, listening. I heard two men in the room talking in not particularly low voices, agreeing with each other that "it shouldn't be long now". By and by a dull *boom* penetrated the hotel; I realized that the bomb had gone off despite being half under water. "There it goes," said the voice of the top hat.

'Another voice within the room, a voice thin as a child's, replied, "Then if you will pay the other half, my dear Mr Devereaux, I will be on my way home."

'"Here it is. Very pleased to do business with you. I hope to see you again in September."

'A moment later Devereaux left the room, and I ambled down the hallway in front of him, as if looking for my room. As he passed me I glimpsed his face and recognized him. He was someone who had been pointed out to me by my brother at his London club. That obviated the need to follow him, as I knew I could find him at my own convenience. I was free to follow the man who was evidently the maker of the bomb. I loitered at the end of the dark hallway. Before long Filbert Abernetty emerged from his room and hurried away down the staircase and out into the Strand. He was a small man with very white skin and very dark hair. His eyes were large and protuberant. His mouth was small, his hands small, his voice high-pitched. He was, all in all, a strange creature. But I must say in his favour that he was exquisitely polite to all whom he encountered, the man at the news stand, the cab driver, the man at the ticket counter in Paddington Station. Also, he dressed well, and in the railway carriage he read Herodotus in the original Greek. I followed him to Bath, followed him through the streets to his clock shop, and I took a room at a nearby hotel.

'The next day I visited his clock shop. I looked at a few watches, then I said that Mr Devereaux had suggested I might find what I wanted here. We had the usual cat-and-mouse conversation, sounding each other out. But the name of Devereaux carried weight, and in the end Abernetty showed me several mechanisms that could set off bombs of various power. "It is easy enough to create big destruction with a huge bomb," he said. "I do not wish to sound immodest, but it was our family who supplied Guy Fawkes and Thomas Wintour with the fuse to set off the thirty-six barrels of gunpowder they had planted beneath Parliament in 1605. But since those crude days we Abernettys have specialized mostly in small bombs with big bangs – bombs that are portable, practical and devastating."

'When I got back to London I did research on his family and found he had not been exaggerating. His ancestor, Malcolm Abernetty, had been a member of the Clockmakers' Company of London in the mid 1600s. In that early day he made clocks and watches, but also mechanisms to set off bombs. In the early 1800s the family moved to Bath, where they are to this day. In the nineteenth century they supplied bombs and bomb timers for anarchists. In the early twentieth century they made bombs for the Irish Republican Army. In recent years their major business has been selling sophisticated explosive devices to guerrilla groups in South America, Africa and the Middle East.'

I was beginning to see where Holmes's logic was leading. 'I am astonished that in Britain we have a family of bomb makers with a tradition going back four hundred years,' I said. 'So you suspect that the man who is Bart's friend is a bomb maker from a long line of bomb makers?'

'That is my fear, Wilson.'

When we turned on to the A44 I called Marianne's mobile. No answer. When we turned on to country roads near Chipping Campden, I called again. Still no answer.

'It's probably just that her battery needs recharging,' I said.

'Yes,' said Holmes, 'no doubt that is the explanation.'

NINETEEN

O mistress mine,
where are you roaming?

As Widcombe Manor hove into view I saw a gleam of red . . . Marianne's car was parked beneath a tree at the side of the drive. In an instant Holmes was out and striding along the narrow, flower-bordered walk that led to the house. I hurried after him. He knocked on the door, then rang the bell. No one answered. We walked to the back and peered into the kitchen window. Through dusty panes we could see only patches of sunlight and the edge of a table. I rapped on the window, then rapped on the back door. Finally I dialled Sir Hugh's landline on my mobile. I could hear the sound of ringing somewhere inside the house, but no one answered.

A bumblebee hummed heavily across the flower beds and vanished in trees, and a bird whistled tiny notes that fell like pebbles into a pool of silence.

Holmes strode off in the direction of the pond. The swans glided towards the middle at his approach. He called, 'Let's have a look at the barn.'

The side door was open. We made our way to the back of the building, where Bart had his workshop and laboratory. 'There is nothing here,' said Holmes. 'They have cleaned it out.'

Everything was gone. The large plasma television monitor on the wall, the computers, the workbench filled with electronic equipment – everything had been removed. All that remained were a cage of dragonflies and a cage of houseflies. I felt sorry for them. I took them outside and opened their cages. The houseflies vanished in an instant, as if they had never existed. The dragonflies seemed bewildered at first, till I shook the cage, and then they roused themselves and hovered as if surprised, and finally shot away into forest gloom beyond the paddock.

'I confess I am worried about Marianne,' I said. 'Where could she be?'

'You are right to worry,' Holmes replied, clenching the briar pipe in his right hand, and frowning. 'My guess is that she is at Castle Mornay. Let's hope that I am right. And let's hope that we can get there in time to save her.'

'My God, Holmes! What are you saying!'

'I am asking, my friend, what is the fastest way to get to Castle Mornay? By plane, by car?'

'Let me think . . . today is Sunday. By the time we get ourselves to Birmingham, park the car, book a plane to Inverness, arrive there, rent a car and drive the rest of the way . . . it's probably six of one and a half dozen of the other. And we have no assurance at this point that we can get a plane out today.'

'Then let us linger no longer!' cried Holmes. 'Let us drive for the Scottish borders.'

But before we set off for Scotland I wanted to be certain that Marianne was not in the house, tied up – or, worse. I smashed the front door twice with my shoulder before the inner bolt splintered through wood. I hit it again and it flung wide open, and then I ran through the house. But I found no one, neither downstairs nor upstairs.

Holmes was already in my car. I drove north on the M6 past Birmingham and Manchester to Carlisle, then on towards Glasgow. As the sun sank in the sky I turned east towards Edinburgh, then turned north and passed over the Firth of Forth Bridge. By then I was getting weary. And the world had changed, become strangely beautiful and bleak, and it was evident we were now in rock-harsh and chilly Scotland. Dusk fell as we crossed the Grampian Mountains. We descended into a little valley, slipped neatly out of the main motorway and into a smaller road that led us to Kingussie, and there we stopped for the night at The Duke of Gordon Hotel.

I knew the hotel. Seventeen years earlier I had ridden my bicycle from Dunnet Head to Lands End, and my father had accompanied me in a car. Each day he had driven ahead ninety miles or so and booked a hotel, and then I had pedalled into town to a room and a supper all organized. He had stopped at Kingussie and booked a room at this hotel, and he and I had walked in the garden together before our supper. Today I was tired from the drive but needed to stretch my legs, so in fading light I strolled where my father and I had strolled, and I imagined him walking beside me, imagined I heard him speaking. But it was no good. He wasn't there. Not even his ghost. In

twilight I returned to the hotel and went upstairs for a short nap.
I am a person for whom even the shortest of naps is an astonishing elixir, and after ten minutes I arose, much refreshed, and
accompanied Holmes down to the dining room. I ordered lamb
cutlets Boswell with mint jelly and roasted potatoes, accompanied by a robust red wine.

Holmes slipped his pipe into the side pocket of his Harris
tweed sport jacket. 'We find ourselves involved in a very strange
case, Wilson. It began as a family affair but I fear it has become
an international plot that could have a stunning and terrible effect
on the world for years to come.'

'You have lost me on both levels,' I said. 'Please be good
enough to fill me in on your conclusions at the family level, for
a start. We have accumulated a vast rubble of details about Lotte
Linger's complicated clan, but I can make very little of it all.'

Holmes finished his appetizer and touched his napkin to his
lips. He looked at me curiously, as if deciding how to explain
things to this particular student. He lay down his napkin and
looked away, and assumed an almost professorial air. 'My dear
fellow,' said he, 'our tale is the tale of a youngest son. Consider
the world that was made for that son. It consisted of two king-
doms, the first in green English countryside, a manor house and
a barn and a pond full of swans and a paddock full of horses.
The second, a rocky Scottish realm crowned with a castle by a
loch. The first was for all year, the second for summer. There
is an older brother, much admired. There is a father whose
opinions seem almost those of a god. And there is a mother,
celebrated, beautiful, bringing the dazzle of celebrity to both
manor and castle. This is a world nearly perfect, and the youngest
son doesn't wish it to change. He loves it all too well: he idol-
izes the older brother, the father, and the mother, and he believes
his two worlds – each a version of fairyland – are made forever.
But then things change. The father dies, the mother remarries,
another child, a girl, enters the scene. By then the youngest son
is fourteen, and he is used to having the world to himself, and
he is stunned by the intrusion. Eventually he grows to hate the
girl. But he also comes to want her. When she passes puberty
he tries to seduce her and is rejected. His hate grows. Meanwhile
the girl's father has left, and yet another man has taken the place
of Lord Gray – a very different man, a softer man, a scholar
who quietly denies what Lord Gray told him was true. This third

father insists that Shakespeare wrote Shakespeare. It sounds a silly cavil to the outside world, perhaps, that the younger son should object to this, but to that son the belief of his stepfather is blasphemy. He loves his mother still, but she has, in a sense, betrayed him, betrayed the family by marrying such a man – she has betrayed his childhood world and put it into the hands of the enemy. He cannot help but love her, but now he mistrusts her. All that remains unchanged of his childhood world is the older brother, still witty, intellectual, aloof, protective, perfect.

'I gather, Wilson, that over the course of the century which I missed, Freud fell out of favour and in the world in which we now find ourselves – with some astonishment, on my part – Freud is regarded more as a curiosity than a source of wisdom. Yet he said many things that are suggestive. Somewhere he writes that the dream of a man always springs from the period of childhood, and that this dream is continually trying to summon childhood back into reality, and to correct the present day by the measure of childhood. Surely this is somewhat true of all of us, is it not? We want the sweetness of things the way they were when we were, for the first time, led by our mother's hand into the garden of the world's delights. Alas, Bart Gray allowed this common dream of mankind to become a ruling passion. As a child he liked tiny flowers and insects, liked to collect only tiny things. And as a man, the same. He specialized in mini-aturization research at Cambridge, and in biological studies. As a child he was cruel, stuffing firecrackers into the mouths of frogs – and like many a scientist he has continued his cruelty to animals in later life. As a child he passionately believed in his father's ideas, however bizarre, and as a man he continued to believe in them. As a child he worshipped his older brother, and as a man he worships him still. He has carried his childhood attitudes into his adult life to an abnormal degree.'

'I follow you, Holmes. I agree that your analysis seems plausible. And then what?'

'And then his obsession with his childhood and family made him not just marginally antisocial but a traitor to his country. He learnt that the castle and the manor were both threatened by the negligent money management of his mother – and by the economic crisis in which the world today finds itself. Both the castle and the manor – the worlds of his youth, the only beautiful worlds he knew – would soon be lost. But this was impossible, could not be allowed, was against nature, against God. Ergo, any action that could save the world about to be destroyed was an action – as any sane man could surely see – not only moral and right, but obligatory. And so he decided to sell the technology he had been developing at Cambridge for the British government to an organization that wishes to destroy not just Britain but all the liberal democracies of the West – he decided to sell it to Al Qaeda.

'But for this,' Holmes went on, popping a little forkful of trout into his mouth, 'he needed help, an intermediary to make the contacts with Al Qaeda, and to manage the demonstrations of the technology, and to make the sale. That man is Lars Lindblad. Lindblad made contact with Katrinka Pushkin – he knew her, according to Lestrade, from his days of selling weapons to insurgents along the Pakistan-Afghanistan border. Lindblad arranged to demonstrate the microbomb technology to Ms Pushkin. He arranged the various demonstrations of Bart's weapons. And how were targets for the demonstrations picked? By paying attention to Alexis Gray's views as to who in this world most deserved pain – his views as expressed in his Bif Carcanson column. No doubt Bart thought Alexis would approve. Because it seems to me, my dear Wilson, that Bart Gray is now living in a world that is completely black and white, with no shades of grey. He shares that world with religious zealots, fascists, political extremists of all kinds – in short, with people whose main interest in life is not to be wise but to be *certain*.

'The Shakespeare letter was but a side issue. When Bart learned that Sir Hugh Blake had found the letter and that he intended to discredit his father, Lord Gray, by publishing it, Bart simply used the resources at hand, in the form of Lars Lindblad, to steal the letter and get it out of circulation. It was at that point, through that inconsequential side issue, that you and I were brought into the case, simply because it happened that your old school chum's niece worked at the place where the letter was stolen. Such are the whims of Chance.'

I tried to calm myself by speaking calmly. I was worried about Marianne. 'And what is our task tomorrow, Holmes?' I took a sip of wine.

Holmes shrugged. 'We will find Marianne Hideaway and the Shakespeare letter.'

'But could it be possible,' I said, 'that they really went to

Brussels, as Bart said. Or, for that matter, that they went some-where altogether else? Everyone has said the castle was closed up five years ago.'

'If Marianne and the letter are not at the castle, you and I will be in a desperate situation. But I have little doubt on that score. Several days ago I telephoned the inn at Kilfinnoch. I pretended to be a photographer interested in taking pictures of the castle. The innkeeper, Mr MacGregor, was not encouraging about the possibility of taking close-up pictures of Castle Mornay. He said that for the past couple of years anyone trespassing on the castle property was quickly accosted by a man – an American – who warned them off. MacGregor told me that the only practical way of approaching Castle Mornay is by boat. The castle sits on a promontory over the lake, but it is not visible from the village. MacGregor avows that the castle has been occupied for the past two years by tenants who never show themselves in the village. A Land Rover has been seen frequently travelling along the mostly unused south lake road, which, after a little distance, becomes a private road on Castle Mornay property. According to MacGregor, Bart Gray has appeared from time to time over the past few years in the bar of MacGregor's inn – in fact, was there just three weeks ago. I have a theory, Wilson, that we may encounter a number of people at Castle Mornay, including a certain Shotgun Abernetty, an American cousin of Filbert Abernetty. I learnt a good bit about this American Abernetty in the Abernetty dossier at Scotland Yard. He is a dubious char-acter who has several times been charged with violent crimes but never convicted.'

'Perhaps he is the American who warns people off,' I suggested.

'Very possibly. I have learnt from Lestrade that Filbert Abernetty is frequently gone from his clock shop in Bath, often for several weeks at a time.'

'The same pattern that Bart Gray seems to have been following.'

'That had occurred to me,' said Holmes.

'It just seems strange that Marianne has not phoned. She should surely have charged her phone by now. Even if she lost it, she would know I must be worried, and she would have borrowed a phone to let me know. That is why I'm a bit concerned. How many people do we expect to find at the castle?'

'Excellent question,' said Holmes. 'Bart, Filbert Abernetty,

Shotgun Abernetty, possibly Marianne Hideaway and Grandpa Gray . . .'

'Heavens, I'd forgotten about the old man!' I said. 'He wasn't at Widcombe Manor, and since it appears he is unable to take care of himself . . . you may be right.'

'It is also barely possible,' said Holmes, 'that Lars Lindblad and Katrinka Pushkin will be there. They may be meeting with Bart if their business arrangement with him – the transfer of technology or of actual hardware – is close to completion. But this we have no way of knowing. And possibly there are others there – if, for instance, technicians were needed, if they have created a bomb factory of some sort. All this is a mystery yet to be cleared up.'

'But Holmes . . .' I paused, pondering how to phrase my question.

'Yes?'

'If he actually kidnapped her, then – but that seems so unlikely!'

'On the contrary, it is very likely. It is not only likely but probable. He is mad, Wilson. You don't seem to grasp that simple fact. The pills – those are what have finally convinced me. The exploding pills have convinced me not only that Bart Gray is mad, but that Marianne Hideaway is in deadly danger, and so are we all. I asked myself, what use could these microbombs be? I have tried to imagine how they might be used by a terrorist movement. Well, there are many possible uses, but if it is true that Bart Gray and Filbert Abernetty have managed to miniaturize a bomb to fit it into a pill capsule, then the danger is enormous. Imagine how many people take medications in the Western world. Many of these medications are manufactured in China and other places where control is not anything like our own governments demand. If microbombs were introduced into the pharmaceutical industry on a large scale, then much of the population would be ready to explode at any given moment. The perpetrators might then merely send out a radio signal to cause a large portion of the population to start bleeding internally. It would be an ultimate form of terror. People would know they couldn't trust even their own bodies. Millions of people. Think what would have happened if Marianne Hideaway had swallowed her vitamin pill before it exploded? Even to a person who never took pills, the world would be a frightening place. Such a person might be riding on the Underground, might hear a few dull pops as Al Qaeda sent out a radio signal, and would see people all around him in the carriage begin bleeding from the mouth and slumping to the floor.'

'You frighten me, Holmes.'

'We must leave very early tomorrow morning, and get to Castle Mornay as quickly as we can,' said Holmes, and his face was uncharacteristically grim as he spoke.

The waiter arrived, smiling and precise and genial. I had planned to finish my meal with crowdie and oatcakes, but suddenly I didn't feel hungry any more.

TWENTY
Castle Mornay

I n grey mist of early morning we floated over the high bridge just north of Inverness. By eight in the morning we were already far up into the Highlands, and were descending a winding road into Kilfinnoch. The Black Bonnet Inn was a stone building overlooking the loch. It was announced by a large white sign hanging from a tall post, and on the panes of the entry door were all the usual RAC, Visa and Tourist Board labels. Mr MacGregor, the proprietor, stood beneath a dark wooden beam and looked over the top of his computer as he welcomed us. He was a short man of fifty or so, brisk to the point of being brusque, energy visible in his every move.

The massively antlered stag head on the wall looked over the scene with glazed eyes as we registered.

'Will you be wanting a boat today, gentleman?' asked MacGregor.

'Later, perhaps,' said Holmes.

'If I'm not mistaken,' said MacGregor, 'you be the gentleman interested in photographing the castle?'

'I am indeed.'

'Aye, Robby MacGregor can always tell such things!' he cried. 'You have the keen, observant look of an artist.'

'Thank you, sir,' said Holmes. 'Is there no way to approach Castle Mornay by a land route?'

'Not easily,' said MacGregor. 'The big American is ever on the watch. It seems a miracle how he knows whenever people approach. Some of the lads have been larking about trying to get on to the Castle premises without being seen, and they canna do it. Many's the time they've tried. A game, it's become. They need only walk on castle property a minute or two, and there appears the big American with his shotgun. Nay, the only way to obtain a land view of the Castle is to climb the backside of Ben Braigh, but a terrible climb is that. You seem very fit gentlemen, but let it be admitted you are older gentlemen. I am a plain, blunt man, I am! Robby MacGregor will tell what he sees. You could do it, you could climb Ben Braigh. Aye, for what one man can do, another can. But I would not advise it. The main road will do you no help, for it will carry you to the north of Ben Braigh where nothing of the castle will be visible. The south lake road you will find 'tis a very rough road indeed, and the dead certainty is that you will be stopped at the edge of the castle property, before you have a proper view. To see the castle from the land is a difficult task.'

'How odd that someone should be so protective of the property,' said Holmes.

'Aye!' cried MacGregor. 'And odd it's been these many a year. At that end of the loch so many an odd thing has occurred that many a good Scot from hereabout won't even fish there any more. It all began when Lord Gray bought the property, and it has been getting worse by the decade! I was a lad when the old owner died, and we learnt that the property was bought by the husband of an actress. Next we knew, the Lord, her husband, was painting targets on oil barrels, floating the barrels in the loch, and firing an elephant gun at them from the parapets. The sound awoke my mother on many a morn, and disturbed her on many a Sunday afternoon, but nothing could be done. The sound was like a cannon, echoing down the lake, and the local people did not like it. But we were powerless. Lotte Linger, not her fault. We felt sorry for her. A lovely lady was Lotte, and she gave wonderful fêtes for all the town each year at the summer solstice, and we young people danced to a pipe band she had imported from Fife. But even that had a tang of the odd, sir! For young Bart behaved in a very strange manner amidst the food and festivities, and he frightened the girls, and made the boys half angry. But what could we do, being guests?'

'How did he make you angry?' asked Holmes, with a genial laugh. 'For example?'

Robby MacGregor slapped the counter. 'Why, he was ever telling us not to touch this or that, not to prowl about the castle grounds as the young always like to do, and as we had done years past, before his coming. He was a pest and a pain, and there was an anger in him that made us wonder, even as we jeered at him beneath our breaths, whether he would seek retribution. He threatened to put my little brother in the dungeon where he would never be found, and poor little Gordy MacGregor was so frightened that he never again went down to that end of the loch till he was a man grown. And in the last few years, no one goes to the end of the loch, or few. There are rumours of monster fish at that end, that follow boats as wolves follow sheep, and roar as never a fish roared. It is said that one boat was sunk by the roar of one of the monster sea trout of Loch Mornay. We'll be soon in the league of Loch Ness, for monster tales.'

'Do you believe such tales, MacGregor?'

'Nay, I believe nothing, and disbelieve nothing. But I know a Welshman hired my aluminium boat, and fished at that end of the loch, and swore a monster fish followed him, and hovered only inches below the surface, and finally came for him with a loud growl such as never a fish has made in sea or loch, with the result that his boat heaved and his Welsh wife went into the water, and when he fished her out he saw his craft was half full of Loch Mornay. He bailed for half an hour before he was able to make headway for my dock. I am reluctant to believe a Welshman, for often they are blowhards, as Shakespeare well knew. But this man was pale, and my boat was dented, and his wife was wet, and I could not do other than to believe his tale, mostly.'

'And that was when?'

'Last year about this time.'

'Anything else?'

'Have you ever known bats to fly at midday, Mr Holmes?'

'Not as I recall.'

'Two lads climbed Ben Braigh a month ago, and from the top they looked down at Castle Mornay with field glasses. They were surprised to see a cloud of bats suddenly issue from the east tower. They then heard gunshots, and saw bats fall into the loch. The lads could not see the shooters, and assumed they must be on the roof of the castle. I know the lads well, Ian and Tam. They are hunters, and trustworthy lads. And they said the shots must have come from a small calibre rifle, not a shotgun. The sound was not a shotgun sound.'

'It would take a very exceptional marksman to consistently hit bats on the fly with a rifle,' said Holmes.

'But every shot brought down a bat,' said MacGregor. 'So the lads said, and so I believe.'

MacGregor answered the ringing telephone and took a reservation. Then he hung up and turned again to Holmes. 'And the matter of the airplane is also odd.'

'Yes?' said Holmes.

'Only rarely does it come, but it is here now, tied up at Castle Mornay pier, a red biplane like something they flew in the thirties, open cockpit. But it makes a strange whooshing sound that mingles with the clatter of the propeller, not like your ordinary airplane. And it can disappear in mid-flight. I once saw it crawling across the sky just over the loch, grinding along as slow as a farm tractor, and then it entered a cloud, one of those white billowy clouds, and we heard a pop, and a whooshing sound, and red rubbish began falling out of the cloud and tumbling end over end into the loch, as if the airplane had popped a strut and collapsed. But where was the rest of the machine? We saw no bodies falling. One of the lads saw a glint of light . . . but I saw nothing at all. It was gone, all but two pontoons and part of a wing that we found floating days later in the loch. But where was the rest? Yet a month later the airplane reappeared, whole and intact, and landed here again. That was just a few days past.'

'A biplane,' mused Holmes.

'You'll spot it by the castle pier . . . then what will it be, gents? Land or loch? I have a map of the area if you choose to climb Ben Braigh. But if you'll listen to MacGregor's advice . . .'

'We'll have a boat,' said Holmes.

MacGregor slapped the counter. 'And very wise you are,' said he. 'You will have nae problem to find your way for the loch is long and narrow. You need only follow the shore for three miles till it bends north, and then you will see Castle Mornay.'

'Have you a rowboat,' asked Holmes, 'with oars, and an outboard motor?'

'We do, Mr Holmes, but it is a wooden boat.'

'Does it row pretty well?'

'It rows very well, my lad. But slowly. And the motor is small.'

'Then that is what we want.'

'Excellent,' cried MacGregor, and he pointed at a boy who was emptying wastebaskets. 'Danny, kindly pull Old Giffey into the loch, and make the wee craft ready to sail, all shipshape and Bristol fashion. Fill the motor with petrol, bring out the oars and life preservers.'

Danny vanished with alacrity.

MacGregor looked searchingly at Holmes and me. 'Will ye gentlemen be wanting a lunch to carry along? A fine cook we have at The Black Bonnet.'

'We're in a hurry,' said Holmes.

'I wouldna hurry too much, lad, for the fog is dense.'

'Ten minutes?' I said.

'MacGregor will never say *no* to any man's challenge!' he cried, and then he shouted, 'Margie!' – and he hurried out the door with one hand over his head as if hailing the invisible cook.

In our room Holmes and I changed into sweaters, jeans, Wellingtons. I put on my Barbour oiled hat, he his Greek fisherman's cap. We slipped into our all-weather jackets and not long afterwards found ourselves stepping down into Old Giffey with our lunch bags in hand.

The lapstrake rowboat was fourteen feet long, a solid old craft that appeared to have been built before the last world war. Oars *thunk*ed as I laid them in the bottom. Only the orange life preservers seemed bright in all the grey world, for everything else was muted in mist, and drained of colour. Even the outline of the boat seemed, at some moments, to merge with the water and vanish.

'It is a bit foggy, Holmes.'

'We must start,' he said.

MacGregor came out and stood on the dock with his hands on his hips, and looked down at us doubtfully. 'Best stay to the shoreline, lads – or ye'll be going in circles.'

Holmes cast us off, the dock drifted away. I pulled the cord. The ten-horse motor began to purr and burble. With a little tilt we turned and were on our way out into Loch Mornay. I steered leftward along the shoreline. Nothing existed but ourselves and the boat; all the world had vanished. When steering blind, a person can grow anxious after only a few seconds. I wondered whether the boat was going straight or turning ever so slightly.

I slowed the engine. From time to time I could glimpse the shore through a rift in the mist. We were travelling very slowly, of necessity, perhaps six miles an hour. I thought that a half hour ought to bring us to the bend in the loch. When a half hour had passed I cut the engine: total silence swept in, and the *whopple* of the waves on the bottom of the boat was the loudest sound we heard.

'Do you have the directions for entering the castle?' he asked.

'Right in my pocket, Holmes. But I have them in memory. They are not complicated. From the pier we go straight towards the castle wall. Marianne said that the door to the basement is the only entrance facing the lake, and seldom used. It is below ground level, down a flight of stone steps. In the old days the door was always kept unlocked. But there is a trick to turning the handle. People who don't know the trick will assume the door must be locked even when it isn't.'

'What is the trick?'

'I don't know the trick,' I said.

'We will have to manage,' he said. 'I think the fog is lifting.'

I could see the near shore now. 'That way should be the castle, directly ahead,' I said, pointing to the right where mist and fog wreathed and turned over the grey flat water. We saw nothing in that direction but the sun, high up, a pale silvery disk.

'Let's use the motor a while longer, Wilson,' he said. 'This fog is a gift.'

I pulled the cord and the little craft pressed ahead, sturdily, through the resistant grey water of the loch. In the blinking of an eye the castle appeared, though it was barely visible at first, like a very faint etching. I cut the motor. Holmes grabbed the oars and began to row. We heard no sound but the creak of the oarlocks, and the dripping of water off the oar blades between strokes, and the warble of the water round the hull. I sat in the stern and watched as Holmes bent to his task. The castle bobbed gently above his right shoulder. I couldn't tell whether the castle was a long way off, or nearly upon us. The scene was hallucinatory.

Then I saw a dragonfly. It kept pace with us precisely.

Holmes was straining at his task, didn't notice the little creature.

But there it was, magically hovering off our starboard side. It faced us and flew sideways. I pointed. Holmes stopped rowing. The dragonfly maintained its position relative to us, as if it were invisibly fastened to the boat.

'Give me the oar, Holmes.'

He shipped the right oar, pulled it out of its oarlock, handed it across. 'Don't tip the boat,' he warned.

I took a swing at the creature but it darted away and hovered just out of reach, a little further from the boat and a little higher up.

'Could that be natural?' I said.

'No,' said Holmes, quietly. 'We are discovered. No need to row now.'

As I turned to pull the starter rope on the outboard motor I was distracted by a flicker of black amidst the grey air. I thought it a trick of the fog. Then I saw it again, and I could not deny to myself that something was circling the boat high up, darting through folds of mist and appearing, veering, reappearing, making large circles round us in swift and wobbly flight.

'It's a bat,' said Holmes, and he grabbed an oar.

I had been about to pull the starter rope, but now desisted.

The bat darted madly in a wide circle, made a dive towards Holmes, and Holmes swung the oar. Miraculously, he smacked the creature, and its wing looked broken as it hit the grey water. It lay wobbling on a wave, then exploded: the rowboat lifted on that side, and bucked as the surge of water passed under us. Holmes was almost thrown out. He fell backwards on to the prow seat.

'You all right?'

'Yes,' he said.

I pulled the starter and the boat thrust ahead. I revved it to top speed and made for the pier. The fog was lifting quickly, the world becoming visible. It was as if an artist had, until now, been lightly sketching outlines of the scene before us in grey pencil, but suddenly had begun to fill it all in to make a solid world. I saw another bat flickering overhead, but as we neared the pier it vanished. Mist shifted and I saw a red biplane tied by the right side of the pier, sleek and sporty. I steered to the left, switched off the motor. Holmes already had the landing rope in his hand.

As we glided in there was not a sound to be heard but the lapping of water. Nor a soul to be seen. We gathered our gear, climbed up the ladder, hurried across the grass towards the looming grey building. We ran half crouched, as if we imagined someone would be shooting at us, and for a moment

my unfortunate tour of duty as a reporter in the Afghan war
flashed through my mind.

Castle Mornay was a square stone edifice with a graceful
round tower on the right. A massive square tower on the left
rose out of the building proper, and it had crenellations around
the top. Very medieval and picturesque was Castle Mornay. The
side we were approaching was a three-storey high wall pierced
at the second storey by arched windows. The graceful round
tower, slender and tapering towards the top, was pierced by only
one arched window very high up. The massive square tower rose
perhaps five stories and had two windows, one above the other.
I noticed a satellite dish mounted incongruously on the side of
the square tower.

Holmes made straight for the sunken staircase, which we found
just where Marianne had described. I followed Holmes down
the worn stone steps to a dark and weather-beaten door. He struggled with the handle for a moment . . . then opened the door.
'Easy enough,' he said over his shoulder.

We stepped down into cold darkness. Holmes closed the door
and we flicked on our pocket torches. We were in a low-ceilinged
space punctuated by thick square pillars. The pillars evidently
held up not only the ceiling above us but the entire castle. We
walked down a slope into a deeper vault, then round to the right.
I saw nothing but little rubbles of round stone here and there,
and a number of bundles of electrical cable running along the
floor and up certain columns, vanishing into gloom. Underfoot
was sometimes hard earth and sometimes slabs of stone. We
were looking for a stairway of stone which led up, according to
Marianne, into a storage room.

'*Liebesträume*,' said Holmes. 'Liszt.'

I could hear it now, faintly. The sound of someone playing
Liszt's *Liebesträume* on the piano. I was tremendously relieved,
felt a rush of joy. 'She must be all right!' I whispered. 'Thank
God.'

'Look there,' whispered Holmes, motioning with his torch
beam towards a grate in the ceiling above.

The rubble floor beneath our feet slanted upward towards the
square grate, through which faint light and music seeped into
our gloomy crypt. We crouched and made our way upward.
Holmes attempted to lift the grate. I lent a hand, and we managed
to move it. The clunking *scrape* as we slid it aside was, I hoped,

masked by the second section of *Liebesträume* as it poured forth from the piano in glorious cascades of sound.

I poked my head up through the hole.

I appeared to be in the corner of a great room of red sandstone.

I could see the end of a grand piano protruding beyond a stone pillar. The pillar blocked my view of the pianist. High up in one wall was a stained glass window. A regally patterned carpet covered the centre of the room. On the carpet sat the piano and the single easy chair that I could see. I squeezed through and crawled out on to the sandstone floor, got to my feet. Then I leant and gave Holmes a hand. The room appeared to be empty except for the person at the piano. We moved cautiously towards the pillar as *Liebesträume* ended with lovingly touched chords, just the sort of expressive interpretation one would expect from an exquisitely sensitive woman.

Full of joy and anticipation, I stepped around the pillar.

TWENTY-ONE
Bats and Microbombs

Lars Lindblad sat with his hands motionless on the keyboard, head half bowed, as the sound died. Then he straightened up, turned, and smiled as if he had been expecting us. 'Good morning, Mr Holmes – Mr Wilson. So good of you to come.'

He rose from the piano and came towards us at a brisk but genial gait, smiling with a polite look of delight. He wore loafers, taupe trousers and an off-white sweater. 'I am Lars Lindblad.'

'And I . . . you know me?' Holmes was momentarily at a loss.

'Of course, Mr Holmes – what civilized man *doesn't* know you?' He reached out and shook Holmes's hand, and then shook mine.

'Most have trouble believing,' said Holmes.

'Oh, I believe implicitly,' said Lindblad. He spoke in a perfectly cultured English accent with only the slightest hint of Swedish – a very mid-channel European accent. He turned up his palms in a gesture of openness. 'But you see, Mr Holmes, I was a biology student at university, after giving up music. I had in mind to be a doctor. I have kept up with the biological sciences, for they are of great interest to me. Anyone who understands the direction of modern biological techniques must realize that the sort of resuscitation you experienced is not only possible, but inevitable. If it hadn't been you, Mr Holmes, it would have been another, and *will* be another. The world is very fortunate that it was a man of your overwhelming talent who was brought back to us, so that you may live out, for at least a while longer, the natural course of your life. It may interest you to know that I have read Dr Coleman's description of how he revived you.'

'How is that possible?' I asked abruptly, still upset at not seeing Marianne at the keyboard. 'It has not been published yet.'

'I have an acquaintance who was asked to peer review Dr Coleman's paper. He was good enough to show it to me.'

'I regret that it must be published,' said Holmes. 'The anonymity of my present life suits me.'

'I wouldn't worry much about that, Mr Holmes,' said Lindblad. 'Most of the world won't believe it anyway – whatever is published, in however authoritative a journal. I have explained the matter, for example, in great detail to my partner in this little venture, Bart Gray, and he will not believe it. I explained to him why he had *better* believe it, for not believing it could well cost him his freedom. I told him that you were the one detective in the history of English crime who would surely undo him unless he took great care. But Bart only laughed and said that, while he knows well the possibility of regrowing organs, he is perfectly certain that you are an imposter *because his brother said you are*! – and so he went his mad way.'

'Do you think him truly mad, Herr Lindblad?' asked Holmes.

Lindblad laughed. His tanned face had a glow as he tilted his head downward. His curly short blond hair, silvered with grey, made him look both young and old. Suddenly he looked up at Holmes with penetrating blue eyes: 'He is the maddest man I've ever met, Mr Holmes. Brilliant, of course. But quite mad. He is certifiable.'

Lindblad strolled to the Yamaha grand, briskly sat, and tossed off the opening passage of the Chopin B minor sonata, in a flourish . . . and then he suddenly stopped and turned to Holmes. 'Would you call a man mad, Mr Holmes, who rigs a bomb in a

piano bench so that whoever plays Debussy's *Clair de Lune* will
be blown to kingdom come – all because he despises a particular half-sister who has played that lovely piece since childhood?'

'*Mad* sounds close enough,' said Holmes.

'Ah, yes. So I am very careful what I play on this piano. Since
my Paris Conservatory days, French music has often been the
only balm to satisfy certain of my moods, yet on this piano I
refuse to play French music of any sort for fear I might happen
upon a passage so similar to one in *Clair de Lune* that it blows
me into eternity.'

'I commiserate, Herr Lindblad,' said Holmes. 'Yet I cannot
feel you are too harshly deprived. For my own part, I would
gladly exchange Debussy for Beethoven, or Ravel for Mozart,
on most days of the week.'

Lindblad laughed. 'And quite right you are.'

'I am willing to postulate that Bart Gray is mad,' said Holmes,
'but as to his being a genius, that is yet to be proved.'

'*Postulate* madness, Holmes?' said Lindblad. 'You are too timid
a theorizer! Would it be madness, do you think, if a brother stuffed
his half-sister full of vitamin pills containing microbombs, then
forced her to eat a quadruple dose of Lomotil tablets to ensure
that she could not void her problems by defecating them; and
would it be madness if he then locked her in a room in this castle
and told her that she would remain there until he decided to push
the button on his radio transmitter in order to prove whether or
not microbombs placed in capsules were sufficient to blow a person
to pieces? Would you call that a symptom of psychosis?'

'My God!' I cried.

'Oh, yes, Mr Wilson,' said Lindblad, turning to me so quickly
that I got a waft of his cologne. 'That is what he has done. The
girl seemed to me so very lovely, so better fit for other uses . . .'
Lindblad shrugged again. 'But madmen know best.'

'Since you so disapprove,' said I, 'can you not do something
about it?'

'I wish I could,' said Lindblad. 'But in the first place, Bart
mistrusts me and did not tell me in which of the many rooms
in this colossal heap the girl is held prisoner. In the second place,
that is not my department.'

He lifted his hands to the keyboard and began to draw forth
into cool castle air the subtle strains of Beethoven's 'Moonlight'
sonata. He turned his head towards Holmes and said, 'I have

always admired you, Holmes, ever since as a child I read of your exploits. I admired your style and tenacity, and often I pretended that I was Professor Moriarty, and that you were after me. What a thrilling and rewarding life that would have been! I only regret that now, after my dream has been almost answered, it must end so quickly. I should like to have been pursued by you across countries and continents, to the far ends of the earth. Instead, it ends all too soon.'

'I apologize for catching you so quickly,' said Holmes.

'Alas, you have not caught me; I have caught you,' said Lindblad softly. 'I fear we can never let you leave this castle, Mr Holmes – even to assure my future sport and amusement.' He shrugged. 'That you have let yourself be caught so easily is a bit disappointing, and tarnishes my childhood image of you. Another ideal of my youth has been seriously damaged, Mr Holmes! But here he comes, your Fate.' He nodded towards the doorway behind us, and the sonorous sullen strains of the 'Moonlight' sonata swelled and subsided like an ebbing sea.

A very large man with a bony head and slumping shoulders walked towards us. He carried a shotgun in one hand and a bull-whip in the other. 'All right, boys, give your mobiles to the Swede and let's move it,' said he, waggling the end of the shotgun towards the door.

'Shotgun Abernetty, I presume?' said Holmes, laying his mobile phone on the piano.

'Presume what you damn please,' said the man. 'But if you don't move fast I'll flick a hunk of ham out of your hide – and it don't look like you have much to spare.' He cracked the whip, a loud POP. 'The boss wants to see you.'

We left the room and walked down a long hallway, and the strains of the 'Moonlight' sonata followed us, growing softer and softer. Our uncouth host, who was about six and a half feet tall and correspondingly meaty, guided us through a maze of stairs and doorways. We passed through a kitchen where a dog was lying on a rug in the corner, sleeping. Our guide, from a distance of twelve feet, cracked the sleeping dog with the end of the whip, and blood appeared on its hip. The dog leapt up and began to whimper and cower; it had but one eye. 'I flicked his other eye out,' said the man. 'I hate cowardly dogs.' He led us at last into a room that appeared to be a laboratory, or work-shop, or menagerie, hard to tell which. Along one wall were large cages of dragonflies, houseflies and bats. On a long bench computer screens glowed. At the operating table in the middle of the room two olive-skinned men dressed in white surgery gowns were bending over a bat, cutting away at its head with a scalpel. In another corner of the large room a man bent over a desk with a watchmaker's magnifying glass plugged into one eye; in his right hand he held a small implement. As he glanced up at us I saw that he was pale-skinned, bulbous-eyed, skinny-headed, and I had no doubt that this was Filbert Abernetty, most recent of a long line of English bomb makers.

'Shotgun,' said this individual, in a small but piercing voice. 'please be so good as to take a pocketful of these transponders –' he pointed at a pile of disks on his desk – 'and place them at fifty-foot intervals all the way to the very top of Ben Braigh. We shall then turn loaded bats loose and see if they go for them. Any bats that the transponders don't detonate, we will detonate remotely, in the usual manner.'

'Dammit,' grunted Shotgun Abernetty, 'Ben Braigh is a long hike.' He walked to the desk and took a big handful of the disks, which were the size of very large watch batteries. He funnelled them into the right pocket of his jeans.

'And one more bit of work . . .' said Filbert.

'Work is my middle name, cousin,' said Shotgun.

'. . . when you have placed the transponders, take a bag of loaded bats to the top of the square tower and release them. If we start hearing explosions on Ben Braigh we will know we have perfected the system.'

'What am I supposed to do with these two yokels?' asked Shotgun, walking back towards us. He jabbed me with the end of the shotgun.

I resisted the impulse to lay him out on the floor with a round-house punch. I must have made a move in that direction, for I felt Holmes touch my shoulder.

'That's not my department,' said Filbert, looking back to his work.

'Where the hell is Bart at?' hollered Shotgun.

One of the men at the operating table turned towards him. 'Bart vill be coming quite soon, sir.' The accent sounded Indian or Pakistani.

That very instant Bart appeared. He walked with a creeping reticence, a smile pasted on his handsome face, a lock of dark hair falling over his brow. His shoulders were slumped slightly forward, as if he didn't want to be quite so tall as he was, or as if he didn't mean to obtrude. But one had the feeling that at any instant he might bare his teeth and spring for the throat. He wore a tweed sport coat over a white, crew-neck sweater, and around his neck was the same necklace of flat blue stones that I had seen before.

'A classic passive-aggressive personality, but so extreme as to be dangerous,' Holmes murmured.

'What did you say?' asked Bart Gray.

'I was observing your manner,' replied Holmes.

'And I am observing your manners, Mr Holmes. They do not strike me as very refined. They strike me as gauche in the extreme. You are trespassing on my property.'

'We merely wished to ask you some questions,' said Holmes.

'Oh! Well! That explains why you have broken into my castle! Excellent! You are a perfect gentleman, after all, Mr Holmes. I understand it all now. Then what are the questions? I am curious.'

'Where is your sister?'

'I don't have a sister.'

'We thought you might know where Marianne Hideaway is,' said Holmes.

'Oh, *her*! She doesn't matter, Mr Holmes. Let me have another question – but no, let's remove to somewhere more comfortable. Come this way, please.'

We walked through another doorway, out of the lab, and along a corridor to a book-lined room that looked out on Ben Braigh to the north. Shotgun Abernetty followed behind. When we entered the room Abernetty said, 'I am supposed to plant these transponders up the mountain. Can I get on with it?'

'I don't want you to do that now,' said Bart.

'Filbert told me . . .'

'I don't care what Filbert told you. I am the Thane of Cawdor here. This is my castle. You are my retainer. You can climb Ben Braigh with your transponders later. Right now I want you to find Alf and Dunwoody and bring them here.'

'They're out in the woods.'

'Bring them in. I need some muscle here. And tell that beautiful wench of Lars's to bring us some tea, quick-time.'

Shotgun Abernetty bowed his head very slightly and touched his forelock with two fingers in a half insolent salute. He left the room with thumping footsteps.

Bart waved his hand gently as if to reveal the room to our view. 'This is my mother's library,' he said. 'Some of my earliest memories are of Mother standing by that window, gazing at Ben Braigh and rehearsing her lines. How beautiful she was!'

'How beautiful she still *is*,' I said.

He looked at me curiously, and with a kind of wonder. 'Yes. Even at her age she is beautiful. No one can fail to notice.'

'I understand she is in Paris at the moment, with your step-father,' said Holmes.

Bart ignored the comment. 'We had such wonderful times here, my mother and father and I, and also my brother, of course. And our servants. It was quite a wonderland. Every summer. But several years ago Mother wearied of the place – I can't think why – and she closed it up. She can be rather abrupt when she wants to be. However, that is past. I intend to hire new servants and invite her back, and I know my brother will come too, for he always loved Castle Mornay – and my hope is that all will be pretty much as it was before at Castle Mornay, once this dreadful business is over.'

'What "dreadful business?"' asked Holmes.

'Sit down, gentlemen. I will explain.'

He waved us into two rich leather chairs near the window. He took the third, crossing his legs and holding on to his top knee with both hands. 'You see, Mr Holmes and Mr Wilson, I feel one ought to work for joy, not for money. So when one is forced to work for money first, and joy only secondarily, I always think it is dreadful. And that is what I have been forced to do. I find quite suddenly that I require substantial sums of money, and as a consequence I am selling some technological trivialities to a terrorist organization based in Saudi Arabia. The Saudis, as you know, have lots of money. And I need lots of money.'

'For money you would betray your countrymen?' asked Holmes.

'I really have no choice.'

Holmes frowned. '*Paucis carior est fides quam pecuniam*,' said he.

'You don't impress me,' said Bart. 'I never studied Latin.'

'Perhaps you should have,' said Holmes. 'Sallust is worth reading.'

'But isn't it illegal, what you are doing?' I asked.

'Oh, certainly,' said Bart. 'Perfectly illegal. That is why it is so profitable.'

I could see where the conversation was leading. Everyone who has ever watched a spy movie could see where it was leading. He would reveal all to us, for he imagined he had us in his power – and truth to tell, I could not help but wonder if perhaps he had. I knew Holmes had made a call to Lestrade to tell him where we were, and that was encouraging. And I hoped Holmes had brought along the Webley service revolver that Scotland Yard (by a special ruling) allowed him to carry. At all events, I thought I might as well find out where we stood with this man by questioning him further. I hoped that I was not intruding too much on Holmes's line of questioning.

'Then aren't you afraid of getting caught?' I said. 'I mean, you are talking to us like this, as if selling minibombs to Al Qaeda were the most natural thing in the world.'

'*Microbombs*, please. The word is microbombs. But my groom collected your mobile phones, did he not? So the conversation is not being recorded,' said Bart. 'So why would I worry? . . . Ah, our refreshments.' He opened his hand, graciously, towards the person now entering.

A striking woman with dark hair brought in a silver tray laden with tea cups, a tea pot, and a plate of biscuits. I recognized her immediately as Katrinka Pushkin.

'Just set it down here, if you will,' said Bart.

'I don't mind serving tea,' said Katrinka. 'I serve my cause in many ways.'

Bart gazed at us and smiled. 'You see how subservient these people can be when they want something? Charming people. Know their place. They are buying my complete system of surveillance and destruction, a system quite unlike anything available anywhere else in the world. Before they take delivery I insist that they serve me a little. Helps build character.'

'Another day of serving you means nothing to me,' said Katrinka. 'Tomorrow all will be accomplished.'

'You see,' said Bart, beaming and for once looking almost genial. 'My brilliance bends even so extraordinary a creature as Katrinka Pushkin to my will – if only momentarily. She madly desires my system, a system made up of surveillance and destruction modules – Surveillance And Destruction Individually Sequenced Modules, to be exact. The SADISM system, as I like to call it.'

'Your whim is to be Macbeth, Mr Gray,' said Katrinka. 'Mine is to be Cleopatra. I do business with Scots only as she did with Romans, to serve my country with beauty and brain.' She shot us each a regal look and left the room. She had a hauteur both charming and threatening.

'Macbeth?' said Holmes. 'You might have picked a safer role – he ends badly.'

'Oh, death doth come to us all,' said Bart Gray. 'I have always thought *Macbeth* is one of Bacon's better plays, and the worthy thane one of Bacon's better villains. All a mortal man can do is be sure one's own death comes quickly – and before that moment be sure to live on his own terms. I have guaranteed myself both of those privileges.' He touched the necklace about his neck. 'Each one of these seeming stones is a microbomb. I need merely say the right word and they will all explode, killing me instantly – together with anyone in the vicinity. That is why I feel quite confident that no one will ever succeed in arresting me.'

'But you'd better hope,' I said, 'that no one guesses the word and shouts it from a distance.'

'It is a word I made up,' laughed Bart Gray, 'and the audio signature is sensitized to my voice only. I am not worried.'

'Where is the Shakespeare letter?' asked Holmes. 'That is my prime question.'

Bart Gray reached into his inner sport coat pocket and drew out a brown manila envelope. 'Right here.'

'Is it a genuine letter?' asked Holmes.

'I have no idea. It may have been written by a man named William Shakespeare. It may have been written in 1592 at Casa Figlio in Florence, as the letter itself indicates. These are fine scholarly points upon which I have no opinion, and in which I have no interest. What I know for sure is that this letter proves nothing about the authorship of the so-called "Shakespeare" plays. That is why I have stolen it. The world is easily deceived, Mr Holmes, and must be protected from gross deception or misconception or misinterpretation.'

'I was under the impression,' said Holmes, 'that your brother, Alexis, and your father, Lord Gray, have already sufficiently protected the world from that particular error. I was under the impression they had already explained the Shakespeare fraud to the world, most brilliantly. Is that not so?'

'Yes, my father has explained in detail why Shakespeare could

not have written the plays, and why it is evident that Francis
Bacon did. And my brother has a book coming out shortly which
will make the explanation even more compelling. It is a shame
you cannot read it.'

'Perhaps I will.'

'No, alas, Mr Holmes – I have work to do and I must insist
that you remain at Castle Mornay a while longer – a good while
longer, in fact.'

'That I cannot do,' said Holmes, and he stood up.

I stood up also.

'I am afraid you must stay, Mr Holmes, and I will tell you
why,' said Bart Gray. As he stood up he drew from his pocket
a small rectangular object, and held it up to our view. 'This
appears to be a television control, but it is not. You see the little
switch on which I have placed my thumb? If I push this switch,
Marianne Hideaway will explode. I promise you, Mr Holmes, I
will push it the instant you do not do exactly as I say.'

'Where is she?' asked Holmes.

'You are too inquisitive, Mr Holmes. She is locked in a little
room. As you soon will be also. For I am about to take you to
a chamber in the Square Tower. Come along, gentlemen – be
quick. Time presses. Oh, and Mr Holmes – our scanning device
shows that you have a revolver in your right coat pocket. Would
you be good enough to lay it on the table beside you, before we
start the long climb to your temporary quarters? Ah, yes, that's
a good fellow. We'll just leave it there, perhaps forever – a
memento of a visit by an inept but memorable charlatan. It will
make a good conversation piece.'

TWENTY-TWO
Open Sesame

The room in which we found ourselves was at the very top
of the Square Tower. It consisted of a stone floor and four
walls. No furniture. A window without glass looked out
towards Loch Mornay. Opposite the window was an oak door,
well-locked, that led to the stairwell.

Holmes crawled around the perimeter of the hard floor on his hands and knees, peering into every irregularity in the stone, looking for listening devices that might be hidden. Next he examined the low ceiling, which consisted of two heavy beams holding up stone and plaster. At last he seemed satisfied. 'I think we can talk,' he said.

A moment later a dragonfly flew in through the open window. It hovered in front of Holmes, then in front of me. The beautiful creature irritated me and I took a swing at it – it darted away, hesitated, then swooped through the window opening and was gone.

Holmes stood close to me, 'Reinforcements should arrive in exactly four hours,' he said, 'if Lestrade got my message.'

'Then let's hope he got it,' I replied. 'But why so late?'

'Matters have progressed faster than I expected.'

The wall was several feet thick. I crawled to the outer window edge and looked down. I felt a little giddy. I turned my head and saw the graceful round tower. I crawled back into the room. By and by we got tired of standing. We sat down on the hard floor and leant our backs against the wall and made ourselves as comfortable as we could.

'Until this moment,' I said, 'I have never really appreciated the advantages of furniture.'

Holmes took his briar pipe from his coat pocket and put it into his mouth, and he stared at the sky beyond the window, contemplating. He had fallen into one of his trances, so I did not trouble him with my thoughts.

I have seldom spent a more miserable two hours.

Finally we heard footsteps on stone, the lock rattling, the door creaking. Shotgun Abernetty stood in the door frame, with a sawn-off shotgun drooping in his left hand and a sneer drooping on his lips. 'Get up,' he said.

I got up stiffly. Holmes was already on his feet.

Abernetty decided to pick on me, the slow one. He gave me a shove. 'Let's go,' he said, 'and no funny business.'

He marched us down the long hard stairs, then through a series of rooms. In the library I noticed Holmes's revolver lying on the table just where he had set it down. For a moment I considered making a dive for it . . . but the moment passed, and I felt disgusted with myself for having missed the opportunity.

Holmes walked a few paces behind me, and Shotgun was a

few paces behind him. 'I have been ordered not to harm you
gentlemen,' said Shotgun, 'for they say you are to be permanent
guests of Castle Mornay. But I don't like taking orders, and I'd
as soon shoot you as look at you. So no funny business.'

He marched us next through the laboratory to a door at the
far end, then down more stone stairs until we reached the vaults
beneath the castle. I could see activity ahead: two dark figures
were lit by a single bulb. The bulb hung from the end of an
extension cord that was looped over a beam. The bulb swayed
slightly, bending the shadows of the two men. The men were
laying a course of bricks across a niche in the outer wall. The
niche was perhaps eight feet wide by three feet deep. A wheel-
barrow of cement was nearby. As we drew near to them it was
clear that the men were making a wall, slapping down cement
and bricks. Already the wall had risen two feet from the stone
floor.

'Step over the brick wall, gentlemen,' said Bart Gray, emerging
suddenly from behind a pillar. 'Everyone has his niche in life,
and that one is yours. You are looking at your new quarters – a
little cramped, perhaps, but cosy.'

Suddenly I wished that I was back in an armoured personnel
carrier in Afghanistan, being shot at by the Taliban. How much
more pleasant a death that would be than this! For it was plain
what Bart Gray had planned for us. Holmes and I stepped over
the wall and stood in the niche. Our backs were to the outer wall
of the castle foundation. Kneeling in front of us were two men,
presumably Alf and Dunwoody, who were slapping down bricks
to make the wall that would erase our existence from the world.
Behind those two stood Shotgun Abernetty, grinning. Behind him
stood Bart Gray, who looked rather out of place in his sport coat
and white cashmere sweater and grey slacks. Bart stroked his
blue necklace with two fingers. Then he pointed at us with a delicate air. 'You know, I always had a fondness for Poe.'

'I can see that,' said I.

'*The Cask of Amontillado* was always my favourite.'

He stepped forward suddenly and leant towards us. He plucked
the briar pipe out of Holmes's breast pocket. 'These little bombs
are rather expensive to make, so I'll have this one back, if you
don't mind.' He slipped the pipe into the breast pocket of his
own sport coat. 'If you had been a better actor, you would have
said the words that would have ended your life more pleasantly

than it now must end. Oh, well. I tried! Yes, and it all works
out for the best . . . for me. We will reprogram this little briar
pipe bomb and use it to eliminate some tedious pipe-smoking
intellectual in Prague or Islamabad – or wherever pipe smoking
is still in fashion. No, no! I have a better idea! I will give it
back to my oppressively ignorant stepfather, Professor Hugh
Blake. Sir Hugh has been off his head for years, despite the best
efforts of my brother and me to set him straight. So maybe the
only cure now is for his head to come completely off.'

He maundered on awhile, telling us about his own tastes in
literature, and how his brilliant brother had formed his view not
only of literature but of the world. Meanwhile, the brick wall
had risen to our waists.

'I will tell you my scheme,' he said, finally. 'All that I have
in store for you.'

'Since you are so sporting,' said Holmes, 'I will tell you my
view of schemes. Perhaps you should have spent less time reading
Poe, more time reading Burns. Do you mind if I quote to you
a stanza from the finest poem in the English language? No, of
course you don't –

> *But mousie thou art no thy lane*
> *In proving foresight may be vain,*
> *The best-laid schemes o' mice and men*
> *Gang aft a'gley,*
> *And lae us nought but grief and pain*
> *For promised joy.'*

Bart Gray smiled. 'Surely you do not consider that better than
the sonnets of Bacon!'

'I do,' said Holmes. 'All in all, Burns's poem is a finer, truer,
more complete poem than any one of the sonnets of . . . well,
you call him Bacon, everyone else calls him Shakespeare.'

'I have never heard anyone say such a thing!' cried Bart Gray.
'It defies common sense. It betrays a great want of taste on your
part, Mr Holmes. Bacon's lines are incomparable:

Shall I compare thee to a summer's day . . .'

'Yes, yes,' said Holmes. 'Many of Shakespeare's sonnets are
entrancing. But though they all have their beauties, none of them
– not sonnet 73, not 29, not 116 – has the reach, the humanity,
the vision that Burns's poem has.'

'Burns better than Bacon! That is laughable,' said Bart Gray.

'I do not say Burns is a better poet than Shakespeare,' said Holmes, 'only that he has the better poem.'

And while those two bandied words about Burns and Bacon and Shakespeare, warring with each other like clever school-boys, the practical world was closing in on us. The course of bricks had reached chest level.

'My scheme,' said Bart, 'which I assure you will not go a'gley, is this: when the second to the last course of bricks is laid, I shall toss this little canister of gas' – he held it up – 'into your cell, to knock you out for a short while, just to allow – you understand – the cement to harden. When you awaken you will be in the dark forever. We will then pile rubble from the castle pilings against the brick wall we are building, to obscure it from view. It will comfort me, in gala days when my castle is once again alight with comrades and laughter, to know you two imposters are slowly turning to skeletons beneath my happy life. I will tell people that one of the finest victories of my life rests forever in the foundations of this very castle. They will think I am speaking in metaphor, of course. They will join me in toasts. They will rejoice with me. My mother will be especially pleased. She loves cryptic statements.'

'You certainly are a curious case, Mr Bart Gray,' said Holmes. 'I don't think I have ever seen your like. When I look at you I cannot tell whether your dominant defect is ignorance or delusions.'

'Ignorance!' laughed Bart Gray. 'That is certainly a novel accusation, particularly coming from a man who has just been outsmarted by me. And what sort of delusions do you imagine dominate me, Mr Holmes?'

'Delusions of adequacy.'

'But no one has ever called me anything but the cleverest of the clever, Mr Holmes. You are quite alone in your opinion.'

'Nevertheless, I am right. For at this very moment you are proving that you are unobservant, imperceptive, and incapable of imaginative thought. The truth is, your lack of intelligence will soon cut short all your schemes, deny Al Qaeda the SADISM system they so desire, end your life, and ensure the sale of this castle to strangers.'

Bart Gray shrunk a little, as though Holmes's concise and forceful statement had wounded him. He began fidgeting, blinking. I wondered what had come over him. 'You are very certain of yourself, Mr Holmes.'

'There is a passage in Epictetus,' said Holmes, 'that you should have paid more . . .'

'Holmes, Holmes!' I cried, for I was unable to restrain myself any longer. The brick wall was rising fast before us. 'Is this the time to be discussing Greek philosophy!'

'Mr Holmes,' said Bart Gray, in a tone of wheedling penitence, a sudden shift from his exuberance of a moment before, 'I am not an evil man, merely an unfortunate one. Like you, I suffer from chronic boredom. Unless I have excitement, action, danger, I feel dull, useless, almost dead. If Chance had put into my path a means of satisfying my desires by doing good, I would have done it. I might, even, have been a great detective – as your hero, Sherlock Holmes, was.'

'I *am* Sherlock Holmes,' said Holmes.

Bart Gray laughed. 'No, you are a grotty little imposter, whom no one believes, and no sane man *could* believe. I sympathize with your tastes in literature, in that you admire the narratives of the great Dr Watson, but I cannot forgive you for denigrating the name of a great soul with your tawdry tricks and disguises, or for tarnishing a great literary tradition of true-life biography.'

'And is that why you have decided to kill me in so cruel a manner?'

Gray laughed. 'You shouldn't object – after all, you are already dead . . . and have been since 1914.'

'Bring in some more bricks,' grunted one of the workmen.

The other workman walked off. Shotgun Abernetty followed him, passing in front of the bulb and making a huge shadow on the wall. By and by I could hear them pulling a pallet of bricks across the stone floor.

Bart Gray pulled the letter from his inside coat pocket. 'Here, let me entertain you with this bit of tripe, as we close the wall on your pale and ridiculous faces.'

'Yes, read it from the beginning,' said Holmes. 'My friend and I will soon be out of here, and I should like to hear just a bit of it before we leave.'

I could scarcely believe my senses. Holmes acted as if the contents of the Shakespeare letter were the most important thing in the world to him. Dunwoody was trowelling cement on to the next tier of bricks, and the other man, Alf, began slapping bricks in place on top of the layer of cement. The wall had risen now to within a foot of the ceiling, and I could see only the letter and fingers and face of Bart Gray as he began to read:

'*Florence, Casa Figlia, March 1592.*

'*My Sweete Emilia,*

'*You do infect me more than plague would do, and would that I had never run so far from it that I am far from you; for though I be here, still I am home at heart, so I have gained little. This eve I crossed the Old Bridge and into the Piazza della Signoria where I did pause in the shadow of the statue of Cosimo . . .*'

And there he stopped reading and tilted the letter to see it in better light below the fold, and then he continued reading. He read and he read. Holmes listened intently to every word, but I did not for I was getting very nervous, and I had suddenly lost my interest in historical holographs. Finally I could stand it no longer, and I said. 'Really, Holmes, do you have a way for us to get out of here?'

'Certainly,' said he. And as he spoke I could see only his eyes and forehead, for the gap was now only eight inches high.

'Then do you think now might be the time to tell me what it is?' I said.

'Absolutely right,' said he.

'What is it then, please, Holmes . . . if you would be so kind.'

Holmes turned his face away from me and looked directly at Bart Gray as he said in a very loud voice, 'Elementary, my dear Watson!'

TWENTY-THREE
Flight

The explosion was tremendous.

I saw Bart's head disappear.

His corpse toppled.

Simultaneously, the wall fell slowly inward, tumbling in slow motion – and I leapt backwards to avoid being crushed.

Bricks were scattered everywhere. Oddly enough, the light bulb still burned.

Dunwoody and Alf were crumpled on the ground, stark dead. Shotgun Abernetty, who had been standing farther back and leaning on a pillar, had been luckier. The pillar apparently had deflected part of the blast. He appeared to be only dazed. He lay draped over the empty pallet of bricks. He was groaning.

'I dared not do it sooner,' said Holmes.

'Why ever not?' I asked.

'I wanted the wall high enough to protect us from the combined blast of the briar pipe and blue necklace, for I assumed that when the pipe went off the necklace would go off also. I hope you did not mind the delay, Wilson.'

'I confess, Holmes, I thought you were carrying your famed *sang froid* a bit far, under the circumstances. But now all is quite clear to me – except, how did you know what words to say to set off the bomb in the pipe?'

'I felt I could count on Bart Gray to go for the commonplace in trying to kill me,' said Holmes. 'And those words are the ones most commonly associated with me, in the popular mind – though I have seldom, if ever, actually said them.'

'But what if you had been wrong!'

Holmes drew the Krueger fountain pen from his shirt pocket. 'I would have used this.'

I laughed in relief. 'Are you all right?'

'Apart from a bruised arm, quite all right.'

As I stepped over the fallen wall I spotted some torn scraps of paper. 'Look here, Holmes! Maybe we can salvage something of the letter.'

'Don't bother,' he said. 'The letter is a fake.'

'Fake!'

'Explain later . . . hurry! Must find Marianne. Let's hope Bart didn't push the switch on her before he blew up.'

Even as Holmes spoke I was on the run, taking the stone stairs two at a time.

'I must tie up the American Abernetty,' called Holmes.

I pushed open the door, entered the lab, and glimpsed the two Indian technicians running out the far side of the room. I then noticed Filbert Abernetty skulking in a corner, peering up over the edge of a counter top. I pounced upon him, grabbed him by the shirt, and simultaneously grabbed a huge canvas bag which was lying nearby. The bag had a zipper across the top. I put the weaselly fellow in a strangle hold, unzipped the bag, and began to stuff him into it. It looked to me like he would just fit.

'No, no,' he cried. 'That's a bat bag!'

'And now it will contain a rodent of another sort!' I cried, incensed that this disgusting little creature had caused so much suffering around the world – he and his family. I zipped him into the bag. For good measure I wired it closed with some of the very wire with which he made bombs. I left him struggling and groaning in his bag on the bomb factory floor.

I ran through the library into the great hall, and there Holmes caught up with me. I said, 'We'll need to break down every door in the castle to find her. I'll take the north side, you the south.'

'Just wait,' he said, and he began to circle the room. He tilted his head this way and that. He circled the room twice. It became apparent to me that he was sniffing.

'What do you smell?' I asked. I feared it was gas, something dangerous.

'This way,' he cried, and darted through a doorway.

I followed Holmes through a maze of rooms; all the while he was sniffing. At one point he knelt by a chair and sniffed the cushion.

'My God, Holmes! This is no time for fooling about,' I cried. 'Let's just search every room, methodically.'

'This way!' he cried, and he darted out another doorway, hurried down a twisting corridor, and finally came to a small door that led to a circular stone staircase – obviously this was the staircase leading to the top of the round tower.

He went ahead of me, sniffing the air. Up and up we circled, round and round, endlessly. 'I'm on the scent – she's up here somewhere!' he cried. And at last we came to the top. By then I was feeling not only exhausted but frantic, for I was not at all sure what horror we might find.

Holmes lifted up the wooden bar, pushed open the door – and a moment later Marianne Hideaway was in my arms, clinging to me, a tear running down her cheek as she kissed me. Then she began to laugh.

'It was quite terrible,' she said. 'I'll be very glad when I can purge all these terrible pills from my body.'

'That will be soon,' I said.

'I am going down to get Shotgun Abernetty,' said Holmes. He fled down the stairs.

I hurried to the window and from my hawk-like position I discerned that the landscape below me was filled with tiny motion: afar off, beyond the winking water of the loch, two figures flickered in and out of view as they ran beneath the trees that lined the private road towards Kilfinnoch. They were the Indian technicians. Close beneath me, two figures hurried towards the pier, each carrying a duffel bag; they flung the bags into the cockpit of the red biplane. The man with silver-blond hair, Lars Lindblad, gave a shout and waved towards the castle, as if telling the girl they had forgotten something. Katrinka Pushkin sprinted back towards the castle, and Lindblad followed her on the run.

'We had better hurry down and help Holmes,' I said to Marianne, and I turned from the window.

She nodded.

Her blonde hair swished and bounced as she passed through the doorway and on to the staircase. Round and dizzyingly round we went, and we tried not to trip as we turned and turned on the too-tiny steps of the tower. We found Holmes in the library – he was just leaning forward, frozen in afternoon light, as he reached for his Webley revolver, which lay on the walnut table where he'd left it.

'My heavens!' said Marianne, gazing at the revolver. 'Are you allowed to carry such a thing, Mr Holmes?'

'It was Holmes's weapon in 1914,' I explained, 'so when he was resuscitated in 2004, a legal paradox arose: there was doubt whether he could be said to have ever been dead, and under the old laws he had legal right—'

'Later, Wilson,' cried Holmes. 'Explanations later!'

'Right,' said I.

'Filbert Abernetty is in a bat bag,' said Holmes.

'I put him there,' I said.

'While I attend to Shotgun Abernetty, see if you and Marianne can drag Filbert outside into the courtyard,' said Holmes. 'Help is on the way.' Holmes then opened the door to the vaults below and – with his Webley at the ready – darted down into the gloom.

Marianne and I dragged the bag containing Filbert Abernetty along the hallway and outside into the sunshine. As we dragged it the last few yards I heard a tiny clatter-bang sound far above my head, like rocks being dumped in a distant dustbin. A few seconds later the sound grew huge, into a *whuffing* clatter-bang, and when I looked up I saw a helicopter battering wind and light over the lake, descending, coming now straight towards us. Amidst furious dust it sank to the courtyard. The last time I'd seen a PUMA was when one had lifted me out of a ravine and carried me to a field hospital in Afghanistan. Several troops with rifles jumped out and ran towards the castle. Three others leapt down and helped us get Filbert Abernetty out of his bag and into the copter.

Shotgun Abernetty loomed in the doorway of the castle. Holmes was right behind him, with a revolver pressed against his back. Holmes marched the big man to the door of the PUMA, and a soldier jerked Shotgun's arms behind his back and clapped cuffs on him, and hustled him into the copter.

Marianne pointed at the jazzy red biplane, which had been untethered from the pier and was floating free. Two heads were in its cockpit, Lindblad behind and the girl in front. The biplane's motor twitched, twitched . . . then caught, and the propeller became a blur.

'We mustn't let them escape!' shouted Holmes, climbing into the copter.

Marianne and I clambered aboard, the helicopter lifted, and in a few instants we were above the level of the castle roof.

Marianne pointed. 'It's Grandpa!'

Grandpa Gray limped across the roof of the castle between the two towers, dragging a rifle. He struggled to lift the rifle. Finally he managed to rest it on one of the crenellations. Standing with his back to the drop-off, he drew a bead on us.

'It's a .600 nitro express!' I hollered.

The pilot nodded – and very suddenly we went UP.

Grandpa Gray fired both barrels. Had we stayed at our original altitude he might have taken down a PUMA with an elephant gun. The roar was tremendous. I saw his legs and his shoes turn upside down as the recoil blew him backwards over the wall.

'My God!' cried Marianne.

Holmes pointed at the red biplane. It was now skimming across the surface of the lake . . . lifting . . . was airborne.

Our helicopter tilted, slid down a hill of air, whirled away in pursuit. In a few moments we caught the little plane, which looked quite jaunty. Lars Lindblad and Katrinka Pushkin wore goggles, and their white scarfs snapped and danced in the slipstream. Lars tossed back his head and laughed as he pointed towards us. Katrinka was smiling – the first time I'd seen her not cool and aloof. Lars flung the biplane into a turn that brought him nearer to us, just ahead of and beneath us. He struggled with something in his cramped cockpit. Finally he pulled the rim of a bag into view. He unzipped the bag, it yawned open – a cloud of bats streamed out . . .

The bats whirled upward in our direction as we approached them from the rear.

Holmes had always been quick – boxing champion at Cambridge and all that – but never have I seen a man of his age move quicker than he did as those bats rose to meet us. In a single lightning motion he grabbed Shotgun Abernetty by the collar and spun him – toppled him – out the open helicopter door.

Abernetty howled like a banshee.

Instantly the bomb-loaded bats veered and went for the transponders in Abernetty's pockets.

As the big man tumbled – handcuffed – through their midst, I saw him explode three times. One explosion blew his left leg off. The leg flew in one direction, the rest of his body in another. His tumbling form accelerated out the bottom of the bat cloud and soon he was out of the reach of the little beasts, who seemed confused as they tried to fly down to reach his vanishing body.

Somebody closed the helicopter door.

'Stay with that plane!' shouted Holmes, pointing to the bright red biplane.

'I've called in a pursuit plane,' said the pilot.

'He's accelerating,' said the co-pilot.

Our copter tilted forward. 'I've never lost a battle or a biplane,' quipped the pilot.

We droned on, our two aircraft locked together at a fixed distance. The hills and lochs of Scotland scrolled beneath us. By and by Lars Lindblad lifted up the bat bag and the wind snatched it away. He touched Katrina's shoulder. She nodded, and she began unwrapping her scarf. His scarf and hers flew away behind like frightened gulls. A clear plastic canopy slid forward and covered their two heads.

Until that moment the canopy had not been visible. What mechanism brought it into view I do not know. Lars Lindblad took off his goggles; Katrinka Pushkin took off hers.

What happened next was difficult to comprehend. The top wing of the biplane appeared to break off. It blew away. The two pontoons below the plane dropped and tumbled towards the glittering water. Simultaneously the propeller fell off and whirled away to the west, still spinning as it vanished.

'Blimey – he's breaking up!' cried a soldier.

The red biplane had vanished and we were staring at a sleek and unexpected craft, still red but utterly changed. It accelerated.

'It's a jet!' cried a crewman.

The red plane shrank away ahead of us, banked, and headed east in the general direction of Sweden.

Our pilot brought the PUMA round in a great circle, and as we rattled through the blue Scottish sky I tried to get my bearings. By and by I recognized Loch Mornay. A few minutes later we were fluttering down into a field behind the Black Bonnet Inn.

Three cars of the local constabulary were parked on the road, growing larger as we descended. Holmes, Marianne and I climbed down and crouched as we hurried across the hard-blowing grass and out from under the blades of the windy PUMA. Several troops hustled the feeble Filbert Abernetty out of the copter and walked him over to the constables, who took him into custody and put him, handcuffed, into one of the vehicles.

The PUMA clattered upward into the suddenly cloud-cluttered sky. And faded away.

Doors slammed. The police cars glided away up on to the road, taking the freakish little bomb maker to his rendezvous with justice.

We three stood in a green field on a little knoll behind the inn, in the cold afternoon sunlight. 'Well, Holmes,' said I, 'at last you have ended the "dreadful Abernetty business". My congratulations!'

'Yes,' he replied. 'And it took me only a hundred and twenty years to do it.'

'Come now, Holmes!'

'But, alas, I've let Lars Lindblad fly out of my fingers.'

'He didn't fly out of your fingers,' I said. 'You never had him in your grasp, nor any real chance at him. He's probably landing in Malmö by now. Or Minsk.'

'He is the pre-eminent criminal of the last half century,' Holmes said, 'and I have missed him! I am not happy with myself!'

'I can't believe he is as dangerous as Moriarty was,' I said, trying to remind him of his past great victory.

'Hard telling,' he mused. 'Lindblad has successfully committed sensational crime after sensational crime for forty years. No law enforcement officer in the world has been able to lay a hand on him! Can you imagine what it would mean for my reputation if I—'

'Are you so vain, Holmes!'

'I fear I am.'

'You mustn't get so excited, Mr Holmes,' said Marianne, touching his arm.

'Holmes was undoubtedly the sort of child,' I said to her. 'who, if ever he took a second at school, would spend the rest of the month sulking.'

'I was,' he admitted.

We walked down the slanting green pasture, all streaked red and shadowed with the dying light of the sun. We stepped on to the road, which was hard underfoot, and walked across to the Black Bonnet Inn. Marianne booked a room. We all took baths and changed clothes, and then we met in the old timbered dining room for an excellent supper of salmon. Afterwards, in the Bonnie Prince Charlie Room, we sat awhile by the fire, and sipped sherry, and talked.

'One thing puzzles me,' I said. 'How did you know where Marianne was hidden?'

'I smelled her.'

'None of your pawky humour, Holmes!'

'That was my method, Wilson, and none other. You may recall that after I was resuscitated I complained of an overwhelming sense of smell.'

'I do recall.'

'At first it was a surprise, later an annoyance, and later still I thought it might be an asset – particularly to a detective. I decided that rather than ignore my increased olfactory power, my *hyperosmia*, I should cultivate it. I had been like a man blessed with massive muscles who had not exercised them. I began walking the streets of London and noting every distinct smell that wafted up my nostril, and I linked each smell to its source, and I described each scent according to a system of my own devising. The normal olfactory human sense is so crude that no sophisticated method of describing scents has ever been devised or, indeed, has ever been necessary. I soon was able to distinguish scores of scents in every breath I took. I recorded them all in a little green notebook.'

'So that's what the cryptic writings in your book were all about!' I said. 'I thought they were something much more sinister.'

'Why should you think anything sinister of me, pray!' He looked astounded.

'Well, when I see you at midnight crawling on your hands and knees in Regent's Park, and your nose to the ground as if you had become a hound, I may be forgiven for imagining dark powers were at work.'

He laughed. 'The explanation is quite simple. Earlier that day I had splashed perfume on the ground at intervals. I waited a few hours and then set myself the task of following the trail – a very crude test, admittedly, and one that any dog would view as beneath contempt . . . but for me, a humble *homo sapien*, it was a beginning.'

'But tell me, Holmes,' I said, 'how do you explain the strychnine and other chemicals? You seemed to be obsessed with some sort of experiment that seemed to be going terribly wrong.'

'My dear fellow,' said he, 'I merely was trying, by chemical means, to make myself more sensitive to smell.'

'More!' cried Marianne.

''Tis true,' Holmes agreed. 'I tried to increase my sense of smell even further by applying various chemical combinations to my olfactory mucosa. The one thing that worked was an application of strychnine. Alas, I noticed signs of strychnine poisoning, and I had to desist. But for one day I was in a hallucinatory world of smells so overwhelming that, like a dog, I almost abandoned eyesight and went by smell alone. I seemed to have no choice! On that day, while following Mrs Cleary's dogs, I found I could stoop behind the dogs where they had sniffed, and smell the very thing they had smelled. Never before had I been able to do that!'

'At the time,' I said, 'I confess I feared you were degenerating into an animal. But now I thank heaven you were so diligent, and were able to detect Marianne's body scent even through the walls of a castle.'

'I did not follow the thread of her body scent at all,' said Holmes. 'Her perfume and face cream were far easier to track. I had smelled them on you, my dear Wilson – as you may recall.'

Marianne laughed, brushed a strand of blonde hair from her cheek.

'It was not a difficult task to remember Chanel Number

Nineteen, Coco Chanel's own favourite, and Lancômbe Rénergie, and to follow the wafting wave they made. The passage reeked of them.'

'Reeked!' cried Marianne, laughing again.

'Only relatively speaking,' said Holmes, raising a hand.

'You are forgiven, Mr Holmes,' she said. 'And thank you for having brought this frightening tale to a safe conclusion.'

'I confess,' said Holmes, 'that I do not relish telling Sir Hugh that I failed to save the letter, and telling him, perhaps even worse, that the letter was a fake.'

'A fake!' gasped Marianne, and she looked horrified. 'He was so certain that it was genuine . . .'

'Despite all his careful research,' said Holmes, 'he overlooked several things that showed the letter was a forgery. But I must put this to him very gently.'

'Why not practise your tactful explanation on Marianne and me?' I said. 'I am curious to know your reasoning.'

'Excellent idea,' said Holmes. 'Cheers.' He sipped sherry. 'Let me begin by mentioning those aspects of the letter which seemed to suggest it was authentic. Mind you, all the evidence I have is what I remember as Bart Gray read the letter while he was walling us up – but I must tell you, the words emblazoned themselves on my mind, and I wrote them down before dinner, to be certain the memory will not fade. Even at this moment I see those few words in my memory as clearly as if I were looking at a photograph of them. Of course, we do not have the orthography to judge by, which would have been important. But what we have, we have. And here it is . . .'

Holmes closed his eyes, leant back in his chair, put his finger tips together as if praying, then began to recite, very deliberately:

'*Florence, Casa Figlia, March 1592.*

'*My Sweete Emilia,*

'*You do infect me more than plague would do, and would that I had never run so far from it that I am far from you; for though I be here, still I am home at heart, so I have gained little. This eve I crossed the Old Bridge and into the Piazza della Signoria where I did pause in the shadow of the statue of Cosimo on his grand steed, for at that instant I heard virginals playing. The music made me think of you, and made me remember how you play upon the stops of my twice-strung heart as prettily as on the ivory.*'

'Bravo, Holmes! I think you have it exactly!' I cried.

Holmes smiled, for he always enjoyed praise. 'There was another sentence or two,' he said, 'that I remember less well, but they went something like this: *In Rome I had many strange adventures. The innkeeper at the inn where I stayed was attacked every year by a disorder that sent him mad, and when it came upon him he began to babble without stop. The disorder struck just as I arrived, and for a month I suffered his furious moods. They told me that his delusions took different forms. One year he thought he was an oil jar, and screamed when anyone came near him with fire. Another year he thought he was a frog and went hopping about. This present year he began to imagine he was a bat, and whenever I returned from my walks in the city he would squeak high-pitched squeaks and flap his arms as if he wanted to fly.*'

'Yes, I remember that, vaguely,' I said.

'Those are not the exact words,' said Holmes, 'but close.'

'Then what is right with the letter,' asked Marianne, 'and what is wrong with it?'

'Many points are convincing,' said Holmes. 'First, there was a plague raging in London in 1592 and 93, and as a result the theatres were ordered closed, and perhaps that was a perfect time for Will Shakespeare, at age twenty-eight, to make the Grand Tour of Europe. His references in the letter to the plague ring true, and are artfully woven into a statement of love. Second, the letter is addressed to Emilia, and this fits with the contention of one Shakespeare scholar, A. L. Rowse, that the "Dark Lady" of the sonnets was Emilia Bassano, a young woman who came from a family of court musicians. Third, the allusion to the playing of the virginals therefore rings true. Fourth, the letter speaks of coming across the Old Bridge – Florence's famous Ponte Vechhio – to the Piazza della Signoria, and of stopping in the shadow of a statue. All this is an accurate depiction of the geography of Florence. Fifth, some may feel the style of the letter rings true to what a young poet would write, for it has almost the rhythm of a poem, and is a bit fantastical and hyperbolical, as Shakespeare so often is. These five things suggest the letter may have been genuine.'

'Yet you say it was not.'

'Couldn't have been,' said Holmes. 'The letter was dated 1592, and also the writer states that he stood in the shadow of the statue of Cosimo on his grand steed. But those two elements are contradictory. The famous equestrian statue of Cosimo by Giambologna was not put up in the Piazza della Signoria until 1594. I am certain of this date because of something that happened at speaker's corner in Hyde Park in 1894, on the three hundredth anniversary of the erection of the statue. I encountered a man railing against the fact that Giambologna had paid an everlasting "tribute to tyranny" by raising the equestrian statue of Cosimo. Scarcely had he said those words than he was shot dead by an anarchist. He fell lifeless off his box and on to the grass almost at my feet. It was an occasion not easily forgotten. Which is why I remember the date so clearly.'

'That sounds pretty conclusive,' I said.

'Yes,' murmured Marianne.

'Still, one would like to have seen the letter,' said Holmes. 'Perhaps the date was poorly written. One would like to have examined the actual script. But there were other things that indicated it was a fake. For instance, that passage about the mad innkeeper in Florence was a false note. Even as Bart Gray read it to us, I knew I had heard it before. It was only a few moments ago, however, as I sat in my bath, that I remembered where I had seen it. The tale is taken almost whole from the autobiography of Benvenuto Cellini. Cellini died twenty-one years before this letter was purportedly written. In his autobiography Cellini tells of being kept prisoner in the Castel Sant'Angelo in Rome, and he speaks of the castellan's yearly delusions, how one year this jailer imagined himself to be a jug of oil, another year a frog, another year a bat. Obviously someone lifted the tale from Cellini and modified it just slightly to fit the Shakespeare letter.'

It was late when we left the Bonnie Prince Charlie room and made our way to our rooms. That night I dreamed that a stranger had come to the inn asking for Marianne Hideaway, and he had left her his card at the front desk. But when I looked at the card, it was blank. This led me to believe that the caller was none other than William Shakespeare. I ran to the door to catch up with him and ask for his autograph – but I saw only a lark leaping up out of the grass and taking flight.

The following morning we had planned to leave for London first thing, but I remembered something important to be done at Castle Mornay. After breakfast we drove around the loch by the main road, and turned on to the drive that led to the castle

grounds. Vehicles from the local constabulary were parked everywhere. The bodies of the dead in the vault had been removed,
and Grandpa Gray's body had been removed from the base of
the wall where he had fallen. The constables were taking pictures
of the crime scene. I first went to the laboratory and saw to it
that the bats were all released, and all the dragonflies. I then
went looking for the little one-eyed dog. I found him hiding
under the desk in the library, hungry and frightened. I finally
convinced him I was a friend – thanks, in part, to the persua-
sive powers of the steak bone in my hand. The little dog followed
me, timidly, out to my car, and he snuggled next to me all the
way to London. Marianne cajoled him to come sit on her lap,
to no avail. Even Holmes tried to make friends with him. No
sale. The little dog would snuggle only next to me as I drove,
and he would let no one else come between us.

TWENTY-FOUR
Nought shall go ill

I t was a June night near the end of spring. Rain was lashing
at our windows and occasional booms of thunder rattled the
panes. Sir Launcelot was lying in his favourite spot near
the cold hearth, head between paws, looking up at me with his
one good eye. Holmes sat in his favourite chair beneath the
lamp by the front window, rereading *Black Holes and Body
Heat*, and making notes in the margins. Occasionally he laughed.
Suddenly he looked at me. 'I tell you Wilson, I entirely disagree
with E. C. Drubbing, but he has a wonderful way of presenting
paradoxes as if they were truths, so that for the briefest instant
one seems to be falling through space and glimpsing something that doesn't exist.'

'You certainly are in a very merry mood these days, Holmes,'
I said.

'It is the glow of success, Wilson – I confess it.'

'You are right to be proud, my dear Holmes,' said I. 'In solving
this last case your brilliance was exceeded only by your bravery.'

I hoped his happy glow would last a week or two longer –

not only for his sake but for my own. For I feared that when his joy faded, his restless mind would begin seeking mysteries close by, and he would set himself the task of discovering my own secret. Even now I saw him gazing absently at me, from time to time, as he looked up from his book.

I rose and went to the window. I gazed out at the world of smear and glisten. Obscure glimpses of our London street appeared through rips and tears in the downpour. The sky lit and flickered like a bad bulb. I went to my chair and opened the side table drawer, then closed it again. I glanced at my watch, then at the window. Dreadful weather. Yet I decided a walk in the rain would be just the thing to help me sort out my dilemma. Also, I had the uneasy feeling that Holmes was observing me, and might be about to draw some conclusion or other about my state of mind. I felt it best to get out of the room before this happened.

'Never worry, Wilson,' said he. 'I'll not intrude on your dilemma – it is none of my business.'

'What!' I cried. 'But you just *have* intruded! You have just broken in on my thoughts, Holmes, and broken your own promise even as you made it!'

He shrugged, sheepishly. 'I apologize, Wilson. I wasn't thinking.'

'Good heavens, Holmes, the problem is that you *were* thinking, that you *never stop* thinking – can't you give a man a rest? One sometimes feels that these intrusions of yours are childish displays designed to make certain everyone is aware of your astonishing powers of observation and deduction.'

'I apologize again,' said he, penitently. 'I can only plead, dear Wilson, that I had no intention to prove anything about my own prowess. What would I be proving, in such an obvious case? Surely, guessing when someone is in love is not a task to test the powers of Sherlock Holmes! Any shop girl can do the same – indeed, any soul in this world can do it! For a poor lovelorn wretch reveals himself, or herself, in a thousand ways at every hour of the day. As to why I made my comment at this partic-ular moment, I can only say that I saw you look into the drawer where you put the letter you received from Rachel Random yesterday, and I saw you then glance at the watch that Marianne Hideaway gave you in thanks for rescuing her from the tower. Then you looked disconsolately out at the rain, then glanced at me with an expression of anxiety on your face, then cast a glance at Sir Launcelot, then looked again at the rain and resolutely took a deep breath. Having seen all this happen in the space of a few seconds, surely it is no great feat to conclude that one or both of those ladies are involved in your thoughts, that love might also be involved, that you feel yourself in a dilemma, that you are hoping I don't discover your problem, and that – despite the rain – you have decided to take a walk with Sir Launcelot to ponder your situation.'

'I am as transparent as glass,' I said, discouraged.

'Who in the grip of love is not?'

'Thank you, Holmes.'

'No need to thank me. I simply state facts. I also commiserate. You are in a dangerous territory.'

'My heavens, you would think at my age I would know better,' I said.

'On the contrary, I would think that any man who knew better had better not be alive at all.'

'I'm surprised to hear you say it, Holmes!'

'I have not pursued love,' he replied. 'But that is not to say I have not felt it. And as to my knowledge of your affairs, never worry that I have any notion of the exact details of your dilemma, for I don't. I have deliberately turned my thoughts away from them, knowing they are none of my affair. I am only cognizant of the most basic of relevant facts – namely, that you are a handsome man who has been spending a good deal of time with a beautiful blonde, also with a beautiful redhead, and also with a beautiful grey-blonde Swedish artist. I can only say, Wilson, that I hope you won't be tempted by the redhead.'

'Why in the world would you offer such an outrageous opinion, Holmes!'

'Because you are a man of sixty-four, and she is a woman of thirty-five.'

'I don't understand.'

'By heaven, Wilson, she is too old for you!'

I burst out laughing. 'Holmes, you are irrepressible when you are in these manic moods!'

The rain had stopped. I mentioned the word *walk* to Sir Launcelot, and he skipped to my side happily, and stared up at the door knob. Soon we two were deep in the dark street, headed over glistening pavement for the park. The full moon emerged and vanished, appearing and disappearing between wracks of clouds that moved as quickly as witches. In the anonymous dark of a London night, calmed by the presence of a faithful and silent companion, I was able to think clearly about my situation – or as clearly as one can ever think about such situations. I decided I really had done the right thing. She was the woman for me. None other. We had told Percy Ffoulkes, of course, and he was delighted. But no use telling Holmes now. The marriage date had not even been set. There would be time enough to inform him later. Meanwhile, he would have the pleasure of trying to uncover the secret, which I had no doubt he would manage to do – though I expected he would chivalrously pretend he hadn't a clue that Rachel Random would soon be my wife.

I returned to the flat feeling at peace, weary, ready to while away the rest of the evening in calm contentment. Instead, I found new excitement.

As I walked in the door Holmes sprang to his feet. 'You just missed him!' he said.

'Who?'

Agitated, he walked to the window and looked out. 'Lestrade. He was just here.'

'On a Saturday night! What possessed him?'

'He brought me this letter.' Holmes waved a sheet of writing paper in the air. 'It is from Lars Lindblad. Shall I read it to you?'

'By all means!'

'It was sent to me care of Scotland Yard.' Holmes sat down at the desk and held the sheet and its envelope under the lamp. He rubbed the sheet between his thumb and forefinger, as if testing its quality. He turned it upside down and held it to the lamp, evidently looking for a watermark. He held it to his nose, fanned his face with it, sniffed both sides of it. At last he seemed satisfied, and made his pronouncement. 'The stationery was bought at The Wren Press in London. At the top of the sheet is a gold embossed Minotaur. The message is handwritten with a medium-tip fountain pen in purple ink, in a Germanic cursive script. The letter may have been written at a supper table, for it smells faintly of basil and on the lower left corner is a smudge of olive oil. No location or date is given, but the postmark on the envelope indicates the letter was sent from Zurich on June eighth. Here is the text:

Dear Mr Holmes,

At last my childhood dreams of being pursued by the legendary Sherlock Holmes have come true – and my childhood anti-hero has proved utterly worthy of my admiration. I congratulate you!

Flinging Shotgun Abernetty from the helicopter was a brilliant ploy, revealing a mind more quick and ruthless than I had imagined. I hope you will believe me, sir, when I say that a surge of joy passed through my body when I saw his ape-like body tumbling through the air, for I realized in that instant that you had utterly foiled my design. You may ask Katrinka Pushkin if, as we banked towards Sweden, I did not shout 'Hurray for Holmes!' The thought of bringing down your helicopter with a bat was so amusing that I could not resist the attempt. I am glad that I did not resist. For I have found again what I value most in life and what, at the age of 60, I had nearly lost: an antagonist worthy of my best game.

What makes a life worth living, Herr Holmes, if not excitement, danger, the possibility of failure? And such a life requires a worthy enemy. I suspect we both share, you and I, the sentiment so well expressed by Mikhail Lermontov, 'I love my enemies, though not in a Christian sense: they amuse me, they quicken my pulses.'

I wish you good health and good luck, Herr Holmes – until we meet again, as I am sure we shall.

Med vänliga hälsningar,
Lars Lindblad.

P.S. You may wish to ask your famed resuscitator, Dr Coleman, to review a disturbing article in the most recent Journal of Scientific Research *published in Leipsic. It suggests that the cells of regenerated organs may begin, after a very little time, to precipitately degenerate. The studies were done, as I recall, on sheep in Herzegovina.*

Holmes looked up and let the letter droop in his hand.

The postscript disturbed me a little. I gazed at my companion, so intensely alive, so close, and yet so strange. And I thought, well, yes, but if he is only cells temporarily and fragilely injected with the appearance of life, so are we all, and we are all disintegrating more rapidly than we can know, subject as we are to 'the thousand natural shocks that flesh is heir to'. But of what use is it to fasten, more than fleetingly, on such obvious truths? Let us, rather, live as if the world were as solid as it seems.

'I wonder what his next grand crime will be,' I said.

'Yes, yes,' mused Holmes. 'I wonder.'

'He is an interesting fellow. Isn't he?'

'Yes. Very.' Holmes sprang suddenly from his chair and, laying the letter on the mantelpiece, poured us each a small glass of Percy's old brandy.

'Are we celebrating something?' I asked. For he had the air of a man about to pronounce words of import.

'You know, Wilson, life is a game . . .'

'Many have said so.'

'. . . a game so bizarre that it occasionally seems to me almost real.'

'I wouldn't go so far as to say it seems real,' said I.

He laughed. 'At all events, you are embarked on an adventure which you are keeping a secret, and I have an enemy awaiting me – that is the important thing.'

'Adventure and romance,' said I. 'What more could we ask?'

Holmes, with a sudden smile, lifted his glass. 'Nothing. We have awaiting us, my dear Wilson, all that two gentlemen of our age could possibly look forward to.'

'We do indeed,' said I.

And Sir Launcelot, catching the spirit of the occasion, leapt up and began barking.